[handwritten: Shanghai 1988]

Mao Dun

The Vixen

Panda Books

Panda Books
First edition 1987
Copyright 1987 by CHINESE LITERATURE
ISBN 0-8351-1608-5
ISBN 7-5071-0000-6/I.1

Published by CHINESE LITERATURE, Beijing (37), China
Distributed by China International Book Trading Corporation
(GUOJI SHUDIAN), P.O. Box 399, Beijing, China
Printed in the People's Republic of China

CONTENTS

Creation

THE small desk by the south window, spread with a dark green cloth, had on its right corner a light blue porcelain vase from which leaned two half-open red roses, like mischievous girls laughing disdainfully at a pile of hard-bound books sitting bolt-upright in the opposite corner, their moralistic appearance making you believe that they definitely were not romances. A silver-plated ink box lay in the upper middle of the desk, well matched by the clean blotter with an old letter stuck in one corner of its leather frame. Another small desk stood under the west window. The crumpled magazines scattered over it had knocked over a triangular green glass thermometer. The nib of the golden fountain pen was kissing the white forehead of a girl on an art postcard. A big drop of ink had congealed on the nib like a black tear lamenting the pen cap's disappearance. A finely carved ivory rabbit, its pink eyes aslant, gazed reproachfully at a small paper fan lying open beside it, because the rude, pushing fan had toppled it. Now it lay there sulkily, revealing the fine green inscription on its white belly: "In memory of Xianxian's twenty-fourth birthday. From her loving husband Junshi." But the character "husband" appeared to have been scraped with a knife.

A sofa with a golden silk cover under the central window in the east wall was flanked by matching armchairs like bodyguards. To the left, against the wall, stood a cabinet with two shelves, the top narrower one with two glass doors backed with purple silk. Opposite this cabinet, to the right of the right arm-chair, was a clothes rack for raincoats, capes, hats and the like. Beyond this was the right window in the east wall, the small square table in front of it spread with a tea-service and a cigarette container. Farther on, in the corner, was a dressing-table and a small door which appeared to lead to the bathroom. Against the north wall stood a wardrobe with an oval mirror-door reflecting the big wooden bed below the window in the middle of the west wall, its gauze mosquito-net and the two people sleeping there. The bedroom door, at an oblique angle to the west of the wardrobe, was tightly closed.

A woman's clothes lay scattered over the sofa. A sky-blue satin gown, black silk sleeveless jacket, white knitted bodice and pink panties with elastic at the legs and waist. These were bundled together as if waiting to be laundered, showing how hastily their mistress had undressed. From under the sofa protruded the polished tip of a girl's grey leather shoe; but its mate was hiding far off under the short-legged dressing-table: she would have to hunt for it. Right of the bed, near the door, was a stand for an imposing reading-lamp with an amber silk shade. Beside this were a dainty handkerchief embroidered in one corner, perfumed · paper, powder-paper, a pocket-mirror, used tram tickets, small silver coins, receipts from a department store, a tiny engagement diary with a gold-embossed leather cover, a brooch and small visiting-cards — and the little things found in a young lady's handbag. An open magazine propped against the reading-lamp had pushed its shade askew and stood there incongruously. On the lamp's bronze base a couple of little doves with outstretched wings had craned their heads as if to guess at the title on the cover: *Women and Politics.*

Sunlight shone through the gauze curtains of the east window, dappling the cream-painted furniture with gold. Suddenly the discordant roar of a fast car sounded down below, waking up one of the sleepers. As he opened his drowsy eyes and stirred, a strong scent assailed his nostrils. Instinctively turning his head he saw his wife still sleeping, her cheeks red as roses. Her bedding kicked off, she was lying on one side wearing only a long woollen vest which reached to her knees. So her arms and legs were exposed to the morning air, and the sunshine filtering through the gauze fell on her white limbs like dancing drops of water.

— If the sun had reached the bed it must be late.

As Junshi thought this, he yawned. He had turned in very early and had no idea when his wife had come home; but he still felt exhausted after waking up at three and being unable to get back to sleep, not dozing off until light glimmered in the window. Then, only half asleep, he had dreamed many short disconnected dreams. He could still remember most of one which struck him as ill-omened. He shut his eyes again to think over that dream, at the same time lightly taking his wife's hand.

Dreams, some say they reproduce the cares of the day, others that they are a subconscious activity; but Junshi believed neither theory. He claimed not to have dreamed since the age of fifteen. His wife doubted this.

"You must dream," she often said. "Most likely after waking up your dreams vanish."

"You're the dreamer," he would retort. "You not only dream in your sleep but with your eyes open."

Now to his surprise he had dreamed, confirming that in the past he hadn't had dreams — he hadn't forgotten them. So he tried to remember these dreams to tell his wife. He wouldn't lightly pass over even such little things, or let his wife suspect him of lying. He wanted at all times to be believed, looked up to and obeyed, to have her accept his love with her whole soul.

He breathed out light-heartedly and re-opened his eyes to stare at the sunlight dancing on the curtains. Then the bundle of clothes on the sofa caught his eye and he surveyed the whole room, his gaze finally coming to rest on his wife's face. For some reason though sound asleep she wore a faint frown and her lips were compressed, just as when she had quarrelled with him yesterday. Of late they had frequently fallen out. Xianxian often refuted him, and he criticized her behaviour even more often. Many of his criticisms seemed to her sheer contrariness. Her friend Miss Li thought this a sign of the progress Xianxian had made recently, whereas Junshi had regressed. Xianxian shared this view, but Junshi wouldn't admit this. At heart he resented Miss Li, thinking she had led his good wife completely astray. So yesterday he had found a pretext to let off steam and sharply disparaged Miss Li. What upset Xianxian most was his saying:

". . . Miss Li behaves just like a slick woman politician. She's busy every day with so-called political activities, but does she know the meaning of politics? I'm not against women taking an interest in politics, Xian-

xian, I used to encourage you to do that, so that now
you have some idea what's involved. But you must be
realistic — ha! You lack the subjective ability, and the
objective conditions aren't ripe. Besides, Miss Li is just
looking upon political activities as films or dances which
are simply fashionable pastimes for modern young
women. She says women must be independent, must
have social status — that's only show talk! In what way
is Miss Li independent? What social status has she?
I know. Her place, her status is dancing in the Carl-
ton or Moon Palace. Now she's dissatisfied with the
status quo and wants to make revolution. Bah, revolution, it used to disgust her, but now she calls new stunts
in cinemas or dance halls revolution. . . ."

What upset Xianxian most was Junshi's attitude —
his conviction that no one else could ever amount to
much. This was worse than his conservatism and his
insinuations. She had really lost her temper. Though
he had later tried to comfort her she had been in a
tizzy for hours.

Watching his wife's expression as she slept, Junshi
recalled the previous day's dispute. He felt Xianxian
was daily becoming more estranged from him, that he
could no longer monopolize her heart and soul. She
had broken away from his moral ascendancy to develop
views of her own. This was hard for someone as
opinionated as Junshi to take. He loved his wife, still
loved her, but had loved most of all the wife who had
modelled her thoughts and actions on his. Unfortunately that golden age had passed, she was no longer the
Xianxian of two years ago.

Junshi could not help sighing over this. He closed
his eyes again to consider how the change had come

about. He recalled that two years ago when they summered in Mt. Mogan, Xianxian had expressed an independent opinion about women's social duties — had that been the start of her present dissidence? It didn't seem likely, she hadn't met Miss Li then; yet it was possible, as since then she had steadily deteriorated. This last half year not only had her views changed, even her behaviour had lost its earlier charm, she tossed her clothes and things about at random as if too busy with important affairs to care for appearances. He instinctively opened his eyes to glance round the room and saw that his domain had shrunk to the desk below the south window. Apart from this neat enclave, the whole chaotic room was Xianxian's domain.

With a heavy heart Junshi went on to recall all Xianxian's disagreements with him over trifles. That holiday in Mt. Mogan when they were in complete accord had been the height of their happiness, yet even then a fateful black thread seemed to have entered their lives. Xianxian's metamorphosis had started, it seemed, with her taste, for by degrees she tired of quiet refinement and demanded strong stimuli, often disagreeing with him over everyday affairs. They would argue over what material to buy, what film to see, what restaurant to go to. They often opted for different things and were unwilling for each to go his or her way, both wanting their proposal to triumph completely. In the end one side was sacrificed. As both disliked the idea of each going his own way they felt it better to take it in turns to win, and of course the winner was very satisfied while the loser had the consolation of a sweet kiss asking for understanding. The first couple of disputes like this really upset them, till they discovered the joy of reconciliation and tacitly accepted these tiffs as essential to their love. So having grown used to this Junshi often told Xianxian:

"This time you've won again. But my fair lady, my spoilt miss, don't imagine your victory's reasonable or lasting."

Then laughing softly Xianxian would nestle in his arms and give him a long kiss. That was the price of her victory, her thanks to her loving husband for giving way to her.

Before long, though, the magic of this lovers' banter wore off. When the kissing became a mechanical routine, the one kissed felt the other's lips were cold, her smile was artificial, and his heart throbbed with the anguish of defeat. The more so as Xianxian came to stick to her views and nearly always insisted on winning. So, reluctantly, each had to go his own way. This was one reason why Junshi's sphere of influence in their room was now reduced to his desk.

Gradually their views had diverged. This was a silent, painful struggle. Junshi had done his utmost, but in vain, to recover his monopoly of his wife's heart. For she had set up a firm barrier against him, and the new influence on her mind, gaining in strength every day, was ousting the old one. This last month Junshi had been conscious several times of his defeat. He realized that his ascendancy over his wife would soon be overthrown, and couldn't understand how he had won her heart and dominated her soul so easily two years ago yet now had lost it imperceptibly, with apparently no hope of recovery. Two years ago her heart had been like a sponge, absorbing all his ideas; now it was as hard as iron and not all his ardour could melt it. "A woman's heart is a mystery," he often thought. He could only resort to satire, in the hope that its acidity would melt the iron in her heart. So Miss Li became his target. He had decided that the change in his wife was entirely due to Miss Li. Sometimes he felt satire inappropriate — feared it might estrange Xianxian even more. But he had no other way. "Ah, a woman's heart is a mystery!" he concluded with a sigh.

Junshi suddenly went into action. Threw off his blanket and rolled to the edge of the bed, forgetting that he was still holding his wife's hand. This woke Xianxian. When she had collected herself she moved closer to her husband and looked over his shoulder at his face.

He shut his eyes and made no move. He felt a soft arm over his chest. Felt his ears tickled by fine fluffy hair. Still he kept his eyes shut, not moving but con-centrating his attention. Presently a warm body pressed down on him and he clearly heard the beat of another heart. Forced to open his eyes, he saw Xianxian prop-ped up on her arms and staring at his face, like a cat watching a rat that was shamming dead. He couldn't but laugh.

"I knew you were just pretending to be asleep."

Xianxian smiled and, relaxing, fell into his arms. Feeling her vitality through the long vest he could hard-ly control himself. But it pained him to think that this soft warm breast, this lovely face with arched eyebrows, these beautiful eyes, entrancing cherry-red lips — this whole captivating woman belonged to him, definitely belonged to him; but hidden deep inside all this was a heart which he could feel beating, and that couldn't count as his! He could be in contact with Xianxian's lovely form, but apart from that there was a formless Xianxian — her soul — with which he had lost contact. Was this what was called the tragedy of love? Did this mean the end of their love?

Unable to shake off his sense of isolation he reflected painfully, ignoring Xianxian's questioning look. Suddenly a hand covered his eyes, its slender fingers in the sun like transparent coral. The bracelet, three rows of seed-pearls, which clasped her soft wrist, was a souvenir of their summer in Mt. Mogan. A few days ago the thread had broken, and it had just been mended. Junshi softly removed her hand. The seed-pearls felt cold and slippery against his fingers. His heart missed a beat. Ah, that pearl bracelet! It recalled their lost happiness on Mt. Mogan. Bless that happiness now gone never to return!

Junshi eyed the seed-pearls for a while in frustration, then looked at Xianxian's face. She was watching him drowsily and pensively.

"Didn't you find our life in the past very happy?"

He spoke slowly as if he had chewed over every word.

"I'm very happy now."

Xianxian smiled as she answered and nestled up to him.

"Don't blurt out whatever comes into your head, Xianxian. Think carefully."

"Then the first year or half year of our marriage or, strictly speaking, the first month was happiest."

"Why?"

She smiled again, bewildered by this cross-examination.

"Why? No reason. Except that everything was a new experience for me. Before that my life had been a white sheet of paper, but then colour was added to it. Thinking back now to my girlhood, it wasn't specially interesting and I'm very hazy about it. It was only after we married, or rather during our honeymoon, that each little thing stands out in my memory."

Junshi nodded with a smile as he pictured the past. But this made him feel depressed. Had their happiness gone for good, never to return?

"How about you? What was your happiest time?"

As Xianxian questioned him she stroked his hair, the tip of her bracelet dangling between his eyebrows.

"I don't disagree with you but I can't approve either. For me the first year or, as you say, first month of our marriage was only the start, not the height of our happiness. I wanted to make an ideal woman of you, and that was the start of making my dream come true, so I was buoyed up by hope but didn't achieve real happiness."

"You've often told me that."

Xianxian interrupted him drily. Though when she heard this talk before she had been "buoyed up by hope", she no longer liked being told that he had shaped her according to his ideal.

"But you've never asked me if I succeeded or failed, Xianxian. My dream did come true, but at the same time I failed. That summer in Mt. Mogan I managed to mould you. Remember what we did on the boulder by the Yinlingshan waterfall? You were very shy, but you sat there in only your vest, the way you are now.

Of course that was a little thing, but it proved that I'd managed to shape you, my dream had come true."

He broke off abruptly, taking Xianxian's arm and staring fixedly at her. Her cheeks burned as she thought back to that episode, and she reproached herself for not having felt at the time that such a novel stimulus was so essential. Nowadays. . . .

"My dream came true, only to go up in smoke! My cup of happiness was already full. Before, our road in life was bright but after that darkness mingled with the brightness. Mt. Mogan was the watershed for us. After we came back you gradually changed. Yes, Xianxian, from then on you changed little by little. You changed into yourself, not the ideal woman I wanted to make you. The books I got you to read didn't mean the same to you as they did to me. I don't know why, because I can't believe that one book can have two different interpretations. You've been influenced, Xianxian, by something apart from books, apart from what I've taught you. And so you've destroyed yourself! Destroyed my ideal!"

Junshi had changed colour and closed his eyes. The shattering of his ideal distressed him; the dream-like past added to his depression.

2

At twenty Junshi had high hopes of the future. He commemorated his twentieth year as the time when his father had died leaving him quite a fortune and he had become a free agent. Though only twenty he was no romantic; his father's homilies had ended his youthful exuberance and made him realistic. By his father's bier he had mapped out his life; with tears for his father in his eyes, he had focussed on his future. Like a traveller planning his journey, he carefully worked out the way to achieve his dream. He wanted to study widely, to find an ideal companion in life, to travel abroad and in the country to investigate local customs, to temper himself to stand hardships and learn self-restraint. In his mid thirties, at the height of his powers, he would have a son and a daughter; then, after forty, he would serve his country and mankind.

Junshi owed these ideals in part to his father. After the failure of the Reform Movement of 1898, his old man had stopped hoping for an official career and concentrated instead on running his business and educating his son. He had passed on to Junshi his theories about national salvation and entrusted this duty to him. Now old, he regretted that in his prime he had been too busy making a living to settle down to a career; he therefore impressed on his son the need to "establish himself in life". He mapped out his future for him and tried to mould him according to his own ideals. He had only half succeeded by the time he died.

Junshi had obviously inherited his father's creative urge. He spent a great deal of time and energy looking for a life-time companion. He had his criteria for an "ideal wife" and used these as a yardstick for potential candidates, deploring the fact that society had produced no "ideal wife" for him. After five or six years his relatives worried about him, his friends looked round for him, but he refused to make up his mind. Finally his "choosiness" became the subject of gossip. When his friends saw him they always asked if he'd settled on someone, but he just shook his head. One day an old classmate raised the subject with him.

"Junshi, you've been looking all these years for a wife and I, to say nothing of others, must have introduced you to at least two dozen girls. Were none of them up to scratch?"

"They were up to scratch but not ideal."

"Isn't up to scratch ideal? What difference is there? Please explain."

"Of course there's a difference." Junshi smiled. "Up to scratch is just passable. That falls far short of ideal. If I'd just wanted someone up to scratch I needn't have waited for seven years."

"Well then, tell me what you mean by ideal."

His old classmate, thoroughly intrigued, lit a cigarette and put his legs up as he waited to be enlightened.

"By ideal I mean she must have the same disposition and views as mine."

Junshi smiled as he said this.

"No other requirements — no other explanation?"

"No. It's as simple as that."

His old classmate looked disappointed. He persisted:

"Well, you should be able to find someone with the same disposition and views. Seems to me Miss Zhang would suit you fine, and you and Miss Wang ought to see eye to eye. Why did you turn them both down?"

"Miss Zhang's quite cultivated, and Miss Wang has a good disposition. But even putting the two of them together still wouldn't be ideal. Both have certain prejudices — academic prejudices and prejudices about other things."

The other stared at him, baffled.

"By prejudices I mean they go to extremes. Yes,

that's the trouble with most modern young women. For instance, freedom of action is necessary, but they tend to be flighty. They should be broad-minded but they concentrate on outside affairs neglecting their duties at home as wives and mothers. Of course traditional ideas are no good, but unfortunately most of them have new-fangled notions which don't make sense."

"Well, that makes it hard, but surely you can find someone?"

His old classmate spoke gravely, thinking: So his ideal is a woman who's not wholly modern nor traditional.

"But don't make the mistake of thinking I want a girl neither wholly modern nor traditional," Junshi added as if reading his friend's mind. "No, I want someone wholly modern, but one who won't go to dangerous extremes."

"That's difficult. Our chaotic society with all its contradictions can't produce girls like that."

Junshi nodded agreement.

"Better marry a foreigner," his classmate proposed, struck by a new idea. "Most English girls should suit you. That's it, Junshi, find yourself an English girl. Since you're thinking of going to Europe, start looking in London."

"That's one way, but it wouldn't do for me. My ideal wife must have a Chinese background with a cultural heritage of five thousand years — she can't be a foreigner."

"Well, Junshi, you'll probably remain a bachelor all your life. Or you'll have to wait for ten or twenty years, by which time Chinese society may be settled enough to produce your ideal wife."

With this melancholy conclusion his classmate wanted to close the discussion; but Junshi had more to say. Raising one thumb to sketch a half circle in the air he went on earnestly:

"No. I've a new plan. I shall look for uncut jade — that's it, uncut jade which I can carve myself. Yes, since society hasn't produced an ideal wife for me, I mean to create one!"

Junshi's eyes were flashing with determination, but his classmate only smiled. Create a wife? Was he joking? However, this was what Junshi had decided. He had already worked it out: A pure, innocent girl born into a family neither new nor old, even if she hadn't studied but was naturally intelligent could always be trained. And any traditional ways she had could easily be changed.

After more than a year Junshi found his uncut jade — Xianxian his young maternal cousin. He had taken the first step towards attaining his ideal.

Xianxian had her father's intelligence and forthrightness, her mother's gentleness and circumspection. Her father had taught her Chinese, her mother housekeeping. An excellent student who rapidly learned whatever she took up, she was greatly influenced by her surroundings. She was really a fine piece of uncut jade. In merely two years she read all the books Junshi assigned her and gained a higher than average understanding of natural sciences, history, literature, philosophy and modern trends of thought. When she and Junshi visited Mt. Mogan she outshone the other wives and daughters of "high-class Chinese" who were summering there. Her refined behaviour, cultivated speech, extensive knowledge, clear head and liveliness all proved that Junshi had surpassed himself in moulding her character.

Still, this process had been difficult.

To start with Xianxian had disliked politics and reading newspapers because her father, a talented and unconventional scholar, considered politics dirty, so naturally she hadn't inherited any political acumen from him. Junshi on the other hand paid close attention to politics, believing that men were political animals and that a girl with no understanding of politics fell short of ideal. He himself had studied all the political theorists from Plato to Hobbes and Rousseau, even including Kropotkin, Marx and Lenin. But he held sound, moderate views, never going to extremes. He wanted to inculcate these views in Xianxian. His attitude to women's suffrage was that of President Roosevelt who said that if the majority of women asked for suffrage he'd let them have it. But the "blue stocking" suffragettes in England struck Junshi as extremists.

Like a stern father who wants his son to win fame he urged Xianxian to read political science, to keep abreast of international trends and memorize important names and dates. He asked her to write a daily review of current events in China, which he then corrected for her. After three months' struggle he managed to interest her in politics.

His second difficulty was Xianxian's happy-go-lucky temperament which needless to say she inherited from her father. This was something Junshi hadn't bargained for. He didn't discover this till one beautiful April afternoon half a year after their marriage. During an outing to Longhua that day they sat down to rest under some peach trees beside the dirt road. Xianxian lifted her face to catch the pink petals fluttering down between her eyebrows, on to her lips and the nape of her neck, and inside her open collar to cling to her breasts. This reminded Xianxian of Junshi's caresses, exciting her as if spring had electrified all her cells, nerves and tiny blood vessels, making her conscious of the slightest touch, the faintest sound, able to remember most insignificant trifles. At the same time countless ideas swirled through her mind and a sweet yet bitter sensation filled her heart. There was no end to what she wanted to say, but not a word could she get out. She just took Junshi's hand and gripped it hard as if this were a form of silent communion.

A ragged drunk, red in the face, with a peach sprig tucked behind one ear, came lurching across the road singing lustily. After shooting a glance at them from his bloodshot eyes he sang even more loudly as he headed west.

"Ha, ha, haha!"

Laughing like a maniac the drunk looked at the corner of the road where a sentry was standing stiff as a wooden puppet. After saying something to him he reeled off to vanish into the peach orchard.

"Ha, ha, haha. . . ."

His laughter as it faded away echoed through the air like the shredding of candy floss. Xianxian relaxed and transferred her gaze from the corner of the road to Junshi's face. On her lips appeared an enigmatic smile.

"A drunk! A drunk roaming in spirit outside the universe!" she exclaimed approvingly. "He's like

Zhuangzi's* Wang Tai whose feet were cut off, or the
man who had no toes, or the one with a big tumour —
they may look repulsive but their goodness shines
through. Did you notice his eyes, Junshi? They showed
his utter content. In his eyes all we admire — wealth,
rank, fame, power and beauty — fades into insignifi-
cance. Because he despises all that. Because to him
there's no difference between rich and poor, noble and
humble, intelligent and stupid, worthy and worthless,
right and wrong, big and small. That's why he's so con-
tented with everything. Dad often says: In his cups a
man begins to be 'complete' and 'genuine'. Only
today have I really understood that. We who pride
ourselves on our intelligence or beauty are just like frogs
at the bottom of a well. We're really too feeble for
words."

Junshi stared at her in amazement, not answering.

"I remember Dad taught me Zhuangzi when I was
eighteen. I was carried away by that part 'Miaogu
Shoots an Immortal'. I felt ashamed then of the way
I'd been praised for my good looks and intelligence,
because I'm really so dreadfully uncouth. Later Dad
said Miaogu's shooting at an immortal most likely stood
for the primeval spirit transcending creation; still I felt
myself unbearably uncouth. It often seems to me that
we should look down on everything as if standing on
the clouds, so that everything seems level, of the same
height. When I've tried to do this for a while I've felt
that I really have transcended the world, forgetting my
own existence and the existence of others."

Xianxian gazed up as if she could see Miaogu's sym-

---

* Zhuangzi (c. 369-286 B.C.) was a Taoist philosopher.

bolic figure coolly riding the wind to the other side of the sky.

Junshi was thinking hard. He had only just discovered this dangerous trancendentalist trend in Xianxian. He recalled that not long ago she had read the debate between the Western schools of monism and dualism, and had written this comment: "If you look on others as different, they are as far apart as Chu and Yue.* If you look on others as the same, all creation becomes one. Isn't that what Zhuangzi said?" He also recalled her reading the disputes of different political schools over the function of the state. She had told him with a smile, "They're all of them both right and wrong." He had thought at the time she was joking, now he realized that she based her views on Zhuangzi: she was standing on the clouds to watch the political disputes in different parts of the world. He decided to give top priority to stopping her from taking things too philosophically.

Since then he had induced her to study evolution, Nietzsche and the great materialists. In view of the deplorable result of making her read the teachings of both sides, he now restricted her to one side only. Although opposed himself to the application of materialism to social science, to cure her idealism and nihilism he resorted to this strong materialist medicine.

And finally he had succeeded.

However, another small rectification was needed. For some reason, though Xianxian was unconventional she was shy about showing emotion. The first time they

---

* A quotation from Zhuangzi. Chu and Yue were two of the Warring States, one in the west the other in the east.

went out together she kept half a foot behind him. If he held her hand in public, she would blush and soon find some pretext to pull it away. Junshi often laughed at this old-fashioned coyness of hers. Under his influence she did become bolder, but still not lively enough for his liking. And in bed she was often passive, which he found dull and insipid. He believed in heredity and feared her bashfulness might make their children timid, so he went all out to change this. Where there's a will there's a way. By the time they visited Mt. Mogan Xianxian had grown lively and uninhibited, able to express her devotion to him in public.

Now the pupil had surpassed her master. In fact sometimes she quite embarrassed Junshi by being so demonstrative and requiring such powerful stimuli.

3

Recalling the last two years as he leaned lazily against the bed-post, Junshi couldn't refrain from thinking bitterly, "You've destroyed yourself! Destroyed my ideal!" The beautiful dream of his twenties was now hazy, misted over. Xianxian was the first to get up. She hopped about the room like a little sparrow, humming a song.

The sunlight had now receded to the back of the sofa. The sound of traffic carried in by the breeze made it clear that it was after nine. Two glasses of hot milk waited quietly, as if smiling, on the table. The big wardrobe mirror reflected its lively mistress. The triple mirror on her dressing-table seemed jealous, as if it alone had the right to reflect her snowy skin.

All the things in the room basking in the May morning sunshine stood lined up in silence to await his orders. They appeared puzzled too by their master's unusual delay in getting up.

The bed gave a soft sigh to complain of having worked overtime.

But Junshi went on staring glumly at the top of the mosquito-net and showed no sign of getting out of bed.

"Are you very tired, Junshi? What's on your mind?" asked Xianxian affectionately.

Sitting on the left armchair she was pulling on a silk stocking. The lower part of her long woollen vest had ridden up slightly, releasing the fragrance of her warm flesh.

Junshi smiled wrily and shook his head in silence.

"Are you still chewing over what I said? Did I annoy you by saying, 'It's you who destroyed your ideal'? Or 'you summoned up a demon but can't control it'. Did that upset you? I was just talking casually, not thinking you'd take it to heart. Silly boy, don't go imagining things. You succeeded. I haven't gone against you. Aren't I going in the direction you mapped out? I may actually be a step ahead of you, but we're going in the same direction."

He made no answer.

"I've done all you asked. Been influenced by you in all my thoughts and actions. Yet you say I've come under someone else's influence. Of course I know you mean Miss Li. But Junshi, why give someone else all the credit; you should be proud of being such a good tutor. You've cured me of my happy-go-lucky ways, made me keen on politics, made me what I am today; but now you disapprove of me. Why, Junshi, silly boy, you're like the Taoist Huang who invoked a devil.

When he chanted his incantations he was only afraid the devil wouldn't come; when it really came he was terrified because it was so vicious, not the devil he had dreamed of."

Xianxian burst out laughing, though she could see that Junshi was glowering. She pulled on her other silk stocking, then went to the bed to take his face in her hands.

"Let's say no more about it," she proposed archly. "Who knows what tomorrow may bring. Tomorrow, no, I ought to say any hour, minute or second now your ideas or mine may change, both of us may change; we may move further apart or we may draw closer together. Who knows? Today's different from yesterday, tomorrow will be different again, and what about after that? We haven't yet dreamed about it; this is today's fashionable trend. But Junshi, you're still clinging to the ideal of your twenties, thinking it holds good for everywhere and all times. That's really ridiculous. Come on, stop giving way to foolish fancies. The past is over and done with, we can discuss the future when it comes, so let's stop daydreaming. We can only grasp the present, only act on our present understanding, Junshi, good boy, Xianxian loves you; let's make it up."

She swiftly pinned him down, her soft firm flesh rubbing against him, her laughter floating out to fill the room. It seemed even the books piled decorously on the desk by the left window could not help feeling flustered. Junshi sensed something forced about her laughter — some hidden grief, regret or reproach. Sure enough, two pearly tears welled up in her lovely eyes, fell by the bridge of his nose, then trickled down to his mouth. As if electrified he clasped her tight and buried his lips in her neck — she had just turned her face away. His feelings were a mixture of sweetness and bitterness, love, resentment and pity. Something like those of a stern father when his prodigal son comes back to kneel at his feet.

But this feeling quickly passed, to be replaced by another.

— Was this what made women such a mystery? So frail? Such sentimentalists? Was this why they seldom developed sound, moderate views but often went too far or not far enough? Did this excitement, tension, hesitation and wretchedness spring from modern thinking? From the confusion and contradictions of their generation? Was this the lassitude, fear and ennui concealed behind active, fervid stimuli?

This reinforced Junshi's conviction that his views were sound and that Xianxian had destroyed herself. For the sake of his ideal and also of Xianxian he must keep up the struggle till the final victory and cure her of those subversive views which only made her wretched. Seeing a ray of hope his courage increased a hundred-fold just as when, ten years ago, he had stood by his father's bier.

He instinctively glanced sideways at Xianxian's face. She was stealing a glance at him too.

She started giggling. Blushed faintly. Her half-closed eyes crinkled in a smile like a charm while the warmth of her flesh was melting him. The enchantress! Symbol of modernism! Junshi began to waver. But reason enabled him to resist temptation, and he knew from experience that this was Xianxian's way of avoiding a scolding. She wasn't going to fool him so easily. He kissed her soft rosy cheek, then told her firmly:

"Xianxian, what you say, like your ideas and actions, is half-baked. We encourage children to be lively, but don't want them to climb on to grown-ups' heads. Children go on playing till the game breaks up in tears; they have no idea when to stop. Recently you've been growing more and more childish, Xianxian. I got you to take an interest in politics, not expecting you to plunge into real politics, not to say unsound, illicit political movements. For instance nowadays everybody talks about 'politics of the whole people,' but they don't expect to achieve this overnight, they just want everyone to learn that expression. Those who try to put it into practice are fools. But that's the way you've been heading, Xianxian. You don't realize how childish it is, or how dangerous. This morning I had a nightmare — I dreamed about you. . . ."

He had to stop at this point, because Xianxian was giggling uncontrollably. He looked doubtfully, disapprovingly into her eyes.

"Go on."

Though she had suppressed her laughter, it was clear from her quivering breasts that she was still laughing inwardly.

"First tell me what you find funny."

"Nothing. Regarding children — if you really want to hear I'll tell you. Listening to you made me think of a way to satisfy children. You tell an eight-year-old, 'Good boy, when you're ten I promise to buy you that.' But a ten-year-old's told to wait till he's eleven. Always promises for next year. And when the child grows bigger he no longer wants that thing, there's no more trouble. Junshi, don't you agree?"

He nodded reluctantly, suspecting her of being caustic.

"I'd love to hear your dream, but I'm sure it was

very long, as long as your life. Keep it till this evening to tell me in detail. Look, the clock says nine twenty. I haven't washed yet. I've an appointment at ten."

Not waiting for an answer she slipped out of Junshi's arms. Her long vest rode up again, revealing her rosy flesh to confront her husband who had sat up abruptly. Not stopping to straighten her vest she ran through the small door by her dressing-table and slammed it shut.

Junshi sat down in front of Xianxian's desk and leafed through the magazine lying untidily there. The way his wife had run out on him hurt him. He couldn't think what she meant by it. She didn't seem all that set on carrying out her present proposals, nor could she free herself from her old habits; after all she was used to a life of luxury. She didn't seem altogether satisfied either by what she called her activities, because after each action she showed hesitation and anxiety. Thus just now she had said incisively, "The past is done with, don't daydream about the future; we must grasp the present and act according to our present understanding." But her hysterical laughter hid unhappiness and tears. He couldn't make her out. Had her attitude to him changed? She still treated him as fondly as ever. If it hadn't changed, at least she no longer wanted him to concern himself with her affairs and had lost patience with his criticisms. Just now she hadn't even wanted to hear his dream.

Ah, he thought, a woman's heart is a mystery.

A mystery? Yes, especially in Xianxian's case. She was a complex character. He carefully analysed the

Xianxian of today, then considered the process by which he had moulded her.

Memories long smothered by dust surfaced one by one; random, disconnected views coalesced bit by bit, finally forcing him to admit that what he had called creation was actually sabotage. And his sabotage tactics had taken root in Xianxian's heart. Had sabotaged her happy acceptance of fate and put materialism in its place; had sabotaged her unconventional aversion to politics, so that now she was a prey to radical views. Had sabotaged her shyness and refinement, so that she had grown sensual and demanded strong stimuli. Apparently she had never related to his thinking. She was easily influenced by her surroundings, yet his views had failed to influence her in the least. When he thought he had succeeded in moulding her, he had just deceived himself. He had failed from the start, not succeeded for one moment. He had thought their honeymoon on Mt. Mogan a success, but that was nonsense. He had worked all this time for nothing.

He recalled Xianxian's remark, "It's you who destroyed your ideal." He had to admit she was right. Miss Li was not to blame.

How could he have been such a fool! He had thought he could step by step realize his dream, whereas he now knew he had step by step destroyed it. Had strained every nerve to create an ideal wife, only to find her nothing of the kind.

— Our chaotic society with all its contradictions can never produce an ideal character.

His old classmate's observation flashed to his mind. He loathed this society. Its chaos and contradictions had sabotaged his ideal. Its atmosphere made it impossible to do anything well. He was in utter despair.

Running water sounded from behind the small door by her dressing-table, telling him that his charming, intelligent young wife was taking a bath.

Junshi turned involuntarily towards that door, distracted by the plash of water. Suddenly a head poked out of the big wardrobe mirror. Whirling round he saw Amah Wang peeping in from the bedroom door which had opened a crack. At sight of Junshi sitting there blankly, still in his pyjamas, she realized this was no time to go in.

A new idea struck Junshi.

Why despair? Though a chaotic, contradictory society was said to be unable to produce moderates with sound ideas, wasn't he living in this society too? How had he been produced? Clearly, society's power over individuals wasn't absolute.

Why should he lose confidence? His efforts over the last two years might have been wasted, but only because he'd been too busy undermining Xianxian to inculcate his own ideas into her. Couldn't he have another try to remould her, to win her back? Sure! Before, he'd used such strong antidotes against her happy-go-lucky and unconventional ways that he'd made her delirious. Well, now he'd use mild healthy ideas to restore her to health. There was hope. While there's life there's hope! All he had to do was recognize his past mistake.

Junshi felt more optimistic than he had for two weeks. This enabled him to make a sober appraisal of his attitude to Xianxian recently. His cutting remarks, he saw now, had been a mistake, had put her back up. And his recent conservative views, due to the circumstances, were no good either, making Xianxian feel that he was really regressing. It had been a mistake too, because of his resentment, to refuse to go to the meetings she attended. He ought to go with her, then voice his dispassionate disapproval to help her see the error of her ways.

Feeling more and more sure of himself, Junshi kept looking at the bathroom door. His new plan worked out, he was waiting for Xianxian's return to try it out on her. He felt as keyed up as a student waiting for an examination paper.

The bedroom door softly opened again. Amah Wang slowly poked in her head, her bright black eyes scanning the room. She tiptoed in to gather up Xianxian's clothes heaped on the sofa, then tiptoed out.

Junshi went on ruminating, reassessing what Xianxian had said. Two sentences he had overlooked now demanded his attention.

— Aren't I going in the direction you mapped out? I may be a step ahead of you, but we're both going in the same direction.

"A step ahead of you." He thought that over. Apparently Xianxian admitted that she'd been influenced by him and followed him, but just now had outstripped him. He abruptly recalled that someone else — most likely Miss Li — had said something similar, implying that he had been Xianxian's guide but had stopped to rest halfway while she had gone on ahead. Was that really the case? Junshi thought too highly of himself to admit it. Refused to believe that he was a spineless fellow who would give up halfway. He reflected: If he was really a middle-of-the-roader, that was because he'd been to one edge of the road, seen something wrong with it and come back to the middle. At all events Xianxian had clearly been influenced by him, as she had admitted as much to her best friend. Yet he had negated that in his recent conclusion and believed that he had used someone else's potent medicine to destroy the original Xianxian and now would have to start all over again.

He was really confused. He believed his conclusion had been quite correct, yet lacked reasons to debunk Xianxian's declaration. Though still buoyed up by optimism he felt rather dubious. He encouraged himself by saying, "I must first solve this riddle; otherwise I won't know how to set to work." But his brain congested by all that hard thinking had run out of inspiration.

The bedroom door opened again. Once more Amah Wang came in, peered round, went to the dressing-table and from one drawer took out a pair of Xianxian's brown leather shoes which she carried off.

Junshi saw Amah Wang come in then go out, and stared for a minute at the bedroom door. Then his glance strayed over Xianxian's desk, finally coming to rest on the ivory rabbit. He picked it up and noticed the word "husband" scratched out by a knife. But this didn't strike him as strange. He remembered Xianxian saying there was something revoltingly traditional about "husband", inevitably suggesting a patriarch, and it should be changed to "sweetheart". So here, too, it was taboo! He couldn't help smiling over her childishness. That made him wonder why she hadn't come out yet.

She'd been gone so long, and it was quite a time since he'd heard the plash of water. He listened carefully. There was no sound from the bathroom. Could she have dozed off in the tub?

Junshi walked to the dressing-table, convinced that Xianxian must be asleep in the tub. He was about to turn the porcelain door-knob when the door suddenly opened. Out came someone carrying towels and a dressing-gown.

Not Xianxian but Amah Wang.

"Oh . . . it's you."

Junshi started. Then at once understood. The bathroom door to the outer room was wide open: Xianxian must have gone downstairs. His wife — his sweetheart — had sneaked away like a rebel from a tailing detective! Now he understood why Amah Wang had come in twice to fetch her clothes and shoes. Why should his wife play such a trick on him?

Seeing Junshi's look of displeasure Amah Wang explained:

"The young mistress finished her bath long ago. Told me to clean the tub."

Junshi's ears were buzzing too much to hear what she said. He recalled his ominous dream. Scented disaster. His effervescent warmth turned suddenly cold. This was a blow to his pride. His heart was pounding a warning.

"Is your mistress downstairs?"

Amah Wang detected his tension from his voice.

"She's gone out. Told me to tell you, sir, she's gone on ahead, she wants you to catch up. And she said if you can't catch up with her she won't wait."

"Oh. . . ."

A moment later a strangled sob burst from Junshi's throat. The little ivory rabbit obsessed him again. By degrees it grew larger and took human shape, gazing at him disdainfully with its pink eyes. He had a hazy notion that it was Xianxian. Finally it vanished, eyes and all. Only the scratches on the word "husband" on its white belly swayed more clearly than ever before him.

February 23, 1928

Translated by Gladys Yang

The Vixen

THE girl's name was Ling, or maybe it was Lin. Who knows? That kind of person never has any definite family name. People call them whatever they like.

The day she arrived, she first walked softly into the room of the old lady to pay her respects. The old lady was munching some water chestnuts her granddaughter had sent, and didn't hear her enter. When she suddenly became aware of the girl kowtowing in front of her, she started with surprise. She considered being shocked like this, at first meeting, a bad omen. It made her feel ill. What's more, the girl's modern hair-do, with its mass of curls, hurt the old lady's eyes. And so, although her son's wife had died some years ago and there was no proper mistress of the house, she refused to recognize this girl as a "wife". Still chewing her water chestnuts, the old lady addressed her contemptuously as "Miss" Ling.

So it was "Miss" Ling! The family matriarch had used the term herself. From then on, this teen-aged girl, Ling, or Lin — or whatever her name was — was permanently relegated to the status of concubine.

Miss Ling had a mother. The Master, her present husband, while in Shanghai on business, had told her mother, "In the future, we shall treat each other as relatives." This was after sleeping with Miss Ling, whom he had met in one of the big department stores,

Miss Ling had no brothers; her mother relied on her
entirely, for support in her old age. All this was made
plain to the Master before Miss Ling left Shanghai with
him.

But now everything had changed. The old lady naturally wouldn't recognize such "relatives". The Master
forgot his promises completely. Whenever there was an
opportune moment, Miss Ling would remark to him
that her mother back in Shanghai must be having a
hard time. But usually, these hints found him deaf
and dumb. At other times he would glare and snort
impatiently:

"What expenses does an old woman have? It's only
been a few months; she couldn't have spent the whole
three hundred dollars I gave her!"

The old lady was very displeased about this gift.
She berated the Master severely, right in front of a
woman servant who had been with the family for years.
"You give three hundred dollars for a smelly
piece of trash you pick up off the streets of Shanghai? You spend money like water! When your own
daughter got married you spent less than three hundred
dollars. The wardrobe trunk you bought her was imitation leather; its lid dropped off the same day. Her
in-laws still sneer at us about it. Anyhow, it was a
very unlucky thing to happen. Three times she's given
birth, but not one baby has lived more than a hundred
days! But you, you scrape together a little cash, running
'black' goods,* and you throw it around any old way!
Carrying on with a slut like that! Heaven might strike
you dead!"

---

* Opium.

The old lady was famous for her nasty disposition, and the Master was a little afraid of her. Besides, now that he thought of it, Miss Ling hardly seemed worth three hundred dollars. She actually wasn't much better than that certain lady he knew right here in town. Regretting the money and smarting from his mother's sharp tongue, the Master took it out on Miss Ling. She had been "Miss" Ling for just two months when she received her first lesson from his fists and feet.

Of course she didn't look the same as when she first came. There was no hairdressing shop in the town, and there certainly was no place to get a permanent wave. Miss Ling's modern curly mop had long since been pressed straight by her pillow. Her hair was now tied together at the back in a bun like a duck's rump. She didn't look any different from any of the town's other girls. Her lipstick was finished, her eyebrow tweezers were broken. You couldn't buy these things in the town, and the Master wouldn't buy them in Shanghai, though he made trips there often. Miss Ling grew less attractive every day, at least she was no longer particularly alluring.

Then the Master discovered something about Miss Ling which made him even more dissatisfied. Two days after the Master beat Miss Ling for the first time, he drank heavily. Although the sun was shining brightly outside, he dallied with her endlessly in their bedroom. Suddenly he noticed faint silvery lines on her abdomen — a telltale sign that a woman has borne a child. The Master was just coming out of a drunken haze. Seeing this sobered him almost completely. He leaped up, flung Miss Ling to the floor and slapped her face twice, hard.

"Stinking whore!" he grated through clenched teeth. "And I thought I was getting the original package! You put on a great show that first night in Shanghai!"

Miss Ling was afraid to utter a word. She wept, muffling her sobs.

When news of this afternoon amorousness reached the old lady's religious ears, the lot of Miss Ling grew harder still. To revile Miss Ling directly or indirectly became the old woman's daily task. At times she worked herself into such a rage that she would forget to observe a Buddhist meat-abstinence day. This would make her even more furious, and she would pound the table and kick over the chairs, cursing Miss Ling till the girl barely dared to breathe. When a weasel stole one of the hens, the old lady blamed that on Miss Ling too. Poking her finger at the girl's face, she swore shrilly.

"Slut! Vixen! Doing those things in broad daylight is a sin! No wonder the weasel got away with our hen! You'll die a horrible death, sinning against the Sun Buddha like that! Shameless hussy!"

2

The Master's business took him to Shanghai at least once a month. Each trip required three days to a week; there was no telling. On these occasions Miss Ling was happier than a condemned man with a last minute reprieve from the axe. Although the old lady's steady stream of abuse was worse than when the Master was at home, at least Miss Ling was freed from those episodes she had grown to fear more and more every day.

The Young Master, about her own age, was as lecherous as his father. Apricot, the little slavey, shivered at the sight of the Young Master like a mouse when it sees a cat. If there was no one else around, the Young Master went after Miss Ling too. He would scratch his finger against the palm of her hand, or pat her face. Miss Ling didn't have the courage to make a row. All she could do was flee, her face crimson. The Young Master would gaze after her, but made no attempt to pursue.

More difficult to cope with was the Master's son-in-law — husband of that daughter the old lady so often mentioned. Just looking at him, the young concubine could tell he was the same kind of rake as the Master. He too addressed her as "Miss" Ling. Even in the presence of an old shrew like the old lady, he had the temerity to pinch the girl's thigh under the table. Miss Ling avoided him in much the same manner as Apricot tried to steer clear of the Young Master.

He had a post of some sort in the local police department. When the Master was away, the son-in-law would become especially diligent about paying his respects to his wife's family. He would call often, with a pistol holster strapped round his waist. Miss Ling knew that the holster contained a gun, and her heart beat fearfully. At times like this she felt that things were better when the Master was at home, and even looked forward to his return.

The town had a "Defence Corps" which the local gentry and landlords had organized, allegedly for protection against "marauding bandits". The Master was the "director" of this corps. Each time he returned with "merchandise" from Shanghai, his "captains" came to

report.   There were two of them, and two pairs of shif-
ty evil eyes would glide over Miss Ling's contours at
every opportunity.

Back from his latest trip, the Master was conferring
with these worthies in his parlour.   Off to one side
were two large packages, wrapped in matting — fruits
of the visit to Shanghai.   The captains had been conferring with him for some time when, abruptly, the
Master became incensed.

"He gets twenty per cent for sitting around doing
nothing, and he's still not satisfied!" he shouted. "So
he wants to make trouble, does he? What kind of fight
can his men put up — those scabby-headed rats! If he
wants to get tough we can get tough too! Tomorrow,
a hundred catties of the stuff is coming on the river
steamer. You fellows be down there and stand guard.
We'll give them a battle if that's what they're after;
they're the ones who are starting this thing! . . . Tomorrow morning, five o'clock! Get up early. It's our public
duty. We shouldn't be afraid of a little trouble!"

"Our men —" one of the captains began hesitantly.

"After we've won," the Master interrupted, "there'll
be an ounce of opium apiece for each and every one!"
His tone was still very angry.

Miss Ling, all ears outside the door, was taken completely unawares when someone came up and pinched
her arm.   She nearly cried out, but caught herself in
time.   The one who had pinched her was the son-in-
law! Lust gleamed in his eyes.   He looked as if he
wanted to swallow her in one gulp. And the Master
was just on the other side of the door! Miss Ling's
heart pounded.

Controlling himself with a visible effort, the son-in-law turned and went into the next room. He conferred in low tones with the Master for several minutes.

"That son of a bitch!" Miss Ling heard the Master explode hoarsely. "We'll take care of him, then! Tomorrow morning, I'll be there too!"

The son-in-law hooted his weird-sounding laugh. It grated on Miss Ling's ears like the cry of an owl.

Until dusk that day, the Master's face was dark iron. He spoke very little. He took his pistol apart, inspected it carefully, put it together again and loaded it. Several times he practised aiming. Miss Ling's legs trembled whenever she had to pass near him. Then, without waiting for dinner, the Master took his gun and went out. There seemed to be a stone pressing in Miss Ling's bosom, and she was growing very frightened.

The old lady sat before a small Buddhist shrine, counting her beads with remarkable rapidity while muttering her prayers. Burning sandalwood in a little bronze urn glowed in front of the shrine.

About eleven that night, the Master finally returned, his face pale and splotchy. His bloodshot eyes looked smaller than usual. His head was steaming with sweat and he reeked of drink. He took out his pistol and thumped it down on the table. With palsied fingers, Miss Ling helped him remove his clothing. Suddenly, laughing boisterously, he grabbed her, lifted her up and tossed her on to the bed. This had often happened before, but this time it was unexpected. Miss Ling couldn't tell what kind of a mood he was in; she lay motionless, not daring to stir. The Master strode up to her and angrily yanked open her garment, the black gleaming pistol clutched in his right hand. Miss Ling went weak with terror. She stared at him, her eyes large and distended. He stripped her, and placed the icy muzzle of the pistol against her breast. Miss Ling was shivering so violently, the whole bed creaked.

"I'll practise on you first," she heard the Master say. "Let's see how good my gun is."

There was a roaring in Miss Ling's ears. Tears coursed down her cheeks.

"Afraid to die, slut? Hah! Don't worry, I still want to play around with you for a while yet!"

Laughing cruelly, the Master flopped into bed, and instantly began to snore, deep in slumber.

Miss Ling huddled to one side of the bed. She was afraid to sleep; she was unable to sleep. If he had only pulled the trigger, she thought, my misery would have been ended, quick and clean. Stealthily she took the pistol, looked at it, then closed her eyes, her heart beating fast. But finally, she put it down again.

Some time after three in the morning, people began beating on the compound gate. The Master raised his head and listened a moment. Picking up his pistol, he ran to the window and pushed it open.

"What are you making such a blasted racket about!" he yelled.

"The men are all here!" a voice replied.

The Master put on the fleece-lined gown, tightened a silk sash around his waist, shoved the pistol into the sash, and hurried out. Miss Ling heard him talking with the crowd outside the gate. He swore savagely, then they all departed.

Miss Ling gazed at the sky. A few scattered stars, one or two frozen grey clouds. She shivered and returned to bed, her mind a blur. I'd better not sleep, she thought as she slipped beneath the covers. But before long she began to doze; her head slid from the back-board down to her shoulder. She dreamed that the Master had shot her. She saw her mother, too. Her mother held her in her arms and cried, her mother cried distractedly. . . . Miss Ling woke with a start. Her mother wasn't there, but someone else was embracing her, murmuring passionately. Her eyes flew open. In the light of the oil lamp burning beside the bed, she saw his face. She blanched.

"Young Master, you —!"

She tried to fight him off. "If you don't go, I'll scream!"

"Go ahead! The old man's gone out to fight the police for opium and the grandmother wouldn't care!" He grappled with her. Although only seventeen, he was much stronger than she.

"You're ruining me. . . ." Miss Ling wept. But finally she let him have his way.

Down the street a loud hubbub of men's voices could be heard approaching. A moment later, thunderous blows began to rain on the compound gate. Miss Ling, terrified, jumped up and ran to lock the bedroom door. The Young Master dashed past her.

"Have you lost your mind?" he demanded. "Wait till I get out of here!" He sped from the room.

Miss Ling hastily put something on, hopped back into bed and pulled the covers over her head. Trembling, she curled herself into a tight ball. There was a tremendous racket going on downstairs. The noise mounted till it was outside the door of the bedroom. She leaped up, took a grip on herself, and opened the door. Five or six men were waiting there, including the Master and his son-in-law.

Two men were carrying the Master. His gown was opened at the chest. The white fleece lining was stained with blood. After putting him on the bed, the others went away, leaving only the son-in-law and one of the captains. The Master was bellowing like an injured bull. The captain looked at his wound, then said to the son-in-law:

"I don't think that wound can be treated here in town. It's queer, him getting shot like that. They were all in front of us, but he was hit from the side. Very strange. And that was no stray bullet. Whoever shot him was aiming for him! Anyhow, we did a fine job on that dog of a police chief!"

From the edge of the bed, Miss Ling saw the son-in-law standing behind the captain. He was concealing a grin.

Downstairs, the old lady could be heard throwing around and cursing.

"It's retribution! Offending against the Sun Buddha! All because of that stinking baggage! I knew she was bad luck the day she came in the door! He doesn't need any doctor; just kill that dirty bitch and he'll get well! Kill her!"

3

Before mid-morning the townspeople were animatedly discussing the ferocity of the robbers. The president of the Chamber of Commerce reported the affair by long-distance telephone to the county authorities. He stated that the chief of police had been killed while "apprehending the criminals" and that the director of the Defence Corps, in the course of "assisting with the arrest", had been severely wounded. Relaying the report to the provincial government, the county converted the robbers into bandits, "between two and three hundred, all heavily armed, who came without warning and quickly disappeared after commission of the offence". On the basis of this information, the provincial authorities sent a company of troops to "eradicate" the bandits.

The day the troops arrived, they marched down the main street. Miss Ling saw them. She didn't know whether they had come to help the Master or to help his son-in-law. For somehow she was positive that it was the son-in-law who had shot the Master. But she kept this conviction to herself, not even mentioning it to the Young Master.

The Master's wound gradually healed. A tiny piece of bullet was still imbedded in his flesh, but the wound had closed. Miss Ling feared that he would soon be completely well and force himself on her again. All too familiar with his lecherous appetite, she was truly afraid.

She privately begged the Young Master to think of a way to rescue her. He only laughed and said there was nothing he could do.

A few days later, and the Master was able to get up and walk around. Miss Ling was so worried she couldn't eat.

But the Master seemed to have something on his mind. He didn't bother much with Miss Ling. One of the captains came frequently to confer. They talked in low tones, the Master frowning continuously. Once, when Miss Ling was serving the Master some bird's-nest soup, she heard the captain say:

"Every day the Chamber of Commerce has to feed them thirty banquet dinners. This has been going on for more than half a month now. It's cost the chamber over two thousand silver dollars. The president of the chamber wants them to leave right away, but the commander of the troops says he was sent here to wipe out the bandits; unless he has a battle with them, he can't go back and report 'mission completed'."

"The hell with his 'mission completed'!" fumed the Master, but his frown deepened.

After a pause, the captain whispered something in his ear. The Master bounded to his feet.

"What!" he yelled. "We gave them thirty ounces of opium yesterday and today they want more? The crooks!"

"That's not the worst of it — they're hijacking us! When our men go out to make deliveries to our big customers, they hold us up on the road and steal our stuff. They've only been here half a month, but they know all the ropes!"

"It's an outrage!" The Master pounded his fist on the table. Veins stood out on his forehead like little fingers.

Miss Ling was as terrified as if the Master again wanted to take his gun and shoot her.

"If they stay another half month, we'll be out of business! You've got to think of something, fast!"

The captain heaved a sigh. The Master sighed too. Then they whispered together for a long time. Miss Ling could see a somewhat happier expression on the Master's face. He kept nodding his head.

"Don't worry about a thing, Your Worship. We'll disguise ourselves well," the captain assured the Master as he was leaving. "There won't be any slip-ups! That village northwest of here will be best. The peasants there have still got a little grain and things left. We might as well 'subsidize' the trip while we're at it."

"Tell our scouts to look sharp. The moment they report that the troops have set out from town, you all get out of there. We don't want a real clash with those soldiers. We'll be the joke of the town if we're exposed!"

After the captain had departed, the Master sat wrapped in thought, looking very serious. Then he dispatched a servant to bring his son-in-law. When she heard the word "son-in-law", Miss Ling felt very uneasy. She was dying to tell her suspicions to the Master, but in the end she said nothing and concentrated on staying out of the way.

The son-in-law talked with the Master for a while, rose and left quickly. He bumped into Miss Ling at the door and smirked at her, revealing big teeth in a wolfish grin. Her hair stood on end. She recoiled from him as from a poisonous snake.

In the evening at dinner, the Master began drinking. Miss Ling's heart became more troubled with each cup she poured him. She had a feeling that tonight was going to be bad. But oddly enough, besides drinking, the Master displayed no other inclinations. He drank from a small cup, sipping slowly and genteelly, putting it down from time to time and listening. At about nine, there was the sound of running feet in the street outside; someone was shouting commands. Obviously very concerned, the Master stopped drinking and lay down on the bed. He directed Miss Ling to knead his legs.

After another interval, rifles began popping in the distance. The Master jumped up and ran to the window. A patch of fire was gleaming to the northwest. The Master watched for a few minutes, then filled himself a big bowl of wine and drank it down. Wagging his head with satisfaction, he stretched forward his two arms. Miss Ling knew this was his signal to be undressed, and she trembled inwardly.

To her surprise, after having her knead his legs a little longer, the Master went to sleep.

The next morning in the kitchen Miss Ling heard the water vendor say that bandits had attacked the village to the northwest the previous night. The troops had fought the raiders for hours and captured many peasants who were in league with them, as well as one wounded bandit. He was now locked up in the police station.

In the front room, the old lady was throwing another tantrum.

"That's what he gets for losing his head over a witch! Now he quarrels with his son-in-law! Anybody who sins against the Sun Buddha. . ."

Carrying a bowl of lotus-seed broth upstairs, Miss Ling could hear the angry voices of the Master and his son-in-law. Just as she reached the door of the room, she heard the Master snarl:

"You're crazy! You dare to talk to me like that!"

"Didn't you get enough that last time you were shot?" hissed the son-in-law. He laughed coldly in a way that sent shivers up Miss Ling's spine.

Though her heart was thumping, she entered the

room. There was a gleaming black pistol in the son-in-law's hand and it was pointing at the Master.   Miss Ling's legs turned to water. Her blood seemed to congeal in her veins.

"Kill me? Hah!" snorted the Master. "Just try, and —"

Bang!

At the sound, Miss Ling collapsed beside the door, her eyes staring. She saw the distorted evil face of the son-in-law as he stepped across her body and went out. Everything faded into darkness after that.

4

It was the Master who had been shot, not Miss Ling. But she became ill, delirious. For two days she ran a high temperature. Her face was brick-red as if she had been drinking heavily, her eyes glassy. She ate nothing. At times she raved unintelligible gibberish. On the third day she was somewhat better, but quite weak.   She felt dizzy, and slept most of the afternoon. Near dark, she awoke with a start, very thirsty. She saw Apricot, the little slavey, leaning over the window sill, looking out. Miss Ling couldn't understand why she was lying in bed; of the recent incident, she remembered nothing. She tried to sit up, but she didn't have the strength.

"Apricot," she said weakly, "what are you looking at? If the Master catches you there, he'll beat you!" She was feeling rather hungry.

The little slavey turned around and grinned at her.

"The Master's dead!" Apricot said with an impish laugh. "See — he was lying right there, blood all over the place!"

Miss Ling shivered. She remembered now. Again her heart beat fast, again her eyes blurred, again she drifted into a vague dream world. She saw the Master poking her breast with the pistol muzzle, she saw his son-in-law take murderous aim at the Master. Last of all, she saw a face — a face with cruelly twisting brows — looking at her avidly. It was the son-in-law! She thought she screamed, but the sound she heard seemed to be coming from the other side of a thick wall. A heavy weight was crushing her bosom. Again she sank into unconsciousness. . . .

When she awoke this time, Miss Ling was sure she was dead. The lamp had already been lit and a man's shadow fell across the bed. Miss Ling recognized the Young Master, standing at her bedside, his back to the lamp. He was leaning very close.

"Am I dead?" she moaned.

"It isn't that easy to die!"

"I ache all over. I think . . . your brother-in-law. . . ."

"He just left. I used a trick to get him out."

"You're a smart little imp!" She let the Young Master kiss her cheek. She was quite hungry.

The Young Master said that his brother-in-law had taken over the post of director of the Defence Corps. He was running everything at home too. Miss Ling was stunned. She asked hesitantly:

"Do you know how the Master died?"

"The old man was careless and shot himself while cleaning his pistol."

"Who says so?"

"My brother-in-law says so, and so does grandmother. She says the old man sinned against the Sun

Buddha, so the spirits made his mind wander and he shot himself. She says you sinned against the Sun Buddha too, and after he died, the old man called you before the king of the underworld to testify. That's why you've been dead for the past couple of days."

Abstractedly, Miss Ling considered this for several minutes, then she shook her head. She put her mouth close to the Young Master's ear.

"It's not like that! The Master didn't kill himself! Now don't tell this to anybody. I saw it with my own eyes — your brother-in-law shot him dead!"

The Young Master gazed at her, only half convinced. "Who cares how he died," he said indifferently. "He's dead, and that's the end of it!"

"Ah, I know your brother-in-law, sooner or later, is going to kill you too! And my turn will also come."

The Young Master said nothing. With a slight frown, he gazed at her searchingly.

"Some day he'll kill us both. If he ever finds out that you and I. . . ." Miss Ling sighed.

Unable to think of any reply, the Young Master lowered his head. She gave him a little shove.

"Don't hang around here. He'll be coming back soon!"

"That's what you think! He took office today. Tonight they're giving him a big feed at the house of that fancy lady in town. A fat chance of him coming back!"

"Bite your tongue — smarty!" Miss Ling murmured. She was too weary to say any more.

The Young Master was a little afraid. After fooling around for a short time, he got up and went away. Miss Ling fell into a deep slumber. She had no idea how long she had been sleeping when someone shook her awake. Voices clamoured on the street; close by, rifles were popping like firecrackers on New Year's Eve. The Young Master, very frightened, was pulling Miss Ling out of bed.

"Real bandits have come!" he cried hysterically. "You hear? They're shooting! They're fighting at the west gate!"

Miss Ling was too terrified to speak. Through the window she could see the slanting rays of the setting sun shining golden in a corner of the courtyard. While the Young Master was urging her to get dressed, he reported breathlessly:

"That day the old man sent his men to the village to the northwest, they robbed and set houses on fire. Then the troops grabbed a lot of the villagers and said they were bandits. Well, now real bandits have come, and the villagers who were falsely accused have joined them! They want to kill our whole family —"

Fierce yells from the street drowned out the rest of his words. Shops quickly put up their shutters. The Young Master left Miss Ling and ran downstairs. Her legs shaking, she stood by the window that looked on to the street. The troops were running in disorder, looting the unboarded shops as they retreated. Bang! Bang! They fired crazily against the shutters of the closed shops. Miss Ling's legs collapsed beneath her. She sat down weakly on the floor. Just then, the Young Master came running back and pulled her to her feet.

"Bandits . . . fought their way into the town!" he panted. "Brother-in-law . . . killed!"

They hurried down the stairs. The old lady was on

her knees, kowtowing before the small shrine. Ignoring her, the Young Master dragged Miss Ling through the back door as fast as she could travel. Where are we going? Miss Ling kept wondering. She thought of her mother in Shanghai, and tears ran down her ashen cheeks.

Suddenly, there were many short whistling sounds. The Young Master was hit by a stray bullet; he fell like a log, pulling Miss Ling down with him. As she crawled closer and looked at him another wild shot went through her chest. Her face twitched. Without a sound, she sprawled on her back and moved no more. The corners of her lips seemed to curl with laughter — and with hatred.

Black smoke rose from the house they had just left. There was a burst of flame. Sparks flew in all directions.

February 29, 1932

Translated by Sidney Shapiro

The Shop of the Lin Family

MISS Lin's small mouth was pouting when she returned home from school that day. She flung down her
books, and instead of combing her hair and powdering
her nose before the mirror as usual, she stretched out
on the bed. Her eyes staring at the top of the bed
canopy, Miss Lin lay lost in thought. Her little cat
leaped up beside her, snuggled against her waist and
miaowed twice. Automatically, she patted his head,
then rolled over and buried her face in the pillow.

"Ma!" called Miss Lin.

No answer. Ma, whose room was right next door,
ordinarily doted on this only daughter of hers. On
hearing her return, Ma would come swaying in to ask
whether she was hungry. Ma would be keeping something good for her. Or she might send the maid out to
buy a bowl of hot soup with meat dumplings from a
street vendor. . . . But today was odd. There obviously were people talking in Ma's room — Miss Lin
could hear Ma hiccuping too — yet Ma didn't even
reply.

Again Miss Lin rolled over on the bed, and raised
her head. She would eavesdrop on this conversation.
Whom could Ma be talking to, that voices had to be
kept so low?

But she couldn't make out what they were saying.
Only Ma's continuous hiccups wafted intermittently to

Miss Lin's ears. Suddenly, Ma's voice rose, as if she were angry, and a few words came through quite clearly:

"— These are Japanese goods, those are Japanese goods, hic! . . ."

Miss Lin started. She prickled all over, like when she was having a hair-cut and the tiny shorn hairs stuck to her neck. She had come home annoyed just because they had laughed at her and scolded her at school over Japanese goods. She swept aside the little cat nestled against her, jumped up and stripped off her new azure rayon dress lined with camel's wool. She shook it out a couple of times, and sighed. Miss Lin had heard this charming frock was made of Japanese material. She tossed it aside and pulled that cute cowhide case out from under the bed. Almost spitefully, she flipped the cover open, and turning the case upside down, dumped its contents on the bed. A rainbow of brightly colour-ed dresses and knick-knacks rolled and spread. The little cat leaped to the floor, whirled and jumped up on a chair, where he crouched and looked at his mistress in astonishment.

Miss Lin sorted through the pile of clothes, then stood, abstracted, beside the bed. The more she examined her belongings, the more she adored them — and the more they looked like Japanese goods! Couldn't she wear any of them? She hated to part with them — besides, her father wouldn't necessarily be willing to have new ones made for her! Miss Lin's eyes began to smart. She loved these Japanese things, while she hated the Japanese aggressors who invaded the north-east provinces. If not for that, she could wear Jap-anese merchandise and no one would say a word.

"Hic —"

The sound came through the door, followed by the thin swaying body of Mrs Lin. The sight of the heap of clothing on the bed, and her daughter, bemused, standing in only her brief woollen underwear, was more than a little shock. As her excitement increased, the tempo of Mrs Lin's hiccups grew in proportion. For the moment, she was unable to speak. Miss Lin, grief written all over her face, flew to her mother. "Ma! They're all Japanese goods. What am I going to wear tomorrow?"

Hiccuping, Mrs Lin shook her head. With one hand she supported herself on her daughter's shoulder, with the other she kneaded her own chest. After a while, she managed to force out a few sentences.

"Child — hic — why have you taken off — hic — all your clothes? The weather's cold — hic — This trouble of mine — hic — began the year you were born. Hic — lately it's getting worse! Hic —"

"Ma, tell me what am I going to wear tomorrow? I'll just hide in the house and not go out! They'll laugh at me, swear at me!"

Mrs Lin didn't answer. Hiccuping steadily, she walked over to the bed, picked the new azure dress out of the pile, and draped it over her daughter. Then she patted the bed in invitation for Miss Lin to sit down. The little cat returned to beside the girl's legs. Cocking his head, with narrowed eyes he looked first at Mrs Lin, then at her daughter. Lazily, he rolled over and rubbed his belly against the soles of the girl's shoes. Miss Lin kicked him away and reclined sideways on the bed, with her head hidden behind her mother's back.

Neither of them spoke for a while. Mrs Lin was busy hiccuping; her daughter was busy calculating "how to go out tomorrow". The problem of Japanese goods not only affected everything Miss Lin wore — it influenced everything she used. Even the powder compact which her fellow students so admired and her automatic pencil were probably made in Japan. And she was crazy about those little gadgets!

"Child — hic — are you hungry?"

After sitting quietly for some time, Mrs Lin gradually controlled her hiccups, and began her usual doting routine.

"No. Ma, why do you always ask me if I'm hungry? The most important thing is that I have no clothes. How can I go to school tomorrow?" the girl demanded petulantly. She was still curled up on the bed, her face still buried behind her mother.

From the start, Mrs Lin hadn't understood why her daughter kept complaining that she had no clothes to wear. This was the third time and she couldn't ignore the remark any longer, but those damned hiccups most irritatingly started up again. Just then, Mr Lin came in. He was holding a sheet of paper in his hand; his face was ashen. He saw his wife struggling with continuous agitated hiccups, his daughter lying on the clothing-strewn bed, and he could guess pretty well what was wrong. His brows drew together in a frown.

"Do you have an Anti-Japanese-Invasion Society in your school, Xiu?" he asked. "This letter just came. It says that if you wear clothes made of Japanese material again tomorrow, they're going to burn them! Of all the wild lawless things to say!"

"Hic — hic!"

"What nonsense! Everyone has something made in Japan on him. But they have to pick on our family to make trouble! There isn't a shop carrying foreign goods that isn't full of Japanese stuff. But they have to make our shop the culprit. They insist on locking up our stocks! Huh!"

"Hic — hic — Goddess Guanyin protect and preserve us! Hic —"

"Papa, I've got an old style padded jacket. It's probably not made of Japanese material, but if I wear it they'll all laugh at me, it's so out of date," said Miss Lin, sitting up on the bed. She had been thinking of going a step farther and asking Mr Lin to have a dress made for her out of non-Japanese cloth, but his expression decided her against such a rash move. Still, picturing the jeers her old padded jacket would evoke, she couldn't restrain her tears.

"Hic — hic — child! — Hic — don't cry — no one will laugh at you — hic — child. . . ."

"Xiu, you don't have to go to school tomorrow! We soon won't have anything to eat; how can we spend money on schools!" Mr Lin was exasperated. He ripped up the letter and strode, sighing, from the room. Before long, he came hurrying back.

"Where's the key to the cabinet? Give it to me!" he demanded of his wife.

Mrs Lin turned pale and stared at him. Her eternal hiccups were momentarily stilled.

"There's no help for it. We'll have to make an offering to those straying demons —" Mr Lin paused to heave a sigh. "It'll cost me four hundred at most. If the Kuomintang local branch thinks it's not enough, I'll quit doing business. Let them lock up the stocks!

That shop opposite has more Japanese goods than I. They've made an investment of over ten thousand dollars. They paid out only five hundred, and they're going along without a bit of trouble. Five hundred dollars! Just mark it off as a couple of bad debts! — The key! That gold necklace ought to bring about three hundred. . . ."

"Hic — hic — really, like a gang of robbers!" Mrs Lin produced the key with a trembling hand. Tears streamed down her face. Miss Lin, however, did not cry. She was looking into space with misty eyes, recalling that Kuomintang committeeman who had made a speech at her school, a hateful swarthy pockmarked fellow who stared at her like a hungry dog. She could picture him grasping the gold necklace and jumping for joy, his big mouth open in a laugh. Then she visualized the ugly bandit quarrelling with her father, hitting him. . . .

"Aiya!" Miss Lin gave a frightened scream and threw herself on her mother's bosom. Mrs Lin was so startled she had no time for hiccups.

"Child, hic — don't cry," Mrs Lin made a desperate effort to speak. "After New Year your papa will have money. We'll make a new dress for you, hic — Those black-hearted crooks! They all insist we have money. Hic — we lose more every year. Your papa was in the fertilizer business, and he lost money, hic — Every penny invested in the shop belongs to other people. Child, hic, hic — this sickness of mine; it makes life hell — hic — In another two years when you're nineteen, we'll find you a good husband. Hic — then I can die in peace! Save us from our adversity, Goddess Guanyin! Hic —"

The following day, Mr Lin's shop underwent a transformation. All the Japanese goods he hadn't dared to show for the past week, now were the most prominently displayed. In imitation of the big Shanghai stores, Mr Lin inscribed many slips of coloured paper with the words "Big Sale 10% Discount!" and pasted them on his windows. Just seven days before New Year, this was the "rush season" of the shops selling imported goods in the towns and villages. Not only was there hope of earning back Mr Lin's special expenditure of four hundred dollars; Miss Lin's new dress depended on the amount of business done in the next few days.

A little past ten in the morning, groups of peasants who had come into town to sell their produce in the market began drifting along the street. Carrying baskets on their arms, leading small children, they chatted loudly and vigorously as they strolled. They stopped to look at the red and green blurbs pasted on Mr Lin's windows and called attention to them, women shouting to their husbands, children yelling to their parents, clucking their tongues in admiration over the goods on display in the shop windows. It would soon be New Year. Children were wishing for a pair of new socks. Women remembered that the family washbasin had been broken for some time. The single washcloth used by the entire family had been bought half a year ago, and now was an old rag. They had run out of soap more than a month before. They ought to take advantage of this "Sale" and buy a few things.

Mr Lin sat in the cashier's cage, marshalling all his

energies, a broad smile plastered on his face. He watched the peasants, while keeping an eye on his two salesmen and two apprentices. With all his heart he hoped to see his merchandise start moving out and the silver dollars begin rolling in.

But these peasants, after looking a while, after pointing and gesticulating appreciatively a while, ambled over to the store across the street to stand and look some more. Craning his neck, Mr Lin glared at the backs of the group of peasants, and sparks shot from his eyes. He wanted to go over and drag them back!

"Hic — hic —"

Behind the cashier's cage were swinging doors which separated the shop itself from the "inner sanctum". Beside these doors sat Mrs Lin releasing hiccups that she had long been suppressing with difficulty. Miss Lin was seated beside her. Entranced, the girl watched the street silently, her heart pounding. At least half of her new dress had just walked away.

Mr Lin strode quickly to the front of the counter. He glared jealously at the shop opposite. Its five salesmen were waiting expectantly behind the counter. But not one peasant entered the store. They looked for a while, then continued on their way. Mr Lin relaxed; he couldn't help grinning at the salesmen across the street. Another group of seven or eight peasants stopped before Mr Lin's shop. A youngster among them actually came a step forward. With his head cocked to one side, he examined the imported umbrellas. Mr Lin whirled around, his face breaking into a happy smile. He went to work personally on this prospective customer.

"Would you like a foreign umbrella, brother? They're

cheap. You only pay ninety cents on the dollar. Come and take a look."

A salesman had already taken down two or three imported umbrellas. He promptly opened one and shoved it earnestly into the young peasant's hand. Summoning all his zeal, the salesman launched into a high powered patter:

"Just look at this, young master! Foreign satin cloth, solid ribs. It's durable and handsome for rainy days or clear. Ninety cents each. They don't come any cheaper. . . . Across the street, they're a dollar apiece, but they're not as good as these. You can compare them and see why."

The young peasant held the umbrella and stood undecided, with his mouth open. He turned towards a man in his fifties and weighed the umbrella in his hand as if to ask "Shall I buy it?" The older man became very upset and began to shout at him.

"You're crazy! Buying an umbrella! We only got three dollars for the whole boatload of firewood, and your mother's waiting at home for us to bring back some rice. How can you spend money on an umbrella!"

"It's cheap, but we can't afford it!" sighed the peasants standing around watching. They walked slowly away. The young peasant, his face brick red, shook his head. He put down the umbrella and started to leave. Mr Lin was frantic. He quickly gave ground.

"How much do you say, brother? Take another look. It's fine merchandise!"

"It is cheap. But we don't have enough money," the older peasant replied, pulling his son. They practically ran away.

Bitterly, Mr Lin returned to the cashier's cage,

feeling weak all over. He knew it wasn't that he was an inept businessman. The peasants simply were too poor. They couldn't even spend ninety cents on an umbrella. He stole a glance at the shop across the way. There too people were looking, but no one was going in. In front of the neighbouring grocery store and the cookie shop, no one was even looking. Group after group of the country folk walked by carrying baskets. But the baskets were all empty. Occasionally, someone appeared with a homespun flowered blue cloth sack, filled with rice, from the look of it. The late rice which the peasants had harvested more than a month before had long since been squeezed out as rent for the landlords and interest for the usurers. Now in order to have rice to eat, the peasants were forced to buy a measure or two at a time, at steep prices.

All this Mr Lin knew. He felt that at least part of his business was being indirectly eaten away by the usurers and landlords.

The hour gradually neared noon. There were very few peasants on the street now. Mr Lin's shop had done a little over one dollar's worth of business, just enough to cover the cost of the "Big Sale 10% Discount" strips of red and green paper. Despondently, Mr Lin entered the "inner sanctum". He barely had the courage to face his wife and daughter. Miss Lin's eyes were filled with tears. She sat in the corner with her head down. Mrs Lin was in the middle of a string of hiccups. Struggling for control, she addressed her husband.

"We laid out four hundred dollars — and spent all night getting things ready in the shop — hic! We got permission to sell the Japanese goods, but business is

dead — hic — my blessed ancestors! . . . The maid
wants her wages —"

"It's only half a day. Don't worry." Mr Lin forced
a comforting note into his voice, but he felt worse than
if a knife were cutting through his heart. Gloomily,
he paced back and forth. He thought of all the business promotion tricks he knew, but none of them seemed any good. Business was bad. It had been bad in
all lines for some time; his shop wasn't the only one
having difficulty. People were poor, and there wasn't
anything that could be done about it. Still, he hoped
business would be better in the afternoon. The local
townspeople usually did their buying then. Surely
they would buy things for New Year! If only they
wanted to buy, Mr Lin's shop was certain of trade.
After all, his merchandise was cheaper than other
shops!

It was this hope that enabled Mr Lin to bolster his
sagging spirits as he sat in the cashier's cage awaiting
the customers he pictured coming in the afternoon.

And the afternoon proved to be different indeed
from the morning. There weren't many people on the
street, but Mr Lin knew nearly every one of them. He
knew their names, or the names of their fathers
or grandfathers. These were local townspeople, and
as they chatted and walked slowly past his shop, Mr
Lin's eyes, glowing with cordiality, welcomed them, and
sent them on their way. At times, with a broad smile
he greeted an old customer.

"Ah, brother, going out to the tea-house? Our little shop has slashed its prices. Favour us with a small
purchase!"

Sometimes, the man would actually stop and come

into the shop.   Then Mr Lin and his assistants would
plunge into a frenzy of activity.   With acute sensitive-
ness, they would watch the eyes of the unpredictable
customer.   The moment his eyes rested on a piece of
merchandise, the salesmen would swiftly produce one
just like it and invite the customer to examine it.   Miss
Lin watched from beside the swinging doors, and her
father frequently called her out to respectfully greet the
unpredictable customer as "Uncle".   An apprentice
would serve him a glass of tea and offer him a good
cigarette.

On the question of price, Mr Lin was exceptionally
flexible.   When a customer was firm about knocking off
a few odd cents from the round figure of his purchase
price, Mr Lin would take the abacus from the hands
of his salesman and calculate personally.   Then, with
the air of a man who has been driven to the wall, he
would deduct the few odd cents from the total bill.

"We'll take a loss on this sale," he would say with
a wry smile.   "But you're an old customer.   We have
to please you.   Come and buy some more things soon!"

The entire afternoon was spent in this manner.   Including cash and credit, big purchases and small, the
shop made a total of over ten sales.   Mr Lin was
drenched with perspiration, and although he was worn
out, he was very happy.   He had been sneaking looks
at the shop across the street.   They didn't seem to be
nearly so busy.   There was a pleased expression on the
face of Miss Lin, who had been constantly watching
from beside the swinging doors.   Mrs Lin even jerked
out a few less hiccups.

Shortly before dark, Mr Lin finished adding up his
accounts for the day.   The morning amounted to zero;

in the afternoon they had sold sixteen dollars and eighty-five cents worth of merchandise, eight dollars of it being on credit. Mr Lin smiled slightly, then he frowned. He had been selling all his goods at their original cost. He hadn't even covered his expenses for the day, to say nothing of making any profit. His mind was blank for a moment. Then he took out his account books and calculated in them for a long time. On the "credit" side there was a total of over thirteen hundred dollars of uncollected debts — more than six hundred in town and over seven hundred in the countryside. But the "debit" ledger showed a figure of eight hundred dollars owed to the big Shanghai wholesale house alone. He owed a total of not less than two thousand dollars!

Mr Lin sighed softly. If business continued to be so bad, it was going to be a little difficult for him to get through New Year. He looked at the red and green paper slips on the window announcing "Big Sale 10% Discount". If we really cut prices like we did today, business ought to pick up, he thought to himself. We're not making any profit, but if we don't do any business I still have to pay expenses anyway. The main thing is to get the customers to come in, then I can gradually raise my prices. . . . If we can do some wholesale business in the countryside, that will be even better! . . .

Suddenly, someone broke in on Mr Lin's sweet dream. A shaky old lady entered the shop carrying a little bundle wrapped in blue cloth. Mr Lin yanked up his head to find her confronting him. He wanted to escape, but there was no time. He could only go forward and greet her.

"Ah, Mrs Zhu, out buying things for the New Year?

Please come into the back room and sit down.   Xiu,
give Mrs Zhu your arm."

But Miss Lin didn't hear.   She had left the swinging doors some time ago.   Mrs Zhu waved her hand in
refusal and sat down on a chair in the store.   Solemnly, she unwrapped the blue cloth and brought out a
small account book.   With two trembling hands she
presented the book under Mr Lin's nose.   Twisting her
withered lips, she was about to speak, but Mr Lin had
already taken the book and was hastening to say:

"I understand.   I'll send it to your house tomorrow."

"Mm, mm, the tenth month, the eleventh month, the
twelfth month; altogether three months.   Three threes
are nine; that's nine dollars, isn't it? — you'll send the
money tomorrow?   Mm, mm, you don't have to send
it.   I'll take it back with me!   Eh!"

The words seemed to come with difficulty from Mrs
Zhu's withered mouth.   She had three hundred dollars
loaned to Mr Lin's shop, and was entitled to three
dollars interest every month.   Mr Lin had delayed payment for three months, promising to pay in full at the
end of the year.   Now, she needed some money to buy
gifts for tomorrow's Kitchen God Festival, and so she
had come seeking Mr Lin.   From the forcefulness with
which she moved her puckered mouth, Mr Lin could
tell that she was determined not to leave without the
money.

Mr Lin scratched his head in silence.   He hadn't
been deliberately refusing to pay the interest.   It was
just that for the past three months business had been
poor.   Their daily sales had been barely enough to
cover their food and taxes.   He had delayed paying her
unconsciously.   But if he didn't pay her today, the old

lady might raise a row in the shop. That would be too shameful and would seriously influence the shop's future.

"All right, all right. Take it back with you!" Mr Lin finally said in exasperation. His voice shook a little. He rushed to the cashier's cage and gathered together all the cash that had been taken in that morning and afternoon. To that he added twenty cents from his own pocket, and presented the whole collection of dollars, pennies and dimes to the old lady. She carefully counted the lot over and over again, then with trembling hands wrapped the money in the blue cloth. Mr Lin couldn't repress a sigh. He had a wild desire to snatch back a part of the cash.

"That blue handkerchief is too worn, Mrs Zhu," he said with a forced laugh. "Why not buy a good white linen one? We've also got top quality wash-cloths and soap. Take some to use over the New Year. Prices are reasonable!"

"No. I don't want any. An old lady like me doesn't need that kind of thing." She waved her hand in refusal. She put her account book in her pocket and departed, firmly grasping the blue cloth bundle.

Looking sour, Mr Lin walked into the "inner sanctum". Mrs Zhu's visit reminded him that he had two other creditors. Old Chen and Widow Zhang had put up two hundred and one hundred and fifty dollars respectively. He would have to pay them a total of ten dollars interest. He couldn't very well delay their money; in fact, he would have to pay them ahead of time. He counted on his fingers — twenty-fourth, twenty-fifth, twenty-sixth. By the twenty-sixth, he ought to be able to collect all the outstanding debts in the countryside. His clerk Shousheng had gone off on a collection trip the day before yesterday. He should be back by the twenty-sixth at the latest. The unpaid bills in town couldn't be collected till the twenty-eighth or twenty-ninth. But the collector from the Shanghai wholesale house to which Mr Lin owed money would probably come tomorrow or the day after. Lin's only alternative was to borrow more from the local bank. And how would business be tomorrow? . . .

His head down, Mr Lin paced back and forth, thinking. The voice of his daughter spoke into his ear:

"Papa, what do you think of this piece of silk? Four dollars and twenty cents for seven feet. That's not expensive, is it?"

Mr Lin's heart gave a leap. He stood stock-still and glared, speechless. Miss Lin held the piece of silk in her hand and giggled. Four dollars and twenty cents! It wasn't a big sum, but the shop only did sixteen dollars' worth of business all day, and really at cost price! Mr Lin stood frozen, then asked weakly:

"Where did you get the money?"

"I put it on the books."

Another debit. Mr Lin scowled. But he had spoiled his daughter himself, and Mrs Lin would take the girl's side no matter what the case might be. He smiled a helpless bitter smile. Then he sighed.

"You're always in such a rush," he said, slightly reproving. "Why couldn't you wait till after New Year!"

3

Another two days went by. Business was indeed very brisk in Mr Lin's shop, with its "Big Sale". They did over thirty dollars in sales every day. The hiccups of Mrs Lin diminished considerably; she hiccuped on the average of only once every five minutes. Miss Lin skipped up and back between the shop and the "inner sanctum", her face flushed and smiling. At times she even helped with the selling. Only after her mother called her repeatedly, did she return to the back room. Mopping her brow, she protested excitedly.

"Ma, why have you called me back again? It's not hard work! Ma, Papa's so tired he's soaking wet; his voice is gone! — A customer just made a five-dollar purchase! Ma, you don't have to be afraid it's too tiring for me! Don't worry! Papa told me to rest a while, then come out again!"

Mrs Lin only nodded her head and hiccuped, followed by a murmur that "Buddha is merciful and kind". A porcelain image of the Goddess Guanyin was enshrined in the "inner sanctum", with a stick of incense burning before it. Mrs Lin swayed over to the shrine and kowtowed. She thanked the Goddess for her protection and prayed for her blessing on a number of matters — that Mr Lin's business should always be good, that Miss Lin should grow nicely, that next year the girl should get a good husband.

But out in the shop, although Mr Lin was devoting his whole being to business, though a smile never left his face, he felt as if his heart were bound with strings. Watching the satisfied customer going out with a package under his arm, Mr Lin suffered a pang with every dollar he took in, as the abacus in his mind clicked a five per cent loss off the cost price he had raised through sweat and blood. Several times he tried to estimate the loss as being three per cent, but no matter how he figured it, he still was losing five cents on the dollar. Although business was good, the more he sold the worse he felt. As he waited on the customers, the conflict raging within his breast at times made him nearly faint. When he stole glances at the shop across the street, he had the impression that the owner and salesmen were sneering at him from behind their counters. Look at that fool Lin! they seemed to be saying. He really *is* selling below cost! Wait and see! The more business he does, the more he loses! The sooner he'll have to close down!

Mr Lin gnawed his lips. He vowed he would raise his prices the next day. He would charge first-grade prices for second-rate merchandise.

The head of the Merchants Guild came by. It was he who had interceded with the Kuomintang chieftains for Mr Lin on the question of selling Japanese goods. Now he smiled and congratulated Mr Lin, and clapped him on the shoulder.

"How goes it? That four hundred dollars was well spent!" he said softly. "But you'd better give a small token to Kuomintang Party Commissioner Pu too. Otherwise, he may become annoyed and try to squeeze you. When business is good, plenty of people are jealous. Even if Commissioner Pu doesn't have any 'ideas', they'll try to stir him up!"

Mr Lin thanked the head of the Merchants Guild for his concern. Inwardly, he was very alarmed. He almost lost his zest for doing business.

What made him most uneasy was that his assistant Shousheng still hadn't returned from the bill collecting trip. He needed the money to pay off his account with the big Shanghai wholesale house. The collector had arrived from Shanghai two days before, and was pressing Mr Lin hard. If Shousheng didn't come soon, Mr Lin would have to borrow from the local bank. This would mean an additional burden of fifty or sixty dollars in interest payments. To Mr Lin, losing money every day, this prospect was more painful than being flayed alive.

At about four p.m., Mr Lin suddenly heard a noisy uproar on the street. People looked very frightened, as though some serious calamity had happened. Mr Lin, who could think only of whether Shousheng would safely return, was sure that the river boat on which Shousheng would come back had been set upon by pirates. His heart pounding, he hailed a passer-by and asked worriedly:

"What's wrong? Did pirates get the boat from Lishi?"

"Oh! So it's pirates again? Travelling is really too dangerous! Robbing is nothing. Men are even kidnapped right off the boat!" babbled the passer-by, a well-known loafer named Lu. He eyed the brightly coloured goods in the shop.

Mr Lin could make no sense out of this at all. His worry increased and he dropped Lu to accost Wang, the next person who came along.

"Is it true that the boat from Lishi was robbed?"

"It must be Ah Shu's gang that did it. Ah Shu has been shot, but his gang is still a tough bunch!" Wang replied without slackening his pace.

Cold sweat bedewed Mr Lin's forehead. He was frantic. He was sure that Shousheng was coming back today, and from Lishi. That was the last place on the account book list. Now it was already four o'clock, but there was no sign of Shousheng. After what Wang had said, how could Mr Lin have any doubts? He forgot that he himself had invented the story of the boat being robbed. His whole face beaded with perspiration, he rushed into the "inner sanctum". Going through the swinging doors, he tripped over the threshold and nearly fell.

"Papa, they're fighting in Shanghai! The Japanese bombed the Zhabei section!" cried Miss Lin, running up to him.

Mr Lin stopped short. What was all this about fighting in Shanghai? His first reaction was that it had nothing to do with him. But since it involved the "Japanese", he thought he had better inquire a little further. Looking at his daughter's agitated face, he asked:

"The Japanese bombed it? Who told you that?"

"Everyone on the street is talking about it. The Japanese soldiers fired heavy artillery and they bombed. Zhabei is burned to the ground!"

"Oh, well, did anyone say that the boat from Lishi was robbed?"

Miss Lin shook her head, then fluttered from the room like a moth. Mr Lin hesitated beside the swinging doors, scratching his head. Mrs Lin was hiccuping and mumbling prayers.

"Buddha protect us! Don't let any bombs fall on our heads!"

Mr Lin turned and went out to the shop. He saw his daughter engaged in excited conversation with the two salesmen. The owner of the shop across the street had come out from behind his counter and was talking, gesticulating wildly. There was fighting in Shanghai;

Japanese planes had bombed Zhabei and burned it; the merchants in Shanghai had closed down — it all was true. What about the pirates robbing the boat? No one had heard anything about that! And the boat from Lishi? It had come in safely. The shopowner across the street had just seen stevedores from the boat going by with two big crates. Mr Lin was relieved. Shousheng hadn't come back today, but he hadn't been robbed by pirates either!

Now the whole town was talking about the catastrophe in Shanghai. Young clerks were cursing the Japanese aggressors. People were even shouting, "Anyone who buys Japanese goods is a son of a bitch!" These words brought a scarlet blush to Miss Lin's cheeks, but Mr Lin showed no change of expression. All the shops were selling Japanese merchandise. Moreover, after spending a few hundred dollars, the merchants had received special authorizations from the Kuomintang chieftains, saying, "The goods may be sold after removing the Japanese markings". All the merchandise in Mr Lin's shop had been transformed into "native goods". His customers, too, would call them "native goods", then take up their packages and leave.

Because of the war in Shanghai, the whole town had lost all interest in business, but Mr Lin was busy pondering his affairs. Unwilling to borrow from the local bank at exorbitant interest, he sought out the collector from the Shanghai wholesale house, to plead with him as a friend for a delay of another day or two. Shousheng would be back tomorrow before dark at the latest, said Mr Lin. Then he would pay in full.

"My dear Mr Lin, you're an intelligent man. How can you talk like that? They're fighting in Shanghai.

Train service may be cut off tomorrow or the day after.
I only wish I could start back tonight! How can I wait
a day or two? Please, settle your account today so that
I can leave the first thing tomorrow morning. I'm not
my own boss. Please have some consideration for me!"

The Shanghai collector was uncompromisingly firm
in his refusal. Mr Lin saw that it was hopeless; he had
no choice but to bear the pain and seek a loan from the
local banker. He was worried that "Old Miser" knew
of his sore need and would take advantage of the situation to boost the interest rate. From the minute he
started speaking to the bank manager, Mr Lin could
feel that the atmosphere was all wrong. The tubercular
old man said nothing when Mr Lin finished his plea,
but continued puffing on his antique water-pipe. After
the whole packet of tobacco was consumed, the manager finally spoke.

"I can't do it," he said slowly. "The Japanese have
begun fighting, business in Shanghai is at a standstill,
the banks have all closed down — who knows when
things will be set right again! Cut off from Shanghai,
my bank is like a crab without legs. With exchange of
remittances stopped, I couldn't do business even with
a better client than you. I'm sorry. I'd love to help
you but my hands are tied!"

Mr Lin lingered. He thought the tubercular manager
was putting on an act in preparation for demanding
higher interest. Just as Mr Lin was about to play along
by renewing his pleas, he was surprised to hear the
manager press him a step farther.

"Our employer has given us instructions. He has
heard that the situation will probably get worse. He
wants us to tighten up. Your shop originally owed us

five hundred; on the twenty-second, you borrowed another hundred — altogether six hundred, due to be settled before New Year. We've been doing business together a long time, so I'm tipping you off. We want
to avoid a lot of talk and embarrassment at the last
minute."

"Oh — but our little shop is having a hard time,"
blurted the dumbfounded Mr Lin. "I'll have to see how
we do with our collections."

"Ho! Why be so modest! The last few days your
business hasn't been like the others! What's so difficult
about paying a mere six hundred dollars? I'm letting
you know today, old brother. I'm looking forward to
your settling your debt so that I can clear myself with
my employer."

The tubercular manager spoke coldly. He stood up.
Chilled, Mr Lin could see that the situation was beyond
repair. All he could do was to take a grip on himself
and walk out of the bank. At last he understood that
the fighting in distant Shanghai would influence his
little shop too. It certainly was going to be hard to get
through this New Year: The Shanghai collector was
pressing him for money; the bank wouldn't wait until
after the New Year; Shousheng still hadn't come back
and there was no telling how he was getting on. So far
as Mr Lin's outstanding accounts in town were concerned, last year he had only collected eighty per cent. From
the looks of things, this year there was no guarantee of
even that much. Only one road seemed open to Mr
Lin: "Business Temporarily Closed—Balancing Books!"
And this was equivalent to bankruptcy. There hadn't
been any of his own money invested in the shop
for a long time. The day the books were balanced and

the creditors paid off, what would be left for him probably wouldn't be enough to stand between his family
and nakedness!

The more he thought, the worse Mr Lin felt. Crossing
the bridge, he looked at the turbid water below. He was
almost tempted to jump and end it all. Then a man
hailed him from behind.

"Mr Lin, is it true there's a war on in Shanghai? I
hear that a bunch of soldiers just set up outside the
town's east gate and asked the Merchants Guild for a
'loan'. They wanted twenty thousand right off the bat.
The Merchants Guild is holding a meeting about it
now!"

Mr Lin hurriedly turned around. The speaker was
Old Chen who had two hundred dollars loaned to the
shop — another of Mr Lin's creditors.

"Oh —" retorted Mr Lin with a shiver. Quickly he
crossed the bridge and ran home.

4

For dinner that evening, beside the usual one meat dish
and two vegetable dishes, Mrs Lin had bought a
favourite of Mr Lin's — a platter of stewed pork. In
addition, there was a pint of yellow wine. A smile
never left Miss Lin's face, for business in the shop was
good, her new silk dress was finished, and because they
were fighting back against the Japanese in Shanghai.
Mrs Lin's hiccups were especially sparse — about one
every ten minutes.

Only Mr Lin was sunk in gloom. Moodily drinking
his wine, he looked at his daughter, and looked at his

wife. Several times he considered dropping the bad news in their midst like a bombshell, but he didn't have that kind of courage. Moreover, he still hadn't given up hope, he still wanted to struggle; at least he wanted to conceal his failure to make ends meet.

And so when the Merchants Guild passed a resolution to pay the soldiers five thousand dollars and asked Mr Lin to contribute twenty, he consented without a moment's hesitation. He decided not to tell his wife and daughter the true state of affairs until the last possible minute. The way he calculated it was this: He would collect eighty per cent of the debts due him, he would pay eighty per cent of the money he owed. Anyhow, he had the excuse that there was fighting in Shanghai, that remittances couldn't be sent. The difficulty was that there was a difference of about six hundred dollars between what people owed him and what he had to pay to others. He would have to take drastic measures and cut prices heavily. The idea was to scrape together some money to meet the present problem, then he would see. Who could think of the future in times like these? If he could get by now, that would be enough.

That was how he made his plans. With the added potency of the pint of yellow wine, Mr Lin slept soundly all night, without even the suggestion of a bad dream.

It was already six thirty when Mr Lin awoke the next morning. The sky was overcast and he was rather dizzy. He gulped down two bowls of rice gruel and hurried to the shop. The first thing to greet his eye was the Shanghai collector, sitting with a stern face, waiting for his "answer". But what shocked Mr Lin particularly was the shop across the street. They too had pasted red and green strips all over their windows; they too were having a "Big Sale 10% Discount"! Mr Lin's perfect plan of the night before was completely snowed under by those red and green streamers of his competitor.

"What kind of a joke is this, Mr Lin? Last night you didn't give a reply. That boat leaves here at eight o'clock and I have to make connections with the train. I simply must catch that eight o'clock boat! Please hurry —" said the Shanghai collector impatiently. He brought his clenched fist down on the table.

Mr Lin apologized and begged his forgiveness. Truly, it was all because of the fighting in Shanghai and not being able to send remittances. After all, they had been doing business for many years. Mr Lin pleaded for a little special consideration.

"Then am I to go back empty-handed?"

"Why, why, certainly not. When Shousheng returns, I'll give you as much as he brings. I'm not a man if I keep so much as half a dollar!" Mr Lin's voice trembled. With an effort he held back the tears that brimmed to his eyes.

There was no more to be said; the Shanghai collector stopped his grumbling. But he remained firmly seated where he was. Mr Lin was nearly out of his wits with anxiety. His heart thumped erratically. Although he had been having a hard time the past few years, he had been able to keep up a front. Now there was a collector sitting in his shop for all the world to see. If word of this thing spread, Mr Lin's credit would be ruined. He had plenty of creditors. Suppose they all decided to follow suit? His shop might just as well close down immediately. In desperation, several times he invited the Shanghai gentleman to wait in the back room where it was more comfortable, but the latter refused.

An icy rain began to fall. The street was cold and deserted. Never had it appeared so mournful at New Year's time. Signboards creaked and clattered in the grip of a north wind. The icy rain seemed like to turn into snow. In the shops that lined the street, salesmen leaning on the counters looked up blankly.

Occasionally, Mr Lin and the collector from Shanghai exchanged a few desultory words. Miss Lin suddenly emerged through the swinging doors and stood at the front window watching the cold hissing rain. From the back room, the sound of Mrs Lin's hiccups steadily gathered intensity. While trying to be pleasant to their visitor, Mr Lin looked at his daughter and listened to his wife's hiccups, and a wave of depression rose in his breast. He thought how all his life he had never known any prosperity, nor could he imagine who was responsible for his being reduced to such dire straits today.

The Shanghai collector seemed to have calmed down somewhat. "Mr Lin," he said abruptly, in a sincere tone, "you're a good man. You don't go in for loose living, you're obliging and honest in your business practices. Twenty years ago, you would have gotten rich. But things are different today. Taxes are high, expenses are heavy, business is slow — it's an accomplishment just to get along."

Mr Lin sighed and smiled in wry modesty.

After a pause, the Shanghai collector continued, "This year the market in this town was a little worse

than last, wasn't it? Places in the interior like this de-
pend on the people from the countryside for business,
but the peasants are too poor. There's really no solution. . . . Oh, it's nine o'clock! Why hasn't your
collection clerk come back yet? Is he reliable?"

Mr Lin's heart gave a leap. For the moment, he
couldn't answer. Although Shousheng had been his
salesman for seven or eight years and had never made
a slip, still, there was no absolute guarantee! And besides he was overdue. The Shanghai collector laughed
to see Mr Lin's doubtful expression, but his laugh had
an odd ring to it.

At the window, Miss Lin whirled and cried urgently,
"Papa, Shousheng is back! He's covered with mud!"

Her voice had a peculiar sound too. Mr Lin jumped
up, both alarmed and happy. He wanted to run out
and look, but he was so excited that his legs were weak.
By then Shousheng had already entered, truly covered
with mud. The clerk sat down, panting for breath,
unable to say a word. The situation looked bad.
Frightened out of his wits, Mr Lin was speechless too.
The Shanghai collector frowned. After a while, Shousheng managed to gasp:

"Very dangerous! They nearly got me!"

"Then the boat was robbed?" the agitated Mr Lin
took a grip on himself and blurted.

"There wasn't any robbing. They were grabbing coo-
lies for the army. I couldn't make the boat yesterday
afternoon; I got a sampan this morning. After we
sailed, we heard they were waiting at this end to grab
the boat, so we came to port further down the river.
When we got ashore, before we had come half a *li*, we
bumped into an army pressgang. They grabbed the

clerk from the clothing shop, but I ran fast and came back by a short cut. Damn it! It was a close call!"

Shousheng lifted his jacket as he talked and pulled from his money belt a cloth-bound packet which he handed to Mr Lin.

"It's all here," he said. "That Huang Shop in Lishi is rotten. We have to be careful of customers like that next year. . . . I'll come back after I have a wash and change my clothes."

Mr Lin's face lit up as he squeezed the packet. He carried it over to the cashier's cage and unbound the cloth wrapping. First he added up the money due on the list of debtors, then he counted what had been collected. There were eleven silver dollars, two hundred dimes, four hundred and twenty dollars in banknotes, and two bank demand drafts — for the equivalent of fifty and sixty-five taels of silver respectively, at the official rate. If he turned the whole lot over to the Shanghai collector, it would still be more than a hundred dollars short of what he owed the wholesale house.

Deep in contemplation, Mr Lin glanced several times out of the corner of his eye at the Shanghai collector who was silently smoking a cigarette. At last he sighed, and as though cutting off a piece of his living flesh, placed the two bank drafts and four hundred dollars in cash before the man from Shanghai. Then Mr Lin spoke for a long time until he managed to extract a nod from the latter and the words "all right".

But when the collector looked twice at the bank drafts, he said with a smile, "Sorry to trouble you, Mr Lin. Please get them cashed for me first."

"Certainly, certainly," Mr Lin hastened to reply. He quickly affixed his shop's seal to the back of the drafts and dispatched one of his salesmen to cash them at the local bank. In a little while, the salesman came back empty-handed. The bank had accepted the drafts but refused to pay for them, saying they would be credited against Mr Lin's debt. Though it was snowing heavily now, Mr Lin rushed over to the bank without an umbrella to plead in person. But his efforts were in vain.

"Well, what about it?" demanded the Shanghai collector impatiently as Mr Lin returned to the shop, his face anguished.

Mr Lin seemed ready to weep. There was nothing he could say; he could only sigh. Except to beg the collector for more leniency, what else could he do? Shousheng came out and added his pleas to Mr Lin's. He vowed that they would send the remaining two hundred dollars to Shanghai by the tenth of the new year. Mr Lin was an old customer who had always paid his debts promptly without a word, said Shousheng. This thing today was really unexpected. But that was the situation; they couldn't help themselves. It wasn't that they were stalling.

The Shanghai collector was adamant. Painfully, Mr Lin brought out the fifty dollars he had taken in during the past few days and handed it over to make up a total payment of four hundred and fifty dollars. Only then did that headache of a Shanghai collector depart.

By that time, it was eleven in the morning. Snowflakes were still drifting down from the sky. Not even half a customer was in sight. Mr Lin brooded a while, then discussed with Shousheng means to be used in collecting outstanding bills in town. Both men were frowning; neither of them had any particular confidence that much of the six hundred dollars due from town

customers could be collected. Shousheng bent close to
Mr Lin's ear and whispered:

"I hear that the big shop at the south gate and the
one at the west gate are both shaky. Both of them owe
us money — about three hundred dollars altogether.
We'd better take precautions with these two accounts.
If they fold up before we can collect, it won't be so
funny!"

Mr Lin paled; his lips trembled a little. Then,
Shousheng pitched his voice lower still, and mumbled
a bit of even more shocking news.

"There's another nasty rumour — about us. They're
sure to have heard it at the bank. That's why they're
pressing us so hard. The Shanghai collector probably
got wind of it too. Who can be trying to make trouble
for us? The shop across the street?"

Shousheng pointed with his pursed lips in the direction of the suspect, and Mr Lin's eyes swung to follow
the indicator. His heart skipping unevenly, his face
mournful, Mr Lin was unable to speak for some time.
He had the numb and aching feeling that this time he
was definitely finished! If he weren't ruined it would
be a miracle: The Kuomintang chieftains were putting
the squeeze on him; the bank was pressing him; his
fellow shopkeepers were stabbing him in the back; a
couple of his biggest debtors were going to default.
Nobody could stand up under this kind of buffeting.
But why was he fated to get such a dirty deal? Ever
since he inherited the little shop from his father, he had
never dared to be wasteful. He had been so obliging;
he never hurt a soul, never schemed against anyone.
His father and grandfather had been the same, yet all
he was reaping was bitterness!

"Never mind. Let them spread their rumours. You don't have to worry," Shousheng tried to comfort Mr Lin, though he couldn't help sighing himself. "There are always rumours in lean years. They say in this town nine out of ten shops won't be able to pay up their debts before the year is out. Times are bad, the market is dead as a doornail. Usually strong shops are hard up this year. We're not the only one having rough going! When the sky tumbles everyone gets crushed. The Merchants Guild has to think of a way out. All the shops can't be collapsing; that would make the market even less like a market."

The snowfall was becoming heavier; it was sticking to the ground now. Occasionally, a dog would slink by; shivering, its tail between its legs. It might stop and shake itself violently to dislodge the snow thickly matting its fur. Then, with tail drooping again, the dog would go on its way. Never in its history had this street witnessed so frigid and desolate a New Year season! And just at this time, in distant Shanghai, Japanese heavy artillery was savagely pounding that prosperous metropolis of trade.

5

It was a gloomy New Year, but finally it was passed. In town, twenty-eight big and little shops folded up, including a "credit A-1" silk shop. The two stores that owed Mr Lin three hundred dollars closed down too. The last day of the year, Shousheng had gone to them and plagued them for hours, but all he could extract was a total of twenty dollars. He heard that afterwards no other collector got so much as a penny out of them; the owners of the two shops hid themselves and couldn't be found. Thanks to the intervention of the head of the Merchants Guild, it wasn't necessary for Mr Lin to hide. But he had to guarantee to wipe off his debt of four hundred dollars to the bank before the fifteenth of the first month, and he had to consent to very harsh terms: The bank would send a representative to "guard" all cash taken in starting from resumption of business on the fifth; eighty per cent of all money collected would go to the bank until Mr Lin's debt to them was paid.

During the New Year holidays, Mr Lin's house was like an ice box. Mr Lin heaved sigh after sigh. Mrs Lin's hiccups were like a string of firecrackers. Miss Lin, although she neither hiccuped nor sighed, moped around in the dazed condition of one who has suffered from years of jaundice. Her new silk dress had already gone to the only pawnshop in town to raise money for the maid's wages. An apprentice had taken it there at seven in the morning; it was after nine when he finally squeezed his way out of the crowd with two dollars in his hand. Afterwards, the pawnshop refused to do any more business that day. Two dollars! That was the highest price they would give for any article, no matter how much you had paid for it originally! This was called "two dollar ceiling". When a peasant, steeling himself against the cold, would peel off a cotton-padded jacket and hand it across the counter, the pawnshop clerk would raise it up, give it a shake, then fling it back with an angry "We don't want it!"

Since New Year's Day, the weather had been beautiful and clear. The big temple courtyard, as was the custom, was crowded with the stalls of itinerant pedlars and the paraphernalia of acrobats and jugglers. People lingered before the stalls, patted their empty money belts, and reluctantly walked on. Children dragged at their mothers' clothing, refusing to leave the stall where fireworks were on sale, until Mama was forced to give the little offender a hard slap. The pedlars, who had come specially to cash in on the usual New Year's bazaar trade, didn't even make enough to pay for their food. They couldn't pay their rent at the local inn and quarrelled with the innkeeper every day.

Only the acrobatic troupe earned the large sum of eight dollars. It had been hired by the Kuomintang chieftains to add to the atmosphere of "peace and normalcy".

On the evening of the fourth, Mr Lin, who had with some difficulty managed to raise three dollars, gave the usual spread for his employees at which they all discussed the strategy for the morrow's re-opening of business. The prospects were already terribly clear to Mr Lin: If they re-opened, they were sure to operate at a loss; if they didn't re-open, he and his family would be entirely without resources. Moreover, people still owed him four hundred dollars, the collection of which would be even more difficult, if he closed down. The only way out was to cut expenses. But taxes and levies for the soldiers were inescapable; there was even less chance of his avoiding being "squeezed". Fire a couple of salesmen? He only had three. Shousheng was his righthand man; the other two were poor devils; besides he really needed them to wait on the customers. He couldn't save any more at home. They had already let the maid go. He felt the only thing to do was to plunge

on. Perhaps, when the peasants, with Buddha's blessing, earned money from their spring raw silk sales, he
still might make up his loss.

But the greatest problem in resuming business was
that he was short of merchandise. Without money to
remit to Shanghai, he couldn't replenish his stock. The
fighting in Shanghai was getting worse. There was no
use in hoping for getting anything on credit. Sell his
reserve? The shop was long since actually cleaned out.
The underwear boxes on the shelves were empty; they
were used only for show. All that was left were things
like wash-basins and towels. But he had plenty of
those.

Gloomily, the feasters sipped their wine. For all
their perplexed reflection, no one could offer any solution to the problem. They talked of generalities for a
while. Then suddenly Asi, one of the salesmen, said:

"The world is going to hell. People live worse than
dogs! They say Zhabei was completely burned out. A
couple of hundred thousand people had to flee, leaving
all their belongings behind. There wasn't any fire in
the Hongkou section, but everybody ran away. The
Japanese are very cruel. They wouldn't let them take
any of their things with them. House rent in safe
quarters in Shanghai has skyrocketed. All the refugees
are running to the countryside. A bunch came to our
town yesterday. They all look like decent people, and
now they're homeless!"

Mr Lin shook his head and sighed, but Shousheng,
on hearing these words, was suddenly struck with a
bright idea. He put down his chopsticks, then raised
his wine cup and drained it in one swallow. He turned to Mr Lin with a grin.

"Did you hear what Asi just said? That means our wash-basins, wash-cloths, soap, socks, tooth powder, tooth brushes, will sell fast. We can get rid of as many as we've got."

Mr Lin stared. He didn't know what Shousheng was driving at.

"Look, this is a heaven-sent chance. The Shanghai refugees should have a little money, and they need the usual daily necessities, don't they? We ought to set up right away to handle this business!"

Shousheng poured himself another cup of wine, and drank, his face beaming. The two salesmen caught on, and they began to laugh. Only Mr Lin was not entirely clear. He had been rather dulled by his recent adversity.

"Are you sure?" he asked, irresolutely. "Other shops have wash-cloths and wash-basins too —"

"But we're the only ones with any real reserve of that sort of stuff. They don't have even ten wash-basins across the street, and those are all seconds. We've got this piece of business right in the palm of our hand! Let's write a lot of ads and paste them up the town's four gateways, any place in town where the refugees are staying — say, Asi, where *are* they living? We'll go put up our stickers there!"

"The ones with relatives here are living with their relatives. The rest have borrowed that empty building in the silk factory outside the west gate." Asi's face shone with satisfaction over the excellent result he had unwittingly produced.

At last, Mr Lin had the whole picture. Happy, his spirits revived. He immediately drafted the wording of the advertisements, listing all the daily necessities which the shop had available for sale. There were over a dozen different commodities. In imitation of the big Shanghai stores, he adopted the "One Dollar Package" technique. For a dollar the customer would get a wash-basin, a wash-cloth, a tooth brush and a box of tooth powder. "Big Dollar Sale!" screamed the ad in huge letters. Shousheng brought out the shop's remaining sheets of red and green paper and cut them into large strips. Then he took up his brush and started writing. The salesmen and the apprentices noisily collected the wash-basins, wash-cloths, tooth brushes and boxes of tooth powder, and arranged them into sets. There weren't enough hands for all the work. Mr Lin called his daughter out to help with writing the ads and tying the packages. He also made up other kinds of combination packages — all of daily necessities.

That night, they were busy in the shop late and long. At dawn they had things pretty much in order. When the popping of firecrackers heralded the opening of business the next morning, the shop of the Lin family again had a new look. Their advertisements had already been pasted up all over town. Shousheng had personally attended to the silk factory outside the west gate. The ad with which he plastered the factory walls struck the eyes of the refugees, and they all crowded around to read it as if it were a news bulletin.

In the "inner sanctum" Mrs Lin, too, rose very early. She lit incense before the porcelain image of the Goddess Guanyin and kowtowed for a considerable time, knocking her head resoundingly against the floor. She prayed for practically everything. About the only thing she omitted was a plea for more refugees to come to the town.

It all worked out fine, just as Shousheng had predict-
ed. Mr Lin's shop was the only one whose trade was
brisk on the first business day after the New Year's
holidays. By four in the afternoon, he had sold over
one hundred dollars' worth of merchandise — the
highest figure for a day ever reached in that town in
the past ten years. His biggest seller was the "One
Dollar Package", and it served as a leader to such items
as umbrellas and rubber overshoes. Business, moreover, went smoothly, pleasantly. The refugees came
from Shanghai, after all; they were used to the ways of
the big city; they weren't as petty as the townspeople
or the peasants from the out-lying districts. When they
bought something, they made up their minds quickly.
They'd pick up a thing, look at it, then produce their
money. There was none of this pawing through all the
merchandise, no haggling over a few pennies.

When her daughter, all flushed and excited, rushed
into the back room for a moment to report the good
business, Mrs Lin went to kowtow before the porcelain
Guanyin again. If Shousheng weren't twice the girl's
age, Mrs Lin was thinking, wouldn't he make a good
son-in-law! And it wasn't at all unlikely that Shousheng had half an eye on his employer's seventeen-year-
old daughter, this girl whom he knew so well.

There was just one thing that spoiled Mr Lin's happiness — completely disregarding his dignity, the local
bank had sent its man to collect eighty per cent of the
sales proceeds. And he didn't know who egged them
on, but the three creditors of the shop, on the excuse
that they "needed a little money to buy rice", all showed up to draw out some advance interest. Not only
interest; they even wanted repayment of part of their

loans too! But Mr Lin also heard some good news — another batch of refugees had arrived in town.

For dinner that evening, Mr Lin served two additional meat dishes, by way of reward to his employees. Everyone complimented Shousheng on his shrewdness. Although Mr Lin was happy, he couldn't help thinking of how his three creditors had talked about being repaid their loans. It was unlucky to have such a thing happen at the beginning of the new year.

"What do they know!" said Shousheng angrily. "Somebody must have put them up to it!" He pointed with his lips at the shop across the street.

Mr Lin nodded. But whether the three creditors knew anything or not, it was going to be difficult to handle them. An old man and two widows. You couldn't be soft with them, but getting tough wouldn't do either. Mr Lin pondered for some time, and finally decided the best thing to do would be to ask the head of the Merchants Guild to speak to his three precious creditors. He asked Shousheng for his opinion. Shousheng heartily agreed.

When dinner was over, and Mr Lin had added up his receipts for the day, he went to pay his respects to the head of the Merchants Guild. The latter expressed complete approval of Mr Lin's idea. What's more, he commended Mr Lin on the intelligent way in which he conducted his business. He said the shop was sure to stand firm, in fact it would improve. Stroking his chin, the head of the Merchants Guild smiled and leaned towards Mr Lin.

"There's something I've been wanting to talk to you about for a long time, but I never had the opportunity. I don't know where Kuomintang Commissioner Pu saw your daughter, but he's very interested in her. Commissioner Pu is forty and he has no sons. Though he has two women at home, neither of them has been able to give birth. If your daughter should join his household and present him with a child, he's sure to make her his wife, Madam Commissioner. Ah, if that should happen, even I could share in the reflected glory!"

Never in his wildest dreams had Mr Lin ever imagined he would run into trouble like this. He was speechless. The head of the Merchants Guild continued solemnly:

"We're old friends. There's nothing we can't speak freely about to each other. This kind of thing, according to the old standards, would make you lose face. But it isn't altogether like that any more; it's quite common nowadays. Your daughter's going over could be considered proper marriage. Anyhow, since that is what Commissioner Pu has in mind, there might be some inconvenience if you refuse him. If you agree, you can have real hope for the future. I wouldn't be telling you this if I didn't have your interests at heart."

"Of course in advising me to be careful, your intentions are the best! But I'm an unimportant person, my daughter knows nothing of high society. We don't dare aspire so high as a commissioner!" Mr Lin had to brace himself up to speak. His heart was thumping fast.

"Ha ha! It isn't a question of your aspirations, but the fact that he finds her suitable. . . . Let's leave it at that. You go home and talk it over with your wife. I'll put the matter aside. When I see Commissioner Pu I'll say I haven't had a chance to speak to you about it, all right? But you must give me an answer soon!"

There was a long pause. Then, "I will," Mr Lin forced himself to say. His face was ghastly.

When he got home, he sent his daughter out of the room and reported to his wife in detail. Even before he finished, Mrs Lin's hiccups rose in a powerful barrage that was probably audible to all the neighbours. With an effort she stemmed the tide and said, panting:

"How can we consent? — hic — Even if it wasn't a concubine he wanted hic — hic — even if he were looking for a wife, I still couldn't bear to part with her!"

"That's the way I feel, but —"

"Hic — we run our business all legal and proper. Do you mean to say if we don't agree he could get away with taking her by force? Hic —"

"But he's sure to find an excuse to make some kind of trouble. That kind of man is crueler than a bandit!" Mr Lin whispered. He was nearly crying.

"He'll get her only over my dead body! Hic! Goddess Guanyin preserve us!" cried Mrs Lin in a voice that trembled. She rose and started to sway out of the room. Mr Lin hastily barred her way.

"Where are you going? Where are you going?" he babbled.

Just then, Miss Lin came in. Obviously she had overheard quite a bit, for her complexion was the colour of chalk and her eyes were staring fixedly. Mrs Lin flung her arms around her daughter and wept and hiccuped while she struggled to say in gasps:

"Hic — child — hic — anybody who tries to snatch you — hic — will have to do it over my dead body! Hic! The year I gave birth to you I got this — sickness —hic — It was hard, but I brought you up till now you're seventeen — hic — hic — Dead or alive, we'll stick to-

gether! Hic! We should have promised you to Shousheng long ago! Hic! That Pu is a dirty crook! He isn't
afraid the gods will strike him down!"

Miss Lin wept too, crying "Ma!" Mr Lin wrung his
hands and sighed. The women were wailing at an
alarming rate, and he was afraid their laments would be
heard through the thin walls and startle the neighbours.
This sort of row was also an unlucky way to commence
the new year. Holding his own emotions in check, he
did his best to soothe wife and daughter.

That night, all three members of the Lin family slept
badly. Although Mr Lin had to get up early the next
morning to go to business, he wrestled with his gloomy
thoughts all night. A sudden sound on the roof sent his
heart leaping with fear that Commissioner Pu had come
to trump up charges against him. Then he calmed himself and considered the matter carefully. His was a
family of proper business people who had never committed any crimes. As long as he did a good business
and didn't owe people money, surely Pu couldn't make
trouble without any reason at all. And now Lin's business was beginning to show some vitality. Just because
he had raised a good-looking daughter, he had invited
disaster! He should have engaged her years ago, then
maybe this problem would never have arisen.... Was
the head of the Merchants Guild sincerely willing to
help? The only way out was to beg for his aid — Mrs
Lin started hiccuping again. Ai! That ailment of hers!

Mr Lin rose as soon as the sky began to turn light.
His eyes were somewhat bloodshot and swollen, and
he felt dizzy. But he had to pull himself together and
attend to business. He couldn't leave the entire mana-

gement of the shop to Shousheng; the young fellow had put in an exhausting few days.

He was still uneasy after he seated himself in the cashier's cage. Although business was good, from time to time his whole body was shaken by violent shivers. Whenever a big man came in, if Mr Lin didn't know him, he would suspect that the man had been sent by Commissioner Pu to spy, to stir up a fuss, and his heart would thump painfully.

And it was strange. Business that day was active beyond all expectations. By noon they had sold nearly sixty dollars' worth of merchandise. There were local townspeople among the customers too. They weren't just buying; they were practically grabbing. The only thing like it would be a bankrupt shop selling its stock out at auction cheap. While Mr Lin was fairly pleased, he was also rather alarmed. This kind of business didn't look healthy to him. Sure enough, Shousheng approached him during the lunch hour and said softly:

"There's a rumour outside that you've cut prices to clear out your left-overs. That when you've collected a little money, you're going to take it and run!"

Mr Lin was both angry and frightened. He couldn't speak. Suddenly two men in uniform entered and barged forward to demand:

"Which one is Mr Lin, the proprietor?"

Mr Lin rose in flurried haste. Before he had a chance to reply, the uniformed men began to lead him away. Shousheng came over to stop them and to question them. They barked at him savagely:

"Who are you? Stand aside! He's wanted for questioning at the Kuomintang office!"

6

That afternoon, Mr Lin did not return. They were busy at the shop, and Shousheng could not get away to inquire personally. He had managed to conceal the truth from Mrs Lin, but one of the apprentices let it leak out, and the lady became frantic almost to the point of distraction. She absolutely refused to let Miss Lin go out of the swinging doors.

"They've already taken your father. They'll be coming back for you next! Hic —"

She called in Shousheng and questioned him closely. He didn't think it advisable to tell her too much.

"Don't worry, Mrs Lin," he comforted. "There's nothing wrong! He only went down to the Kuomintang office to straighten out the question of our creditors. Business is good. What have we got to be afraid of!"

Behind Mrs Lin's back, he told Miss Lin quietly, "We still don't really know what this is all about." He urged her to look after her mother; he would attend to the shop. Miss Lin didn't have the faintest idea what to do. She agreed to everything Shousheng said.

Between waiting on the customers and thinking up answers to Mrs Lin's constant questions, it was impossible for Shousheng to find time to inquire about the fate of Mr Lin. Finally, at twilight, word was brought by the head of the Merchants Guild: Mr Lin was being held by the Kuomintang chieftains because of the rumour that he was planning to abscond with the shop's money. Besides what Mr Lin owed the bank and the wholesale house, there were also his three poor creditors to be considered. The total of six hundred and fifty dollars which they had put up was in jeopardy. The

Kuomintang was especially concerned over the welfare of these poor people. So it was detaining him until he settled with them.

Shousheng's face was drained of colour. Dazed, he finally managed to ask:

"Can we put up a guarantee and have him released first? Unless we get him out, how are we going to raise the money?"

"Huh! Release him on a guarantee! You can't become his guarantor if you go there without money in your hands!"

"Mr Guild Leader, think of something, I beg you. Do a good deed. You and Mr Lin are old friends. I beg you to help him!"

The head of the Merchants Guild frowned thoughtfully. He looked at Shousheng for a minute, then led him to a corner of the room and said in a low voice:

"I can't stand by with folded arms and watch Mr Lin remain in difficulty. But the situation is very strained now! To tell you the truth, I've already pleaded with Commissioner Pu to intervene. Commissioner Pu only wanted Mr Lin to agree to one thing, and would be willing to help him. I've just seen Mr Lin at the Kuomintang office where I urged him to consent, and he did so. Shouldn't that be the end of the matter? Who would have thought that dark pock-marked fellow in the Kuomintang would be so nasty? He still insists —"

"Surely he wouldn't go against Commissioner Pu?"

"That's what I thought! But the pock-marked fellow kept mumbling and grumbling till Commissioner Pu was very embarrassed. They had a terrible row! Now you see how awkward things are?"

Shousheng sighed. He had no idea. There was a pause, then he sighed again and said:

"But Mr Lin hasn't committed any crime."

"Those people don't talk reason! With them, might makes right! Tell Mrs Lin not to worry; Mr Lin hasn't been mistreated yet. But to get him out she'll have to spend a little money!"

The head of the Merchants Guild held up two fingers, then quickly departed.

Though he racked his brains, Shousheng could see no other alternative. The two salesmen plagued him with questions, but he ignored them. He was wondering whether he should report the words of the head of the Merchants Guild to Mrs Lin. Again they had to spend money! While he didn't know whether Mrs Lin had any private resources of her own, he was quite clear as to the financial condition of the shop: After the local bank got through deducting its eighty per cent from the cash earned during the past two days, all that was left for the shop was about fifty dollars. A lot of good that would do! The head of the Merchants Guild had indicated a bribe of two hundred dollars. Who knew whether that would be enough! The way things were, even if business should improve even more, it still wouldn't be any use. Shousheng felt discouraged.

From the back room, someone was calling him. He decided to go in and size up the situation, and then determine what should be done. He found Mrs Lin leaning on her daughter's arm.

"Hic — just now — hic — the head of the Merchants Guild came — hic —" she panted. "What did he say?"

"He wasn't here," lied Shousheng.

"You can't fool me — hic — I — hic — know every-

thing. Hic — your face is scared yellow! Xiu saw him
— hic!"

"Be calm, Mrs Lin. He says it's all right. Commissioner Pu is willing to help —"

"What? Hic — hic — What? Commissioner Pu is
willing to help! — Hic, hic — Merciful goddess —
hic — I don't want his help! Hic, hic — I know —Mr
Lin — hic, hic — is finished! Hic — I want to die too!
There's only Xiu — hic — that I'm worried about! Hic,
hic — take her with you! — Hic! You two go and get
married! Hic — hic — Shousheng — hic — you take
good care of Xiu and I won't worry about anything!
Hic! Go! They want to grab her! — Hic — the savage
beasts! Goddess Guanyin, why don't you display your
divine power!"

Shousheng stared. He didn't know what to say. He
thought Mrs Lin had gone mad, yet she didn't look the
least abnormal. His heart beating hard, he stole a glance
at Miss Lin. She was blushing scarlet; she kept her
head down and made no comment.

"Shousheng, Shousheng, somebody wants to see you!"
an apprentice came running in and announced.

Thinking it was the head of the Merchants Guild or
some such personage, Shousheng rushed out. To his surprise, he found Mr Wu, proprietor of the shop across
the street, waiting for him. What does he want? wondered Shousheng. He fixed his eyes on Mr Wu's face.

Mr Wu inquired about Mr Lin, and then, all smiles,
said he was sure it was "not serious". Shousheng felt
there was something fishy about his smile.

"I've come to buy a little of your merchandise —"
The smile had disappeared from Mr Wu's face and the
tone of his voice changed. He produced a sheet of paper

from his sleeve. It was a list of over a dozen items —
the very things Mr Lin was featuring in his "One Dollar
Package". One look and Shousheng understood. So that
was the game!

"Mr Lin isn't here," he said promptly. "I haven't
the right to decide."

"Why not talk to Mrs Lin? That'll be just as good!"

Shousheng hesitated to reply. He was beginning to
have an inkling of why Mr Lin had been detained.
First there was the rumour that Mr Lin was planning
to run away, then Mr Lin was arrested, and now the
competitor's shop had come to gouge merchandise.
There was an obvious connection between these events.
Shousheng became rather angry, and a bit frightened.
He knew that if he agreed to Mr Wu's request, Mr Lin's
business would be finished, and the heart's blood that
he himself had expended would be in vain. But if he refused, what other tricks would be forthcoming? He simply didn't dare to think.

"I'll go and talk to Mrs Lin, then," he offered tentatively. "But she only operates on a cash basis."

"Cash? Ha, Shousheng, of course you're joking?"

"That's the kind of person Mrs Lin is. I can't do
anything with her. The best thing would be for you to
come again tomorrow. The head of the Merchants
Guild just told me that Commissioner Pu is willing to
take a hand in the matter. Mr Lin probably will be
back tonight," said Shousheng with cold deliberateness.
He shoved the list back in Mr Wu's hand.

His face twitching, the latter hastily forced the list
on Shousheng again.

"All right, all right, if it has to be cash then it's cash.
I'll take the goods tonight. Cash on delivery."

Scowling, Shousheng walked into the back room and told Mrs Lin about the shop across the street wanting to gouge merchandise.

"When the head of the Merchants Guild was here, he really said Mr Lin was fine; he hasn't been through any hardships. But we'll have to spend some money to get him out. There's only fifty dollars in the shop. Now this fellow across the street wants goods — from the looks of his list, about a hundred and fifty dollars' worth. Why not let him have them? The important thing is to get Mr Lin back as soon as possible!"

Upon hearing that they had to spend money again, tears gushed from Mrs Lin's eyes, and her hiccups truly shook the heavens with their intensity. Beyond words, she could only wave her hand, while her head, which she rested on the table, resounded alarmingly against the wooden top. Shousheng could see that he was getting nowhere, and he quietly withdrew.   Miss Lin caught up with him outside the swinging doors. Her face was deathly white, her voice trembling and hoarse.

"Ma is so angry she can't think straight," Miss Lin whispered urgently.   "She keeps saying they've already killed papa! You, you hurry up and agree to what Mr Wu wants. Save papa, quick! Shousheng, brother, you —" At this point, her face suddenly flamed scarlet, and she flew back into the room.

In a daze, Shousheng stared after her for a full half minute, then he turned away, determined to take the responsibility for selling the merchandise to their competitor. At least Miss Lin agreed with him on what should be done.

The table had already been laid for dinner in the shop, but Shousheng had no appetite. As soon as Mr

Wu arrived with the money, Shousheng took one hundred dollars in his hand and concealed another eighty dollars on his person, and rushed off to find the head of the Merchants Guild.

Half an hour later Shousheng returned with Mr Lin. Bursting into the "inner sanctum", they nearly startled Mrs Lin out of her wits. When she saw that it was really Mr Lin in the flesh, she agitatedly prostrated herself before the porcelain Guanyin and kowtowed vigorously, pounding her head so loudly that it drowned out the sound of her hiccups. Miss Lin stood to one side, her eyes staring. She looked as if she wanted to laugh and cry at the same time. Shousheng took out a paper-wrapped packet and set it on the table.

"This is eighty dollars we didn't have to use."

Mr Lin sighed. When he finally spoke, his voice was dull.

"You should have let me die there and be done with it. Spending more money to get me out! Now we've got no money, we're all going to die anyhow!"

Mrs Lin jumped up from the ground, excited and wanting to speak. But a string of hiccups blocked the words in her throat. Miss Lin wept quietly, with suppressed sobs. Mr Lin did not cry. He sighed again and said in a choked voice:

"Our merchandise has been cleaned out! We can't do any business, they're pressing us hard for debts —"

"Mr Lin!"

It was Shousheng who shouted. He dipped his finger in the tea, then wrote on the table the one word — "Go".

Mr Lin shook his head. Tears flowed from his eyes.

He looked at his wife, he looked at his daughter, and again he sighed.

"That's the only way out, Mr Lin! We can still scrape together a hundred dollars in the shop. Take it with you; it'll be enough for a month or two. I'll take care of what has to be done here."

Although Shousheng spoke quietly, Mrs Lin overheard him. She curbed her hiccups and interjected:

"You go too, Shousheng! You and Xiu. Leave me here alone. I'll fight to the death! Hic!"

Mrs Lin suddenly appeared remarkably young and healthy; she whirled and ran up the stairs. "Ma!" called Miss Lin, and dashed after her mother. Mr Lin stared at the stairway, bewildered. He felt he had something important to say, but he was too numb to recall what it was.

"You and Xiu go together," Shousheng urged softly. "Mrs Lin will worry if Xiu stays here! She says they want to snatch —"

Tears in his eyes, Mr Lin nodded. He couldn't make up his mind.

Shousheng felt his own eyes smarting. He sighed and walked around the table.

Just then, they heard Miss Lin crying. Startled, Mr Lin and Shousheng rushed up the stairs. Mrs Lin was coming out of her room with a paper packet in her hand. She went back into the room when she saw them, and said:

"Please come in, both of you. Listen to what I've decided." She pointed at the packet. "In here is my private property — hic — about two hundred dollars. I'm giving you two half. Hic! Xiu, I give you in marriage to Shousheng! Hic — tomorrow, Xiu and her fa-

ther will leave together. Hic — I'm not going! Shousheng will stay with me a few days, and then we'll see.
Who knows how many days I have left to live — hic —
So if you both kowtow in my presence, I can set my
mind at ease! Hic —"

Mrs Lin took her daughter by one hand and Shousheng by the other, and ordered them to "kowtow".
Both did so, their cheeks flaming red; they kept their
heads down. Shousheng stole a glance at Miss Lin.
There was a faint smile on her tear-stained face. His
heart thumped wildly, and two tears rolled down from
his eyes.

"Good. That's the way it'll be." Mr Lin heaved a
sigh. "But Shousheng, when you stay here and deal
with those people, be very, very careful!"

7

The shop of the Lin family had to close down at last.
The news that Mr Lin had run away soon spread all
over town. Of the creditors, the local bank was the
first to send people to put the stock into custody. They
also searched for the account books. Not one was to
be found. They asked for Shousheng. He was sick
in bed. They grilled Mrs Lin. Her reply was a string
of explosive hiccups and a stream of tears. Since she
after all enjoyed the social position of "Madam Lin",
there was nothing they could do with her.

By about eleven a.m., the horde of creditors in the
Lin shop were quarrelling with a tremendous din. The
local bank and the other creditors were wrangling as to
how to divide the remaining property. Although the

stock was nearly gone, the remainder and the furniture and fixtures were enough to repay the creditors about seventy per cent; but each was fighting for a ninety, or even one hundred, per cent for himself. The head of the Merchants Guild had talked until his tongue was a little paralysed, to no avail.

Two policemen arrived and took their stand outside the shop door. Clubs in hand, they barked at the crowd that had gathered to see the excitement.

"Why can't I go in? I've got a three hundred dollar loan in this shop! My savings!" Mrs Zhu argued with a policeman, twisting her withered lips. Tottering, she was elbowing her way through the mass. The blue veins on her forehead stood out as thick as little fingers. She kept pushing. Then suddenly she saw Widow Zhang, with her five-year-old baby in her arms, pleading with the other policeman to let her enter. He looked at the widow out of the corner of his eye, and while feigning to tease the child, furtively rubbed the back of his hand against the widow's breasts.

"Sister Zhang —" Mrs Zhu gasped loudly. She sat down on the edge of the stone steps, forcibly moving her puckered mouth.

Tears in her eyes, Widow Zhang took an aimless step, which brought into her line of vision Mrs Zhu panting on the edge of the stone stairs. She practically stumbled over to Mrs Zhu and sat down beside her. Then, Widow Zhang began to cry and lament:

"Oh, my husband, you've left me alone! You don't know how I'm suffering! The wicked soldiers killed you — it was three years ago the day before yesterday. ... That cursed Mr Lin — may he die without sons or grandsons! — has closed his shop! The hundred and fifty dollars that I earned by the toil of my two hands has fallen into the sea and is gone without a sound! Aiya! The lot of the poor is hard, and the rich have no hearts —"

Hearing his mother cry, the child also began to wail. Widow Zhang hugged him to her bosom and wept even more bitterly.

Mrs Zhu did not cry. Her sunken red-rimmed eyes glared, and she kept saying frantically:

"The poor have only one life, and the rich have only one life. If they don't give me back my money, I'll fight them to the death!"

Just then, a man pushed his way out of the shop. It was Old Chen. His face was purple. He was cursing as he jostled through the crowd.

"You gang of crooks! You'll pay for this! One day I'll see you all burning in the fires of Hell! If we have to take a loss, everybody should take it together. Even if I got only a small share of what's left, at least that would be fair —"

Still swearing vigorously, he spotted the two women.

"Mrs Zhang, Mrs Zhu, what are you sitting there crying for!" he shouted to them. "They've finished dividing up the property. My one mouth couldn't out-argue their dozen. That pack of jackals doesn't give a damn about what's reasonable. They insist that our money doesn't count —"

His words made Widow Zhang weep more bitterly than ever. The playful policeman abruptly walked over to her. He poked her shoulder with his club.

"Hey, what are you crying about? Your man died a long time ago. Which one are you crying for now!"

"Dog farts!" roared Old Chen furiously. "While those

people are stealing our money, all a turd like you can do is get gay with women!" He gave the policeman a strong push.

The policeman's nasty eyes went wide. He raised his club to strike, but the crowd yelled and cursed at him. The other policeman ran over and pulled Old Chen to one side.

"It's no use your raising a fuss. We've got nothing against you. The Merchants Guild has ordered us to guard the door. We've got to eat. We can't help it."

"Old Chen, go make a complaint at the Kuomintang office!" a man shouted from the crowd. From the sound of it, it was the voice of Lu, the well-known loafer.

"Go on, go on!" yelled several others. "See what they say to that!"

The policeman who had mediated laughed coldly. He grasped Old Chen by the shoulder. "I advise you not to go looking for trouble. Going there won't do you any good! You wait till Mr Lin comes back and settle things with him. He can't deny the debt."

Old Chen fumed. He couldn't make up his mind. The idlers were still shouting for him to "go". He looked at Mrs Zhu and Widow Zhang.

"What do you say? They're always screaming down there how they protect the poor!"

"That's right," called one of the crowd. "Yesterday they arrested Mr Lin because they said they didn't want him to run away with poor people's money!"

Almost involuntarily, Old Chen and the two women were swept along by the crowd down the street to the Kuomintang office. Widow Zhang was crying as she walked, and cursing the wicked soldiers who had killed her husband, and praying that Mr Lin should die without sons or grandsons, and reviling that dirty dog of a policeman!

As they neared the office, they saw four policemen standing outside the gate with clubs in their hands. The policemen yelled to them from a distance:

"Go home! You can't go in!"

"We've come to make a complaint!" shouted Old Chen, who was in the first rank of the crowd. "The shop of the Lin family has closed down, and we can't get hold of the money we put up —"

A swarthy pock-marked man jumped out from behind the policemen and howled for them to attack. But the policemen stood their ground, restricting themselves to threats. The crowd in back of Old Chen began to clamour.

"You cheap mongrels don't know what's good for you!" screamed the pock-marked man. "Do you think we have nothing better to do than bother about your business? If you don't get out of here, we're going to fire!"

He stamped and yelled at the policemen to use their clubs. In the front ranks, Old Chen was struck several times. The crowd milled in confusion. Mrs Zhu was old and weak, and she toppled to the ground. In her panicky haste, Widow Zhang lost her slippers. Pushed and buffeted, she also fell down. Rolling and crawling, she avoided many leaping and stamping feet. She scrambled up and ran for all she was worth. It was then she realized that her child was gone. There were drops of blood on the upper part of her jacket.

"Aiya! My precious! My heart! The bandits are killing people! Jade Emperor God save us!"

Wailing, her hair tumbled in disorder, she ran quickly. By the time she fled past the closed door of the shop of the Lin family, she was completely out of her mind.

June 18, 1932

Translated by Sidney Shapiro

Spring Silkworms

OLD Tongbao sat on a rock beside the path that skirted the canal, his long-stemmed pipe lying on the ground next to him. Though it was only a few days after "Clear and Bright Festival" the April sun was already very strong. It scorched Old Tongbao's spine like a basin of fire. Straining down the canal path, the men towing the fast junk wore only thin tunics, open in front. They were bent far forward, pulling, pulling, pulling, great beads of sweat dripping from their brows.

The sight of others toiling strenuously made Old Tongbao feel even warmer; he began to itch. He was still wearing the tattered padded jacket in which he had passed the winter. His jacket had not yet been redeemed from the pawn shop. Who would have believed it could get so hot right after "Clear and Bright"?

Even the weather's not what it used to be, Old Tongbao said to himself, and spat emphatically.

Before him, the water of the canal was green and shiny. Occasional passing boats broke the mirror-smooth surface into ripples and eddies, turning the reflection of the earthen bank and the long line of mulberry trees flanking it into a dancing grey blur. But not for long! Gradually the trees reappeared, twisting and weaving drunkenly. Another few minutes, and they were again standing still, reflected as clearly as before. On the gnarled fists of the mulberry branches, little fingers of tender green buds were already bursting forth.

Crowded close together, the trees along the canal seemed to march endlessly into the distance. The unplanted fields as yet were only cracked clods of dry earth; the mulberry trees reigned supreme hero this time of the year! Behind Old Tongbao's back was another great stretch of mulberry trees, squat, silent. The little buds seemed to be growing bigger every second in the hot sunlight.

Not far from where Old Tongbao was sitting, a grey two-storey building crouched beside the path. That was the silk filature, where the delicate fibres were removed from the cocoons. Two weeks ago it was occupied by troops; a few short trenches still scarred the fields around it. Everyone had said that the Japanese soldiers were attacking in this direction. The rich people in the market town had all run away. Now the troops were gone and the silk filature stood empty and locked as before. There would be no noise and excitement in it again until cocoon selling time.

Old Tongbao had heard Young Master Chen — son of the Master Chen who lived in town — say that Shanghai was seething with unrest, that all the silk weaving factories had closed their doors, that the silk filatures here probably wouldn't open either. But he couldn't believe it. He had been through many periods of turmoil and strife in his sixty years, yet he had never seen a time when the shiny green mulberry leaves had been allowed to wither on the branches and become fodder for the sheep. Of course if the silkworm eggs shouldn't ripen, that would be different. Such matters were all in the hands of the Old Lord of the Sky. Who could foretell His will?

"Only just after Clear and Bright and so hot al-

ready!" marvelled Old Tongbao, gazing at the small
green mulberry leaves. He was happy as well as surprised. He could remember only one year when it was
too hot for padded clothes at Clear and Bright. He was
in his twenties then, and the silkworm eggs had hatched
"two hundred per cent"! That was the year he got married. His family was flourishing in those days. His
father was like an experienced plough ox — there was
nothing he didn't understand, nothing he wasn't willing
to try. Even his old grandfather — the one who had
first started the family on the road to prosperity —
seemed to be growing more hearty with age, in spite of
the hard time he was said to have had during the years
he was a prisoner of the "Long Hairs".*

Old Master Chen was still alive then. His son, the
present Master Chen, hadn't begun smoking opium yet,
and the "House of Chen" hadn't become the bad lot
it was today. Moreover, even though the House of Chen
was of the rich gentry and his own family only ordinary
tillers of the land, Old Tongbao had felt that the des-
tinies of the two families were linked together. Years
ago, "Long Hairs" campaigning through the countryside had captured Tongbao's grandfather and Old
Master Chen and kept them working as prisoners for

---

* In the middle of the nineteenth century, China's oppressed
peasants rose against their feudal rulers in one of the longest
(1851-1864) and bitterest revolutions, it was defeated only with the
assistance of the armed forces of England, France and the United
States of America.

The Qing rulers hated and feared the "Long Hairs", as they
called the Taiping Armymen, and fabricated all sorts of lies about
them in a vain attempt to discredit them with the people.

Old Tongbao, although going steadily downhill economically,
was a typical rich peasant. Like others of his class, he felt and
thought the same as the feudal landlord rulers.

nearly seven years in the same camp. They had escaped together, taking a lot of the Long Hairs' gold with them — at least so people claimed to this day. What's more, at the same time Old Master Chen's silk trade began to prosper, the cocoon raising of Tongbao's family grew successful too. Within ten years grandfather had earned enough to buy three acres of rice paddy, two acres of mulberry grove, and build a modest house. Tongbao's family was the envy of the people of East Village, just as the House of Chen ranked among the first families in the market town.

But afterwards, both families had declined. Today, Old Tongbao had no land of his own, in fact he was over three hundred silver dollars in debt. The House of Chen was finished too. People said the spirit of the dead Long Hair had sued the Chens in the underworld, and because the King of Hell had decreed that the Chens repay the fortune they had amassed on the stolen gold, the family had gone down financially very quickly. Old Tongbao was rather inclined to believe this. If it hadn't been for the influence of devils, why would Master Chen have taken to smoking opium for no good reason at all?

What Old Tongbao could never understand was why the fall of the House of Chen should affect his own family? They hadn't really taken any of the Long Hairs' gold. True, his father had related that when grandfather was escaping from the Long Hairs' camp he had run into a young Long Hair on patrol and had to kill him. What else could he have done? It was "fate"! Still from Tongbao's earliest recollections, his family had prayed and offered sacrifices to appease the soul of the departed young Long Hair time and time again. That little wronged spirit should have left the nether world and been reborn long ago by now! Although Old Tongbao couldn't recall what sort of man his grandfather was, he knew his father had been hard-working and honest — he had seen that with his own eyes. Old Tongbao himself was a respectable person; both Asi, his elder son, and his daughter-in-law were industrious and frugal. Only his younger son, Aduo, was inclined to be a little flighty. But youngsters were all like that. There was nothing really bad about the boy. . . .

Old Tongbao raised his wrinkled face, scorched by years of hot sun to the colour of dark parchment. He gazed bitterly at the canal before him, at the boats on its waters, at the mulberry trees along its banks. All were approximately the same as they had been when he was twenty. But the world had changed. His family now often had to make their meals of pumpkin instead of rice. He was over three hundred silver dollars in debt. . . .

Toot! Toot-toot-toot. . . .

Far up the bend in the canal a boat whistle broke the silence. There was a silk filature over there too. He could see vaguely the neat lines of stones embedded as reinforcement in the canal bank. A small oil-burning river boat came puffing up pompously from beyond the silk filature, tugging three larger craft in its wake. Immediately the peaceful water was agitated with waves rolling toward the banks on both sides of the canal. A peasant, poling a tiny boat, hastened to shore and clutched a clump of reeds growing in the shallows. The waves tossed him and his little craft up and down like a seesaw. The peaceful green countryside was filled with the chugging of the boat engine and the stink of its exhaust.

Hatred burned in Old Tongbao's eyes. He watched the river boat approach, he watched it sail past and glared after it until it went tooting around another bend and disappeared from sight. He had always abominated the foreign devils' contraptions. He himself had never met a foreign devil, but his father had given him a description of one Old Master Chen had seen — red eyebrows, green eyes and a stiff-legged walk! Old Master Chen had hated the foreign devils too. "The foreign devils have swindled our money away," he used to say. Old Tongbao was only eight or nine the last time he saw Old Master Chen. All he remembered about him now were things he had heard from others. But whenever Old Tongbao thought of that remark — "The foreign devils have swindled our money away" — he could almost picture Old Master Chen, stroking his beard and wagging his head.

How the foreign devils had accomplished this, Old Tongbao wasn't too clear. He was sure, however, that Old Master Chen was right. Some things he himself had seen quite plainly. From the time foreign goods — cambric, cloth, oil — appeared in the market town, from the time the foreign river boats increased on the canal, what he produced brought a lower price in the market every day, while what he had to buy became more and more expensive. That was why the property his father left him had shrunk until it finally vanished completely; and now he was in debt. It was not without reason that Old Tongbao hated the foreign devils!

In the village, his attitude toward foreigners was well known. Five years before, someone had told him: The new Kuomintang government says it wants to "throw out" the foreign devils. Old Tongbao didn't believe it. He heard those young propaganda speech-makers of the Kuomintang when he went into the market town. Though they cried "Throw out the foreign devils", they were dressed in Western style clothing. His guess was that they were secretly in league with the foreign devils, that they had been purposely sent to delude the countryfolk! Sure enough, the Kuomintang dropped the slogan not long after, and prices and taxes rose steadily. Old Tongbao was firmly convinced that all this occurred as part of a government conspiracy with the foreign devils.

Last year something had happened that made him almost sick with fury: Only the cocoons spun by the foreign strain silkworms could be sold at a decent price. Buyers paid ten dollars more per load for them than they did for the local variety. Usually on good terms with his daughter-in-law, Old Tongbao had quarrelled with her because of this. She had wanted to raise only foreign silkworms, and Old Tongbao's younger son Aduo had agreed with her. Asi, his elder son, though he didn't say much, had also favoured this course. This year, Old Tongbao had to compromise. Of the five trays they would raise, only four would be silkworms of the local variety; one tray would contain foreign silkworms.

"The world's going from bad to worse! In another couple of years they'll even be wanting foreign mulberry trees! It's enough to take all the joy out of life!"

Old Tongbao picked up his long pipe and rapped it angrily against a clod of dry earth. The sun was directly overhead now, foreshortening his shadow till it looked like a piece of charcoal. Still in his padded jacket, he was bathed in heat. He unfastened the jacket and swung its opened edges back and forth a few times to fan himself. Then he stood up and started for home.

Behind the row of mulberry trees were paddy fields. Most of them were as yet only neatly ploughed furrows of upturned earth clods, dried and cracked by the hot sun. Here and there, the early crops were coming up. In one field, the golden blossoms of rape emitted a heady fragrance. And that group of houses way over there, that was the village where three generations of Old Tongbao's family were living. Above the houses, white smoke from many kitchen stoves curled lazily upwards into the sky.

After crossing the mulberry grove, Old Tongbao walked along the raised path between the paddy fields, then turned and looked again at that row of trees bursting with tender green buds. A twelve-year-old boy came bounding along from the other end of the fields, calling as he ran:

"Grandpa! Ma's waiting for you to come home and eat!"

It was Little Bao, Old Tongbao's grandson.

"Coming!" the old man responded, still gazing at the mulberries. Only twice in his life had he seen these finger-like buds appear on the branches so soon after Clear and Bright. His family would probably have a fine crop of silkworms this year. Five trays of eggs would hatch out a huge number of silkworms. If only they didn't have another bad market like last year, perhaps they could pay off part of their debt.

Little Bao stood beside his grandfather. The child

too looked at the soft green on the gnarled fist branches. Jumping happily, he clapped his hands and chanted:

Green, tender leaves at Clear and Bright,
The girls who tend silkworms,
Clap hands at the sight!

The old man's wrinkled face broke into a smile. He thought it was a good omen for the little boy to respond like this on seeing the first buds of the year. He rubbed his hand affectionately over the child's shaven pate. In Old Tongbao's heart, numbed by a lifetime of poverty and hardship, hope began to stir again.

2

The weather remained warm. The rays of the sun forced open the tender, finger-like, little buds. They had already grown to the size of a small palm. Around Old Tongbao's village, the mulberry trees seemed to respond especially well. From a distance they gave the appearance of a low grey picket fence on top of which a long swath of green brocade had been spread. Bit by bit, day by day, hope grew in the hearts of the villagers. The unspoken mobilization order for the silkworm campaign reached everywhere and everyone. Silkworm rearing equipment that had been laid away for a year was again brought out to be scrubbed and mended. Beside the little stream which ran through the village, women and children, with much laughter and calling back and forth, washed the implements.

None of these women or children looked really healthy. Since the coming of spring, they had been eating only half their fill; their clothes were old and torn. As a matter of fact, they weren't much better off than beggars. Yet all were in quite good spirits, sustained by enormous patience and grand illusions. Burdened though they were by daily mounting debts, they had only one thought in their heads — If we get a good crop of silkworms, everything will be all right! ... They could already visualize how, in a month, the shiny green leaves would be converted into snow-white cocoons and the cocoons exchanged for clinking silver dollars. Although their stomachs were growling with hunger, they couldn't refrain from smiling at this happy prospect.

Old Tongbao's daughter-in-law was among the women by the stream. With the help of her twelve-year-old son, Little Bao, she had already finished washing the family's large trays of woven bamboo strips. Seated on a stone beside the stream, she wiped her perspiring face with the edge of her tunic. A twenty-year-old girl, working with other women on the opposite side of the stream, hailed her.

"Are you raising foreign silkworms this year too?"

It was Sixth Treasure, sister of young Fuqing, the neighbour who lived across the stream.

The thick eyebrows of Old Tongbao's daughter-in-law at once contracted. Her voice sounded as if she had just been waiting for a chance to let off steam.

"Don't ask me; what the old man says, goes!" she shouted. "Asi is dead set against him, so he let us raise one batch of foreign breed! The old fool only has to hear the word 'foreign' to send him up in the air! He'll take dollars made of foreign silver, though; those are the only 'foreign' things he likes!"

The women laughed. From the threshing ground on

the other side of the stream a strapping young man approached. He reached the stream and crossed over on
the four logs that served as a bridge. Seeing him, his
sister-in-law dropped her tirade and called in a high
voice:

"Aduo, will you help me carry these trays? They're
as heavy as dead dogs when they're wet!"

Without a word, Aduo lifted the six big trays and set
them, dripping, on his head. Balancing them in place,
he walked off, swinging his hands in a swimming mo-
tion. When in a good mood, Aduo refused nobody. If
any of the village women asked him to carry something
heavy or fish something out of the stream, he was usually quite willing. But today he probably was a little
grumpy, and so he walked empty-handed with only six
trays on his head. The sight of him, looking as if he
were wearing six layers of wide straw hats, his waist
twisting at each step in imitation of the ladies of the
town, sent the women into peals of laughter. Lotus,
wife of Old Tongbao's nearest neighbour, called with
a giggle:

"Hey, Aduo come back here. Carry a few trays for
me too!"

Aduo grinned. "Not unless you call me a sweet
name!" He continued walking. An instant later he
had reached the porch of his house and set down the
trays out of the sun.

"Will 'kid brother' do?" demanded Lotus, laughing
boisterously. She had a remarkably clean white complexion, but her face was very flat. When she laughed,
all that could be seen was a big open mouth and two
tiny slits of eyes. Originally a slavey in a house in town,
she had been married off to Old Tongbao's neighbour

— a prematurely aged man who walked around with a sour expression and never said a word all day. That was less than six months ago, but her love affairs and escapades already were the talk of the village.

"Shameless hussy!" came a contemptuous female voice from across the stream.

Lotus' piggy eyes immediately widened. "Who said that?" she demanded angrily. "If you've got the brass to call me names, let's see you try it to my face! Come out into the open!"

"Think you can handle me? I'm talking about a shameless, man-crazy baggage! If the shoe fits, wear it!" retorted Sixth Treasure, for it was she who had spoken. She too was famous in the village, but as a mischievous, lively young woman.

The two began splashing water at each other from opposite banks of the stream. Girls who enjoyed a row took sides and joined the battle, while the children whooped with laughter. Old Tongbao's daughter-in-law was more decorous. She picked up her remaining trays, called to Little Bao and returned home. Aduo watched from the porch, grinning. He knew why Sixth Treasure and Lotus were quarrelling. It did his heart good to hear that sharp-tongued Sixth Treasure get told off in public.

Old Tongbao came out of the house with a wooden traystand on his shoulder. Some of the legs of the uprights had been eaten by termites, and he wanted to repair them. At the sight of Aduo standing there laughing at the women, Old Tongbao's face lengthened. The boy hadn't much sense of propriety, he well knew. What disturbed him particularly was the way Aduo and Lotus were always talking and laughing together.

"That bitch is an evil spirit. Fooling with her will bring ruin on our house," he had often warned his younger son.

"Aduo!" he now barked angrily. "Enjoying the scenery? Your brother's in the back mending equipment. Go and give him a hand!" His inflamed eyes bored into Aduo, never leaving the boy until he disappeared into the house.

Only then did Old Tongbao start work on the tray-stand. After examining it carefully, he slowly began his repairs. Years ago, Old Tongbao had worked for a time as a carpenter. But he was old now; his fingers had lost their strength. A few minutes' work and he was breathing hard. He raised his head and looked into the house. Five squares of cloth to which sticky silk-worm eggs were adhered, hung from a horizontal bamboo pole.

His daughter-in-law, Asi's wife, was at the other end of the porch, pasting paper on big trays of woven bamboo strips. Last year, to economize a bit, they had bought and used old newspaper. Old Tongbao still maintained that was why the eggs had hatched poorly — it was unlucky to use paper with writing on it for such a prosaic purpose. Writing meant scholarship, and scholarship had to be respected. This year the whole family had skipped a meal and with the money saved, purchased special "tray pasting paper". Asi's wife pasted the tough, gosling-yellow sheets smooth and flat; on every tray she also affixed three little coloured paper pictures, bought at the same time. One was the "Platter of Plenty"; the other two each showed a militant figure on horseback, pennant in hand. He, according to local belief, was the "Guardian of Silkworm Hatching".

"I was only able to buy twenty loads of mulberry leaves with that thirty silver dollars I borrowed on your father's guarantee," Old Tongbao said to his daughter-in-law. He was still panting from his exertions with the traystand. "Our rice will be finished by the day after tomorrow. What are we going to do?"

Thanks to her father's influence with his boss and his willingness to guarantee repayment of the loan, Old Tongbao was able to borrow the money at a low rate of interest — only twenty-five per cent a month! Both the principal and interest had to be repaid by the end of the silkworm season.

Asi's wife finished pasting a tray and placed it in the sun. "You've spent it all on leaves," she said angrily. "We'll have a lot of leaves left over, just like last year!"

"Full of lucky words, aren't you?" demanded the old man, sarcastically. "I suppose every year'll be like last year? We can't get more than a dozen or so loads of leaves from our own trees. With five sets of grubs to feed, that won't be nearly enough."

"Oh, of course, you're never wrong!" she replied hotly. "All I know is with rice we can eat, without it we'll go hungry!" His stubborn refusal to raise any foreign silkworms last year had left them with only the unsalable local breed. As a result, she was often contrary with him.

The old man's face turned purple with rage. After this, neither would speak to the other.

But hatching time was drawing closer every day. The little village's two dozen families were thrown into a state of great tension, great determination, great struggle. With it all, they were possessed of a great hope, a hope that could almost make them forget their hungry bellies.

Old Tongbao's family, borrowing a little here, getting a little credit there, somehow managed to get by. Nor did the other families eat any better; there wasn't one with a spare bag of rice! Although they had harvested a good crop the previous year, landlords, creditors, taxes, levies, one after another, had cleaned the peasants out long ago. Now all their hopes were pinned on the spring silkworms. The repayment date of every loan they made was set for the "end of the silkworm season".

With high hopes and considerable fear, like a soldier going into a hand-to-hand battle to the death, they prepared for their spring silkworm campaign!

"Grain Rain" day — bringing gentle drizzles — was not far off. Almost imperceptibly, the silkworm eggs of the two dozen village families began to show faint tinges of green. Women, when they met on the public threshing ground, would speak to one another agitatedly in tones that were anxious yet joyful.

"Over at Sixth Treasure's place, they're almost ready to incubate their eggs!"

"Lotus says her family is going to start incubating tomorrow. So soon!"

"Huang 'the Priest' has made a divination. He predicts that this spring mulberry leaves will go to four dollars a load!"

Old Tongbao's daughter-in-law examined their five sets of eggs. They looked bad. The tiny seed-like eggs were still pitch black, without even a hint of green. Her husband, Asi, took them into the light to peer at them carefully. Even so, he could find hardly any ripening eggs. She was very worried.

"You incubate them anyhow. Maybe this variety is a little slow," her husband forced himself to say consolingly.

Her lips pressed tight, she made no reply.

Old Tongbao's wrinkled face sagged with dejection. Though he said nothing, he thought their prospects were dim.

The next day, Asi's wife again examined the eggs. Ha! Quite a few were turning green, and a very shiny green at that! Immediately, she told her husband, told Old Tongbao, Aduo ... she even told her son Little Bao. Now the incubating process could begin! She held the five pieces of cloth to which the eggs were adhered against her bare bosom. As if cuddling a nursing infant, she sat absolutely quiet, not daring to stir. At night, she took the five sets to bed with her. Her husband was routed out, and had to share Aduo's bed. The tiny silkworm eggs were very scratchy against her flesh. She felt happy and a little frightened, like the first time she was pregnant and the baby moved inside her. Exactly the same sensation!

Uneasy but eager, the whole family waited for the eggs to hatch. Aduo was the only exception. We're sure to hatch a good crop, he said, but anyone who thinks we're going to get rich in this life, is out of his head. Though the old man swore Aduo's big mouth would ruin their luck, the boy stuck to his guns.

A clean dry shed for the growing grubs was all prepared. The second day of incubation, Old Tongbao smeared a garlic with earth and placed it at the foot of the wall inside the shed. If, in a few days, the garlic put out many sprouts, it would mean that the eggs would hatch well. He did this every year, but this year he was more reverential than usual, and his hands trembled. Last year's divination had proved all too accurate. He didn't dare to think about that now.

Every family in the village was busy "incubating". For the time being there were few women's footprints on the threshing ground or the banks of the little stream. An unofficial "martial law" had been imposed. Even peasants normally on very good terms stopped visiting one another. For a guest to come and frighten away the spirits of the ripening eggs — that would be no laughing matter! At most, people exchanged a few words in low tones when they met, then quickly separated. This was the "sacred" season!

Old Tongbao's family was on pins and needles. In the five sets of eggs a few grubs had begun wriggling. It was exactly one day before Grain Rain. Asi's wife had calculated that most of the eggs wouldn't hatch until after that day. Before or after Grain Rain was all right, but for eggs to hatch on the day itself was considered highly unlucky. Incubation was no longer necessary, and the eggs were carefully placed in the special shed. Old Tongbao stole a glance at his garlic at the foot of the wall. His heart dropped. There were only two small green shoots! He didn't dare to look any closer. He prayed silently that by noon the day after tomorrow the garlic would have many, many more.

At last hatching day arrived. Asi's wife set a pot of rice on to boil and nervously watched for the time when the steam from it would rise straight up. Old Tongbao lit the incense and candles he had bought in anticipation of this event. Devoutly, he placed them before the idol of the Kitchen God. His two sons went into the fields to pick wild flowers. Little Bao chopped a lamp-wick into fine pieces and crushed the wild flowers the men brought back. Everything was ready. The sun was entering its zenith; steam from the rice pot puffed straight upwards. Asi's wife immediately leaped to her feet, stuck a "sacred" paper flower and a pair of goose feathers into the knot of hair at the back of her head and went to the shed. Old Tongbao carried a wooden scalepole; Asi followed with the chopped lamp-wick and the crushed wild flowers. Daughter-in-law uncovered the cloth pieces to which the grubs were adhered, and sprinkled them with the bits of wick and flowers Asi was holding. Then she took the wooden scalepole from Old Tongbao and hung the cloth pieces over it. She next removed the pair of goose feathers from her hair. Moving them lightly across the cloth, she brushed the grubs, together with the crushed lamp-wick and wild flowers, on to a large tray. One set, two sets ... the last set contained the foreign breed. The grubs from this cloth were brushed on to a separate tray. Finally, she removed the "sacred" paper flower from her hair and pinned it, with the goose feathers, against the side of the tray.

A solemn ceremony! One that had been handed down through the ages! Like warriors taking an oath before going into battle! Old Tongbao and family now had ahead of them a month of fierce combat — with no rest day or night — against bad weather, bad luck and anything else that might come along!

The grubs, wriggling in the trays, looked very healthy. They were all the proper black colour. Old Tongbao and his daughter-in-law were able to relax a little. But when the old man secretly took another look at his garlic, he turned pale! It had grown only four measly shoots! Ah! Would this year be like last year all over again?

3

But the "fateful" garlic proved to be not so psychic after all. The silkworms of Old Tongbao's family grew and thrived! Though it rained continuously during the grubs' First Sleep and Second Sleep, and the weather was a bit colder than at Clear and Bright, the "little darlings" were extremely robust.

The silkworms of the other families in the village were not doing badly either. A tense kind of joy pervaded the countryside. Even the small stream seemed to be gurgling with bright laughter. Lotus' family was the sole exception. They were only raising one set of grubs, but by the Third Sleep their silkworms weighed less than twenty catties. Just before the Big Sleep, people saw Lotus' husband walk to the stream and dump out his trays. That dour, old-looking man had bad luck written all over him.

Because of this dreadful event, the village women put Lotus' family strictly "off limits". They made wide detours so as not to pass her door. If they saw her or her taciturn husband, no matter how far away, they made haste to go in the opposite direction. They feared that even one look at Lotus or her spouse, the briefest conversation, would contaminate them with the unfortunate couple's bad luck!

Old Tongbao strictly forbade Aduo to talk to Lotus.

"If I catch you gabbing with that baggage again, I'll disown you!" he threatened in a loud, angry voice, standing outside on the porch to make sure Lotus could hear him.

Little Bao was also warned not to play in front of Lotus' door, and not to speak to anyone in her family.

The old man harped at Aduo morning, noon and night, but the boy turned a deaf ear to his father's grumbling. In his heart, he laughed at it. Of the whole family, Aduo alone placed little stock in taboos and superstitions. He didn't talk with Lotus, however. He was much too busy for that.

By the Big Sleep, their silkworms weighed three hundred catties. Every member of Old Tongbao's family, including twelve-year-old Little Bao, worked for two days and two nights without sleeping a wink. The silkworms were unusually sturdy. Only twice in his sixty years had Old Tongbao ever seen the like. Once was the year he married; once when his first son was born.

The first day after the Big Sleep, the "little darlings" ate seven loads of leaves. They were now a bright green, thick and healthy. Old Tongbao and his family, on the contrary, were much thinner, their eyes bloodshot from lack of sleep.

No one could guess how much the "little darlings" would eat before they spun their cocoons. Old Tongbao discussed the question of buying more leaves with Asi.

"Master Chen won't lend us any more. Shall we try your father-in-law's boss again?"

"We've still got ten loads coming. That's enough for one more day," replied Asi. He could barely hold himself erect. His eyelids weighed a thousand catties. They kept wanting to close.

"One more day? You're dreaming!" snapped the old man impatiently. "Not counting tomorrow, they still have to eat three more days. We'll need another thirty loads! Thirty loads, I say!"

Loud voices were heard outside on the threshing ground. Aduo had arrived with men delivering five loads of mulberry branches. Everyone went out to strip the leaves. Asi's wife hurried from the shed. Across the stream, Sixth Treasure and her family were raising only a small crop of silkworms; having spare time, she came over to help. Bright stars filled the sky. There was a slight wind. All up and down the village, gay shouts and laughter rang in the night.

"The price of leaves is rising fast!" a coarse voice cried. "This afternoon, they were getting four dollars a load in the market town!"

Old Tongbao was very upset. At four dollars a load, thirty loads would come to a hundred and twenty dollars. Where could he raise so much money! But then he figured — he was sure to gather over five hundred catties of cocoons. Even at fifty dollars a hundred, they'd sell for two hundred and fifty dollars. Feeling a bit consoled, he heard a small voice from among the leaf-strippers.

"They say the folks east of here aren't doing so well with their silkworms. There won't be any reason for the price of leaves to go much higher."

Old Tongbao recognized the speaker as Sixth Treasure, and he relaxed still further.

The girl and Aduo were standing beside a large basket, stripping leaves. In the dim starlight, they worked quite close to each other, partly hidden by the pile of mulberry branches before them. Suddenly,

Sixth Treasure felt someone pinch her thigh. She knew well enough who it was, and she suppressed a giggle. But when, a moment later, a hand brushed against her breasts, she jumped; a little shriek escaped her.

"Aiya!"

"What's wrong?" demanded Asi's wife, working on the other side of the basket.

Sixth Treasure's face flamed scarlet. She shot a glance at Aduo, then quickly lowered her head and resumed stripping leaves. "Nothing," she replied. "I think a caterpillar bit me!"

Aduo bit his lip to keep from laughing aloud. He had been half starved the past two weeks and had slept little. But in spite of having lost a lot of weight, he was in high spirits. While he never suffered from any of Old Tongbao's gloom, neither did he believe that one good crop, whether of silkworms or of rice, would enable them to wipe off their debt and own their own land again. He knew they would never "get out from under" merely by relying on hard work, even if they broke their backs trying. Nevertheless, he worked with a will. He enjoyed work, just as he enjoyed fooling with Sixth Treasure.

The next morning, Old Tongbao went into town to borrow money for more leaves. Before leaving home, he talked the matter over with his daughter-in-law. They decided to mortgage their grove of mulberries that produced fifteen loads of leaves a year as security for the loan. The grove was the last piece of property the family owned.

By the time the old man ordered another thirty loads, and the first ten were delivered, the sturdy "little darlings" had gone hungry for half an hour. Putting forth their pointed little mouths, they swayed from side to side, searching for food. Daughter-in-law's heart ached to see them. When the leaves were finally spread in the trays, the silkworm shed at once resounded with a sibilant crunching, so noisy it drowned out conversation. In a very short while, the trays were again empty of leaves. Another thick layer was piled on. Just keeping the silkworms supplied with leaves, Old Tongbao and his family were so busy they could barely catch their breath. This was the final crisis. In two more days the "little darlings" would spin their cocoons. People were putting every bit of their remaining strength into this last desperate struggle.

Though he had gone without sleep for three whole days, Aduo didn't appear particularly tired. He agreed to watch the shed alone that night until dawn to permit the others to get some rest. There was a bright moon and the weather was a trifle cold. Aduo crouched beside a small fire he had built in the shed. At about eleven, he gave the silkworms their second feeding, then returned to squat by the fire. He could hear the loud rustle of the "little darlings" crunching through the leaves. His eyes closed. Suddenly, he heard the door squeak, and his eyelids flew open. He peered into the darkness for a moment, then shut his eyes again. In addition to the crunching of the leaves he heard a peculiar rustling sound. The next thing he knew, his head had struck against his knees. Waking with a start, he heard the door screen bang and thought he saw a moving shadow. Aduo leaped up and rushed outside. In the moonlight, he saw someone crossing the threshing ground toward the stream. He caught up in a flash, seized and flung the intruder to the ground. Aduo was sure he had nabbed a thief.

"Aduo, kill me if you want to, but don't give me away!"

The voice made Aduo's hair stand on end. He could see in the moonlight a queer flat white face and round piggy eyes. But the eyes were fixed upon him quite without fear. Aduo snorted.

"What were you after?"

"A few of your family's 'little darlings'!"

"What did you do with them?"

"Threw them in the stream!"

Aduo's face darkened. He knew that in this way she was trying to put a curse on the lot. "You're pure poison! We never did anything to hurt you."

"Never did anything? Oh, yes you did! Yes, you did! Our silkworm eggs didn't hatch well, but we didn't harm anybody. You were all so smart! You shunned me like a leper. No matter how far away I was, if you saw me, you turned your heads. You acted as if I wasn't even human!"

She got to her feet, the agonized expression on her face terrible to see. Aduo stared at her. "I'm not going to beat you," he said finally. "Go on your way!"

Without giving her another glance, he trotted back to the shed. He was wide awake now. Lotus had only taken a handful and the remaining "little darlings" were all in good condition. It didn't occur to him either to hate or pity Lotus, but the last thing she had said remained in his mind. It seemed to him there was something eternally wrong in the scheme of human relations; but he couldn't put his finger on what it was exactly, nor did he know why it should be. In a little while, he forgot about this too. The lusty silkworms, though eating and eating, by some magic were never full!

Nothing more happened that night. Just before the sky began to brighten in the east, Old Tongbao and his daughter-in-law came to relieve Aduo. They took the trays of "little darlings" and looked at them in the light. The silkworms were turning a whiter colour, their bodies gradually becoming shorter and thicker. Old Tongbao and his daughter-in-law were delighted with the excellent way they were developing.

But when, at sunrise, Asi's wife went to draw water at the stream, she met Sixth Treasure. The girl's expression was serious.

"I saw that slut leaving your place shortly before midnight," she whispered. "Aduo was right behind her. They stood here and talked for a long time! Your family ought to look after things better than that!"

The colour drained from the face of Asi's wife. Without a word, she carried her water bucket back to the house. First she told her husband about it, then she told Old Tongbao. It was a fine state of affairs when a baggage like that could sneak into people's silkworm sheds! Old Tongbao stamped with rage. He immediately summoned Aduo. But the boy denied the whole story; he said Sixth Treasure was dreaming. The old man then went to question Sixth Treasure. She insisted she had seen everything with her own eyes. The old man didn't know what to believe. He returned home and looked at the "little darlings". They were as sturdy as ever, not a sickly one in the lot.

But the joy that Old Tongbao and his family had been feeling was dampened. They knew Sixth Treasure's words couldn't be entirely without foundation. Their only hope was that Aduo and that hussy had played their little games on the porch rather than in the shed!

Old Tongbao recalled gloomily that the garlic had only put forth three or four shoots. The future looked dark. Hadn't there been times before when the silkworms ate great quantities of leaves and seemed to be growing well, yet dried up and died just when they were ready to spin their cocoons? Yes, often! But Old Tongbao didn't dare let himself think of such a possibility. To entertain a thought like that, even in the most secret recesses of the mind, would only be inviting bad luck!

4

The "little darlings" began spinning their cocoons, but Old Tongbao's family was still in a sweat. Both their money and their energy were completely spent. They still had nothing to show for it; there was no guarantee of their earning any return. Nevertheless, they continued working at top speed. Beneath the racks on which the cocoons were being spun fires had to be kept going to supply warmth. Old Tongbao and Asi, his elder son, their backs bent, slowly squatted first on this side then on that. Hearing the small rustlings of the spinning silkworms, they wanted to smile, and if the sounds stopped for a moment their hearts stopped too. Yet, worried as they were, they didn't dare to disturb the silkworms by looking inside. When the silkworms squirted fluid in their faces as they peered up from beneath the racks, they were happy in spite of the momentary discomfort. The bigger the shower, the better they liked it.*

Aduo had already peeked several times. Little Bao had caught him at it and demanded to know what was going on. Aduo made an ugly face at the child, but did not reply.

After three days of "spinning", the fires were extinguished. Asi's wife could restrain herself no longer. She stole a look, her heart beating fast. Inside, all was white as snow. The brush that had been put in for the silkworms to spin on was completely covered over with cocoons. Asi's wife had never seen so successful a "flowering"!

The whole family was wreathed in smiles. They were on solid ground at last! The "little darlings" had proved they had a conscience; they hadn't consumed those mulberry leaves, at four dollars a load, in vain. The family could reap its reward for a month of hunger and sleepless nights. The Old Lord of the Sky had eyes!

Throughout the village, there were many similar scenes of rejoicing. The Silkworm Goddess had been beneficent to the tiny village this year. Most of the two dozen families garnered good crops of cocoons from their silkworms. The harvest of Old Tongbao's family was well above average.

Again women and children crowded the threshing ground and the banks of the little stream. All were much thinner than the previous month, with eyes sunk in their sockets, throats rasping and hoarse. But everyone was excited, happy. As they chattered about the

---

* The emission of the fluid means the silkworm is about to spin its cocoon.

struggle of the past month, visions of piles of bright silver dollars shimmered before their eyes. Cheerful thoughts filled their minds — they would get their summer clothes out of the pawnshop; at Dragon Boat Festival perhaps they could eat a nice fat fish. . . .

They talked, too, of the farce enacted by Lotus and Aduo a few nights before. Sixth Treasure announced to everyone she met, "That Lotus has no shame at all. She delivered herself right to his door!" Men who heard this laughed coarsely. Women muttered a prayer and called Lotus bad names. They said Old Tongbao's family could consider itself lucky that a curse hadn't fallen on them. The gods were merciful!

Family after family was able to report a good harvest of cocoons. People visited one another to view the shining white gossamer. The father of Old Tongbao's daughter-in-law came from town with his little son. They brought gifts of sweets and fruit and a salted fish. Little Bao was happy as a puppy frolicking in the snow.

The elderly visitor sat with Old Tongbao beneath a willow beside the stream. He had the reputation in town of a "man who knew how to enjoy life". From hours of listening to the professional story-tellers in front of the temple, he had learned by heart many of the classic tales of ancient times. He was a great one for idle chatter, and often would say anything that came into his head. Old Tongbao therefore didn't take him very seriously when he leaned close and queried softly:

"Are you selling your cocoons, or will you spin the silk yourself at home?"

"Selling them, of course," Old Tongbao replied casually.

The elderly visitor slapped his thigh and sighed, then rose abruptly and pointed at the silk filature rearing up behind the row of mulberries, now quite bald of leaves.

"Tongbao," he said, "the cocoons are being gathered, but the doors of the silk filatures are shut as tight as ever! They're not buying this year! Ah, all the world is in turmoil! The silk houses are not going to open, I tell you!"

Old Tongbao couldn't help smiling. He wouldn't believe it. How could he possibly believe it? There were dozens of silk filatures in this part of the country. Surely they couldn't all shut down? What's more, he had heard that they had made a deal with the Japanese; the Chinese soldiers who had been billeted in the silk houses had long since departed.

Changing the subject, the visitor related the latest town gossip, salting it freely with classical aphorisms and quotations from the ancient stories. Finally he got around to the thirty silver dollars borrowed through him as middleman. He said his boss was anxious to be repaid.

Old Tongbao became uneasy after all. When his visitor departed, he hurried from the village down the highway to look at the two nearest silk filatures. Their doors were indeed shut; not a soul was in sight. Business was in full swing this time last year, with whole rows of dark gleaming scales in operation.

He felt a little panicky as he returned home. But when he saw those snowy cocoons, thick and hard, pleasure made him smile. What beauties! No one wants them? — Impossible. He still had to hurry and finish gathering the cocoons; he hadn't thanked the gods properly yet. Gradually, he forgot about the silk houses.

But in the village, the atmosphere was changing day by day. People who had just begun to laugh were now all frowns. News was reaching them from town that none of the neighbouring silk filatures were opening their doors. It was the same with the houses along the highway. Last year at this time buyers of cocoons were streaming in and out of the village. This year there wasn't a sign of even half a buyer. In their place came dunning creditors and government tax collectors who promptly froze up if you asked them to take cocoons in payment.

Swearing, curses, disappointed sighs! With such a fine crop of cocoons the villagers had never dreamed that their lot would be even worse than usual! It was as if hailstones dropped out of a clear sky. People like Old Tongbao, whose crop was especially good, took it hardest of all.

"What is the world coming to!" He beat his breast and stamped his feet in helpless frustration.

But the villagers had to think of something. The cocoons would spoil if kept too long. They either had to sell them or remove the silk themselves. Several families had already brought out and repaired silk reels they hadn't used for years. They would first remove the silk from the cocoons and then see about the next step. Sixth Treasure was planning to do the same. Old Tongbao discussed the matter with his son and daughter-in-law.

"We won't sell our cocoons; we'll spin the silk ourselves!" said the old man. "Nobody ever heard of selling cocoons until the foreign devils' companies started the thing!"

Asi's wife was the first to object. "We've got over five hundred catties of cocoons here," she retorted. "Where are you going to get enough reels?"

She was right. Five hundred catties were no small amount. They'd never finish spinning the silk themselves. Hire outside help? That meant spending money. Asi agreed with his wife. Aduo blamed his father for planning incorrectly.

"If you listened to me, we'd have raised only one tray of foreign breed and no locals. Then the fifteen loads of leaves from our own mulberry trees would have been enough, and we wouldn't have had to borrow!"

Old Tongbao was so angry he couldn't speak.

At last a ray of hope appeared. Huang the Priest had heard somewhere that a silk house below the city of Wuxi was doing business as usual. Actually an ordinary peasant, Huang was nicknamed "The Priest" because of the learned airs he affected and his interest in Taoist "magic". Old Tongbao always got along with him fine. After learning the details from Huang, Old Tongbao conferred with his elder son Asi about going to Wuxi.

"It's about 270 *li* by water, six days for the round trip," ranted the old man. "Son of a bitch! It's a goddam expedition! But what else can we do? We can't eat the cocoons, and our creditors are pressing hard!"

Asi agreed. They borrowed a small boat and bought a few yards of matting to cover the cargo. It was decided that Aduo should go along. Taking advantage of the good weather, the cocoon selling "expeditionary force" set out.

Five days later, the men returned — but not with an empty hold. They still had one basket of cocoons. The silk filature, which they had reached after a 270-*li* journey by water, had offered extremely harsh terms — Only thirty-five dollars a load for foreign breed, twenty for local; thin cocoons not wanted at any price. Although their cocoons were all first class, the people at the silk house had been extremely fussy, and rejected one whole basket. Old Tongpao and his sons received a hundred and ten dollars for the sale, ten of which had to be spent as travel expenses. The hundred dollars remaining was not even enough to pay back what they had borrowed for that last thirty loads of mulberry leaves! On the return trip, Old Tongbao became ill with rage. His sons carried him into the house.

Asi's wife had no choice but to take the ninety odd catties they had brought back and reel the silk from the cocoons herself. She borrowed a few reels from Sixth Treasure's family and worked for six days. All their rice was gone now. Asi took the silk into town, but no one would buy it. Even the pawnshop didn't want it. Only after much pleading was he able to persuade the pawnbroker to take it in exchange for a load of rice they had pawned before Clear and Bright.

That's the way it happened. Because they raised a good crop of spring silkworms, the people in Old Tongbao's village got deeper into debt. Old Tongbao's family raised five trays and gathered a splendid harvest of cocoons. Yet they ended up owing another thirty silver dollars and losing their mortgaged mulberry trees — to say nothing of suffering a month of hunger and sleepless nights in vain!   November 1, 1932

Translated by Sidney Shapiro

A Ballad of Algae

WHEN the northwest wind had blown for two days on end you could scarcely hear a dog bark in the tiny village. A leaden sky met the gaze everywhere, except where at the eastern horizon a strip of vague yellow appeared weakly yet wilfully to be attempting to melt away the sky's leaden cover.

Seven or eight low houses crouched like beetles on the ground. The stacks of fresh rice straw resembled withered wild fungi; close beside them and on the river-bank some distance away tallow trees denuded of leaves reared their newly snapped forked branches in dignified contention with the northwest wind. These kindly mothers to the peasantry generally needed no laborious tending, and when winter came and their black nuts burst into white tips, they gave up their covering of slender fingers and submitted to a thousand knife wounds to make good the peasants' lives with those oil-rich nuts.

Twisting westwards like a black python, the river crawled past paddy-fields criss-crossed with dykes and past irregularly shaped mulberry orchards, widening towards the west until it merged with the horizon. As summer turned into autumn, this merry, goodly stream became sewn over with coin-like, floating duckweed and threads of waterweed, but had now been swept clean of both by the northwest wind, and its naked torso wrinkled in the bitter cold, into waves fragmented like fish scales, turning black with fury.

Caixi, a strapping fellow approaching forty, came out of one of the low houses, strode to the east end of the threshing ground and looked up at the sky all around. The vague yellow on the eastern horizon was now hidden behind the great, chinkless lead cover of the sky. Caixi looked then sniffed to test the humidity of the air.

"It's going to snow, damn it!" he mumbled to himself and went back indoors. A gust of wind from the northwest scurried whistling across the river from the mulberry orchards, lifting the lower hem of his torn quilted cotton jacket. A mangy yellow dog that had just come out of the house tucked its head in quickly and arched its back, each hair seeming to rise on its own.

"Oho, you creatures don't like the cold either, then!" he said, grabbed it by the scruff of the neck and, as if searching for an object on which to vent all the energy in his body, pitched it smoothly on to the threshing ground.

The dog landed, rolled into a somersault and without one bark fled back indoors, its tail between its legs. Laughing heartily, Caixi followed it.

"Xiusheng!" Caixi's manly tone at once set the air in the house ringing. "The weather's changing. Get in the hornwort — today!"

The dingy black object wriggling in the corner was Xiusheng, the "householder", for all that he was Caixi's nephew. Ten years younger than Caixi, he looked a

great deal older. A tiller of the soil, he had been afflict-
ed with jaundice from childhood. He was engaged in
filling two sacks with ground rice, checking that the
weight was even.

"Today?" he replied, straightening up. "I was going
into town to sell the rice."

"You can do that tomorrow! What are you going to
do if there's a heavy fall of snow? And what about
the money from selling the tallow nuts the time before
last? All gone, is it?"

"Ages ago. It was your idea to redeem the winter
clothes. Now we've no oil, we're out of salt, and yesterday the headman was round dunning us for Master
Chen's interest, one yuan fifty; I said at the time, pay
him back his interest and we can redeem the clothes bit
by bit later, didn't I? But no, you lot —"

"Ah!" shouted Caixi irritably. "In any case, if we
miss today our share of the hornwort will be lost, won't
it?" And he retreated bellowing into the back of the
house.

Xiusheng shot a dubious look at the sky outside. He
too expected snow, and the hornwort would be piled
up already in the narrow bends of the stream after the
past two days of northwest wind, and snow or no snow,
if he waited another day the others would have got to
it before him; yet he couldn't forget the village headman's "Have the money ready tomorrow or I'll have
the rice as security, all right?", and once the headman
got his hands on the rice, three yuan worth would be
down to one fifty.

"The rice has to be sold, and the hornwort has to be
got in," thought Xiusheng as he tentatively hefted the
sacks on the carrying pole. Putting them down, he de-

cided to ask if any of the neighbours was going to town
and could take the rice along and sell it for him.

2

At the back of the house, Caixi leaned into the sheep
shed, his bedroom, grabbed a blue cloth belt from the
bed board and fastened it tightly around his waist. He
felt much warmer. It had been two years since they
had kept sheep there, Xiusheng having no extra cash
to buy lambs, but the peculiar acrid smell of sheep
lingered. Caixi, who liked cleanliness, not only frequently aired the upper board on which he slept but swept
the mud floor where the sheep had slept until it was
spotless, not because of the smell, whose faint redolence
he quite liked, but because of the musty mould which
often attacked such dank places.

As no snow had yet fallen, he went for two bundles
of fresh straw to add to his bedding. He was just leaving the sheep shed on his way to a nearby rick when he
heard a humming noise from the rick itself, beside which
he saw a pail full of water in the mud and immediately
caught a faint but familiar whiff of sheep. Realizing at
once who it was, he bounded across at the double, and
there indeed was Xiusheng's wife moaning as she squatted by the rick of straw.

"What's up with you?" He caught hold of the sturdy
young woman to haul her to her feet but let go when
he saw how she was cradling her distended belly in both
hands. "Is it the pains?" he asked anxiously. "Is it on
its way?"

She nodded, then shook her head, struggling to speak.

"I doubt it. It's too early! Just the sickness, I should think. I just went for a bucket of water, got as far as here and then my stomach — the pain was awful."

Caixi turned to look at the pail of water with an air of indecision.

"He got cross with me again last night," she said, making an effort to push herself up. "He cursed and kicked me in the side down there. I think that was just the sickness. It went away again after a bit, but just now —"

She heaved a sigh with some effort then squatted down again against the rick.

"What, and you never let on?" cried Caixi angrily. "You just let him? Brave of him, isn't it, taking it out on you? What did he say?"

"He said the kid wasn't his and he didn't want it."

"Hm! He's got a damn nerve to say that, when he's not man enough to plant his own seed!"

"He said one of these days the knife'll go in clean and come out red. I'm afraid he may mean it."

"He'd never dare," laughed Caixi. "He hasn't got the guts." Xiusheng's hydropic, bloodless face and dry, stick-like arms flashed before his eyes; the contrast with this vivacious woman before him in the exuberance of her youth, the strong odour of whose flesh resembled that of sheep, convinced him that they were ill-matched, that this sturdy woman, stronger than most lads when it came to work, had no business putting up with the blows and curses of her sickly swine of a husband.

He saw why she did put up with the humiliation, though; she was in a way conscious of being unworthy of him and tried to make it up to him with hard work and patient submission. But was this the way? Caixi was perplexed. He could see no other way for them to get on. In any case, Xiusheng was not to blame for his own frailty.

"Still," he sighed, I'm not going to let him lash out over anything just as he wants. Supposing he harms the baby? Whether it's his or mine, it all comes down to the same thing. You're the one that's bringing it into the world, and it's a chip off the family block. Hey, are you feeling any better now?"

She nodded and attempted to stand, her full form making her movements as ungainly as if she had been carrying a big drum. Caixi supported her by the arm, and then the strong stimulant of her scent assailing his nostrils drove him to hold her tightly in his arms.

He retrieved the pail and went indoors without her.

3

Hornwort was collected to prepare fertilizer for the coming spring. On the lower Yangzi this was applied once in spring when the seedlings were transplanted and again in July or August when they had reached waist height. In the region where Xiusheng lived, the second application was thought more important, and for this bean cake was necessary. One year there had been an "incident" in the area that produced bean cake, and prices rose every year, outstripping peasant means and bankrupting the dealers.

Poor peasants had then had to rely on a single application, the earlier one that they called the "first spreading", the best material for which was held to be the river waterweed referred to locally as "hornwort".

Hornwort had to be gathered in winter when a north-west wind had been blowing; it was easiest then, when the wind had piled it up together. But winter was hardly the pleasantest time to be out in the severe cold.

Deprived of bean cake, the peasants had no choice but to wrestle doggedly for their lives.

Caixi and Xiusheng propelled their "bareback" boat in a westerly direction. They knew from experience that the most hornwort was to be found in a fork some twenty *li* from the village, but also that two village boats had set out ahead of them, so that to reach their goal they would have to go ten *li* west then turn south for ten more at double speed. This was Caixi's idea.

They made their way downstream against the still powerful northwest wind, Caixi poling and Xiusheng rowing.

The wind played with the free end of Caixi's blue cloth belt, wrapping it around the bamboo punt pole again and again. He grasped it without breaking rhythm and wiped the sweat from his face, then with a brushing noise the pole met the frozen earth of the bank and the lip of the boat sputtered with silver spray. With a powerful and long drawn out, deep-chested cry, Caixi whirled the pole nimbly through the air into the water on the other side of the boat, leaned on its end for a two-handed thrust, heaved it out again and whirled all twelve feet of it dripping over his head once more.

The pole danced with ever greater animation as Caixi, seeming to have found an object for his anger, trickled all over with the hot sweat of victory.

The river began to widen out after something like ten *li*. Endless expanses of harvested paddy-fields stretched before the eye. The branch stream snaked through the intricate chessboard of the tilled earth like a glittering belt studded here and there with the thatched housings of waterwheels. The sparse grey cluster was hamlets from which rose vague white smoke.

And near and far across this simple farmland rose the proud, verdant cemetaries of the rich.

Waterfowl broke fluttering from the dry reedbank and scattered abruptly to land far out of sight.

Caixi, holding his pole across the bows of the boat, was struck with the novelty of this familiar scene. Mutely, Nature was communicating with him. He felt something in his breast that wanted to get out.

He gave a long cry for the bleak land.

His cry was dispersed by the northwest wind. Slowly, he put the pole down. Dry reeds rustled along the bank. The strokes of the oar from the stern were sharply audible though sluggish and listless.

Caixi went aft and gave Xiusheng a hand with the oar. Water, as though defeated, hissed past.

Before long they had reached their destination.

"Now let's get on with it! They'll be here in no time, and there'll be no peace with everybody grabbing for it."

As he spoke, Caixi lifted the massive clamp that they used to gather the hornwort. They stood one on either side of the bows holding it open between them, stabbed it down into the thick bank of weed, clamped it closed, then with vigorous twists hauled it up and tossed the mess of weed and mud into the bottom of the boat.

As though woven together, the weed of the river resisted the strength of the men tearing at it. Mud and splinters of ice added to the weight. Caixi's protruding

chin knotted forcefully as he stirred and twisted with
determination; he shouted with triumph every time it
came up, and the thick clamp of bamboo creaked and
bent like a bow.

"Harder, Xiusheng! Faster!" Caixi spat on his hands,
rubbed them and full of beans applied himself to raising
his weed clamp.

Xiusheng's puffy face was oozing with sweat too,
though he was moving at only half Caixi's rate and got
only half the weed that Caixi got with each sweep of
his clamp. Still his shoulders ached, his heart pumped
wildly in his chest, and from time to time he whimpered
softly.

The hornwort, with its accompaniment of mud and
ice, gradually built up in the bottom of the boat, which
settled lower in the water; whenever Caixi planted his
feet firmly to bring up another full load, the boat veered
outwards and icy water washed over the bows to soak
his straw-shod feet. He was in shirtsleeves, having removed the torn jacket, but the blue belt stayed tightly
around his waist; from head to waist he gave off heat
in billows like a kitchen steamer.

4

The creaking of oars and the sound of voices were borne
gradually nearer on the wind. A felt hat flashed from
the clump of dry reeds not far ahead. Then a small boat
made its laborious way out, then another.

"Aha, there you all are!" cried Caixi merrily, as he
strained to heave a clampful of weed into the boat;
then with a sly smile he raised up the bamboo clamp,
smashed it down into a thick clump that he had had his

eye on for some time, opened it as wide as it would go and stirred as hard as he could.

"Well, I'm blowed! Where did you come from? How come we didn't bump into you on the way?" shouted a man in the newly arrived boat as it ploughed into the bank of hornwort.

".Us?" said Xiusheng, knocking off and panting. "We —" But Caixi butted in with vitality ringing in his voice.

"We flew down from the sky, didn't we? Ha, ha!"

As he spoke, he brought his clamp down a second and a third time.

"Don't talk so big. You're old hands at bog-trotting, as we all know," laughed the newcomer, clumsily extracting his thick hornwort clamp of bamboo.

Caixi continued hurriedly to lay into his selected area without replying, then put up his clamp and looked first into his boat then at the stream with its carpet of tatters, which his experienced eye told him was only a surface layer mixed mostly with duckweed and fine liverwort.

Putting down the clamp, he hoisted up the end of his belt, wiped away the sweat that covered his face and went nimbly aft.

The mud that had splashed on to the stern was frozen almost solid, and Caixi's torn padded jacket was stuck firmly to the planks; he prised it up, slung it round his shoulders and squatted down.

"We're done," he said. "It's all yours, the whole streamful."

"Tchah! It's all very well to be gracious when you've skimmed the cream off," retorted one of the newcomers as he set to work.

The calm backwater was bustling in no time.

Xiusheng lifted a plank and took out the coarse flour rolls they had brought with them. They too were frozen as hard as stones. He bit bravely into one. Caixi ate too, though reflectively with his face to the sky; he was reckoning whether any of the nearby waterways had a lot of hornwort on them.

Dark cloud gathered thickly, and the northwest wind dropped somewhat. A distant steam whistle announced the passage of the passenger packet on the main stream.

"It can't be noon already, surely? Wasn't that the steamboat?"

There was a hubbub as the weed gatherers looked up at the sky.

"We'd better be off home then, Xiusheng." said Caixi, standing up and grasping the oar.

This time Xiusheng took the pole. Caixi gave a wild laugh as they emerged from the sidestream. "North, go north! There's bound to be some in the dead end."

"There too?" said Xiusheng, surprised. "We'll have to spend all night in the boat."

"Never mind that. Can't you see the weather's going to change? If we fill the boat today we shan't have to worry!" replied Caixi decisively and with a few thrusts of the oar directed the boat into a small cross-stream.

Xiusheng went silently aft and helped him row. But he had used up what strength he had and did not so much row as allow himself to be rowed by the oar, which in Caixi's hands became a living dragon.

The water slapped and splashed, and some unplaceable birds started up from the bleached, withered reeds with a wailing call.

Caixi's iron arms moved along as regularly as a lever;

sweat drenched his face, and there was joy in his eyes. He began a song that the villagers often sang:

> She was eighteen or nineteen with tits nice and
> plump
> That quivered and shook when she wiggled her
> rump
> As she set off to market while dawn was still cold,
> And her hubby was hung on one end of her pole.
> It was twenty-five *li* there and twenty-five back,
> But her fancy man stopped her, though she didn't
> slack.
> It was by the sheep shack
> That he grabbed her and rolled her right on to her
> back.*

Xiusheng took the entire song as meant for himself. His puffy face went ashen, and his legs trembled a little. Suddenly he crumpled at the waist, his hands lost contact with the dragon-like oar, and he subsided backwards and sat down on the planking.

"What? Xiusheng!" asked Caixi in surprise, halting in the middle of the song without stopping his hands moving in the slightest.

Xiusheng hung his head and did not answer.

"You're a useless lad," said Caixi pityingly. "Have a rest, then." Caixi seemed to remember something and levelled his eyes at the horizon; in a while the song welled up again from his throat.

"Caixi!" Suddenly Xiusheng was on his feet. "Do you have to? I may be useless, I may be sickly, and I

---

* A satire on rich peasants who married their infant sons to older wives who would work for them but tended to look else-where for male companionship.

may get nothing done, but while there's a breath in my body I'll starve to death before I stand by while my wife cheats on me!"

Never before had he displayed such openness or decision. Caixi was momentarily at a loss. He looked at Xiusheng's face livid with anger and pain and was smitten with remorse; it was true that the song, though current for ages, came sufficiently close to the circumstances of their particular triangle for it to grate understandably on Xiusheng's ears. He felt that he should not have sung with such gusto in front of Xiusheng as if purposely to taunt him and put him down. But hadn't he talked about starving to death first? In fact, Caixi put in a great deal of work living with Xiusheng. Was Xiusheng now exerting his position as head of the family and telling him to go? At this point in his train of thought Caixi became angry himself.

"Right then, if I go I go!" said Caixi coldly, and his rowing slowed involuntarily.

Xiusheng, who seemed not to have expected such a reaction, squatted down again dejectedly.

"But," added Caixi, again coldly but more seriously, "don't you go hitting your wife any more! A woman like that, and you still don't appreciate her? And she's carrying a child that'll carry on our name."

"You keep out of it!" Xiusheng leaped up wildly, his voice so shrill that it seemed on the verge of being lost. "She's my wife, and if I kill her it's me that'll get the chop!"

"Would you? Try it!" Caixi rounded on him sharply, his fists tightly balled and his eyes fixed on Xiusheng's face.

Xiusheng seemed to be trembling all over: "I will, if

I want. I'm fed up with life. From one year's end to the next they're pressing you for grain, collecting your taxes, dunning you for debts, running you into the ground. You eat for today, and there's none for tomorrow. You pawn your summer clothes and you can't get your winter ones out of hock. And you haven't even got your health. I'm fed up with it! Life's misery!"

Slowly, Caixi's head lowered, his fists relaxed, and his heart ached and stung and burned. With no one at the oar, the boat had swung across the stream: Caixi subconsciously took hold of the oar and gave it a thrust without however taking his eyes off his poor nephew.

"Come on, Xiusheng. It's no use just complaining. And another thing: none of your troubles are anything your wife's forced on you; she puts up with them and helps you cope. She doesn't answer back when you curse at her, and she doesn't raise her hand when you beat her. And when you got sick this year she lost a few nights' sleep looking after you."

As Xiusheng listened frustratedly, his eyes gradually filled with tears, and as if he were melting, he collapsed back into a squatting position on the planking, hanging his head; after a while he murmured to himself mournfully:

"It'd clear things up if I died. No one would care anyway, and you two would be happier."

"Xiusheng, don't you think it's wrong to talk like that? Don't take on so. Nobody wants you to die. We all live or die together!"

"Hm! Nobody wants me to die, eh? May not say so, but that's the thought."

"Who do you mean?" Caixi turned to face him, and his hands on the oar stopped moving.

"Someone here or someone at home."

"Now then, don't you go wronging a good woman. She's as conscientious about you as can be."

"Conscientious? I suppose it's conscientious of her to put a cap on me!" His voice rose again, not in anger but with apathetic lack of self-confidence and a callous turn.

"Ah!" said Caixi simply, then fell silent. Bad as he sometimes felt about what went on between himself and Xiusheng's wife, he strongly disapproved of Xiusheng's view of the matter. It did not, in his opinion, have anything to do with a woman's conscience if she went with other men because of a starveling husband. Xiusheng's wife was exactly as she had been except for the fact that she slept with another man. She was still Xiusheng's wife and did everything that was her duty to the best of her ability, and she did it well.

Yet though Caixi thought this, he had not the ability to express it in words; still, seeing how Xiusheng suffered and how he had misunderstood the "good woman", he felt it a matter of necessity to clear things up.

Irritated by this predicament, Caixi vented his anger by rowing harder, wielding his oar in a blind fury, oblivious even of the direction he was taking.

"Oh, to hell with it, it's snowing!" he cried instinctively, turning skywards a face that burned with vexation.

"Hey!" said Xiusheng as if in reply, raising his head.

The wind was rising, whirling snowflakes near and far, its eddies blurring their vision. In the maze of waterways that cut across the mosaic of fields, every sure indicator of direction, the shrines, the pavilions, the cemeteries, the stone bridges, even the great immemorial trees, was swept into obscurity by the thickly falling snow.

"Xiusheng, let's get home quick!" cried Caixi, leaping to the bows and snatching up a bamboo punt pole, with thrusts of which to left and right he propelled the boat into one of the small cross-channels. The broader river was round the next bend. Caixi thought he could see in the snow ahead two boats that ought to belong to the villagers who had gone for the hornwort.

Caixi leaped back to the stern, where Xiusheng, pale in the face and gritting his teeth, was churning the big oar all on his own. He snatched it and told Xiusheng to "draw in tight".*

"Oho!" bellowed Caixi with all the vigour his lungs could muster, as the oar moved like an angry monster in his hand and spray bounded over the bows.

For all that, Xiusheng was not even up to "pulling in tight".

"Leave it. I can do it myself!" said Caixi.

With the speed and regularity of a thoroughbred, Caixi's iron arms churned the oar powerfully and smoothly. The wind was dropping, but the flakes of snow were getting bigger.

Caixi kept one hand on the oar as with the other he removed his torn padded jacket, then looking round saw Xiusheng huddled in a heap, already covered in snow, took the jacket and covered him with it.

"Poor fellow!" he thought. "Sick, penniless and down at heart." He was mortally ashamed of the way he had treated his own nephew. He had come to live with him a year ago with the best intentions of working for him as best he could, and then some devil had driven him

---

* i.e. to haul on the oar cable, a less strenuous job.

into an affair with the wife that put another complexion altogether on his motives and was the sole reason for Xiusheng's misery and the beatings and curses she came in for.

The thought was like ice water on his back.

"Had I better go?" he asked himself, then thought again and replied: "No. Xiusheng could never manage all the work on the land, not even with his wife to help him, and she's strong enough. And then there's the child."

"That flower of a child! They have to have a proper life, both of them, and how the hell will they get that if I go?" he shouted inwardly, his prominent chin knotted and his eyes blazing.

He rowed savagely, as if there was a fire within him; in a minute he had caught up with the two boats, and in another had left them far, far behind.

5

The snow had stopped by dusk the same day, and the hamlet was transformed into a world of silver. Snow mantled the cottage tiles. Where the eaves were in disrepair finger-like icicles hung down from roofs under which people huddled as though stored away in an icebox, to awaken with cold at midnight and hear the old north wind howling over their heads.

Dawn broke, and the sun shed its golden radiance on the bitterly cold village. A couple of dogs were rolling on the threshing ground. A couple of women were breaking ice at the river bank to draw water; three hornwort boats pressed tightly together as if frozen into a block. Some people thought to declare war on the severe cold and move the weed from the boats to the trench that had been dug in the fields to receive it, but with the mud and water it contained, it had frozen harder than iron, and they rubbed their hands after hacking at it with metal rakes a few times.

"My hands are all numb, damn it!" they said. "I doubt if anybody but Caixi could shift that."

But the heroic figure of Caixi did not appear on the threshing ground.

He returned from town when the sun was quite high. He had gone to get medicine from the little Chinese pharmacy that accommodated the poor, who could tell the one assistant who ran it what was wrong with the patient, and he would sell them two or three hundred cash worth of a herbal remedy that would neither cure nor kill. Caixi said Xiusheng had a fever and received a febrifuge containing plaster of Paris.

Something had disturbed the villagers.

Between three and five of them, as he saw with surprise from some way off, were conferring outside Xiusheng's door. "He can't have got worse, can he?" thought Caixi, breaking into a run.

His heart thumped when he heard Xiusheng's wife cry for help. The abrupt passage from brilliant sunlight as he ran indoors robbed him of the use of his eyes, and it was only the instinct of his ears that told him that over in the corner where their bed was a tussle was going on.

Xiusheng was sitting up in bed, and his wife was half prostrate, half kneeling as she clasped his hands and lower body for dear life.

As his sight came back, Caixi's heart relaxed, but he remained confused.

"What's happening? Are you hitting her again?" he asked, repressing his anger.

She released her grip and stood up, smoothing her ruffled hair, then said disjointedly:

"He insists on joining the road crew! He says he's fed up with living, he hasn't any money and he'll risk his life! Just think, yesterday he had a temperature and groaned all night. He's in no condition to. I said talk about it when you get back, the headman wouldn't hear of it, and he wouldn't either. Then he went crazy when I wouldn't let him get up. He said we'd all be better off dead, and he grabbed me by the throat and set about beating me."

At this point Caixi noticed that there was someone else in the room, the headman that she had mentioned, the illustrious bigshot at the bottom of all the trouble. He was requisitioning three days' labour on the roads, and no one could get out of it.

One or two of the spectators had come in through the door and were standing around wittering. Caixi pushed Xiusheng back on to the bedclothes.

"What's there to get worked up about? She means well, you know," he said.

"I don't want to live. I've no money, but I've got my life!"

Xiusheng was still being stubborn, though his voice was weak.

Caixi turned to the headman.

"Xiusheng's really ill," he said. "I've spent the whole morning getting medicine for him," — here he dangled the packet in the headman's face — "and you can't demand work from a sick man."

"No," said the headman, stony-faced, "but I can have a substitute or cash. One yuan for every day without a substitute. If everybody malingered no public work would get done!"

"Then how come Chief Chen's son didn't work on the last labour gang and didn't pay either? The bloke didn't even report sick. It's all in your hands, isn't it?"

"Don't talk rubbish! Is he going to sign up or pay? Three days makes three yuan!"

"Caixi," interrupted Xiusheng sternly, "I'm going! I've no money, but I've got my life! If I die on the way, they'll at least give me a coffin to rest in!"

Like a wounded beast, Xiusheng removed the quilt and rose quivering to his feet.

"Not one copper!" Caixi threw down the medicine packet and took the headman's chest in his pincer-like grip. "Get out of here, you bastard!"

Xiusheng had been grabbed by his wife and two neighbours. The headman cursed and blustered outside the door, threatening to report them to the "bureau". Caixi went over to Xiusheng, took him in his arms like a child and put him to bed.

"But Caixi, what are we going to do if he reports us and you get arrested?" sobbed Xiusheng, his face burning violently.

"Let him. Let the heavens fall, Caixi'll still be here!" he answered firmly and decisively.

Xiusheng's wife undid the packet of medicine and emptied the four or five herbs into a crock. When she was through, she picked up the plaster of Paris, took a few pinches as if unsure what to do with it, then finally put it in the crock too.

6

The sun, at the zenith, conferred warmth on the hamlet.

Remnants of snow streaked the threshing ground like pig's caul. The hornwort was being moved from the boats.

One of those moving it was Caixi. Wearing only a thin jacket caught tightly by the blue belt and with the sleeves rolled up high, he was pitching into the semi-frozen weed and mud with a rake like some stalwart of old and loading it into wooden buckets. It would be put in the prepared troughs interlayered with the compost they had gathered.

"Damn it!" called a neighbour from another boat. "Even the rake's stuck. Hey, Caixi!"

"Oh, Caixi!" said someone from a third boat. "Can you take this load over for us? It's on your way in any case."

Caixi, his face covered in sweat, jumped across and lent a helping hand.

The mud was steaming in the sun, as was the sweat on their bodies. Sparrows twittered in the tallow trees.

They stepped up the work, looking forward to getting the hornwort out of the way before sundown and hoping for another fine day tomorrow so that they could boat farther out where there was more.

As they laughed, shouted and worked, they extemporized meaningless snatches of song, and Caixi's bellow kept rising above the voices solemnly and vigorously like an appeal or a show of strength.

February 26, 1936

Translated by Simon Johnstone

Second Generation

HE smoothed the sheet of paper and picked up his pen. Although he couldn't see the door from where he sat, he heard it open quietly. From the sound of the footsteps he knew that his son Xiang had come into the room.

The clock on the chest of drawers opposite the desk said only twelve or thirteen minutes past eleven. Is it running slow again? he wondered, and put down his pen.

"Papa, I have to go to the Chamber of Commerce Building this afternoon."

"Oh," he replied, his mind on the article he was writing. A phrase occurred to him and he pondered over it. His son, getting no response, turned to leave.

To the Chamber of Commerce, eh? he thought, his son's remark finally registering. His wife had complained yesterday that Xiang was always going off with his schoolmates. Sometimes they even walked as far as Wenmiao Park — nearly seven miles, there and back. She thought it was too much for a boy his age.

"What are you going to do at the Chamber of Commerce?" asked the father.

"Have a meeting." An irrepressible suggestion of a smile tugged at the corners of the boy's mouth.

Ah, he remembered now — today was May Thirtieth.*

So you've reached the stage of taking part in campaigns already, he mused. He scrutinized his son's face.

"I'm going with two others. They're both in my class," said the boy. He wouldn't have told even this much had he not been afraid that his father wouldn't let him go alone. He had always been very close-mouthed about his "private affairs".

"Do you know the way?"

"Yes. At least the boys I'm going with do."

"All right. But you're not to walk. Take the bus both ways. I'll give you fare money." He returned to his article. Only a few words were needed to finish the paragraph. Then he could have lunch.

As he wrote, he could hear his son take a book from the shelves in the next room and walk down the stairs.

The paragraph concluded, he read it through. He shook his head and put his pen on the desk.

Taking twenty cents to give Xiang for fare, he also went downstairs.

Xiang was sitting in the wicker chair with the shrewd smile he always wore when he thought adults were making too much fuss.

The boy's mother was ironing clothes. "Xiang wants to go to a mass meeting outside the Chamber of Commerce. Did you give him permission?" she asked. "He knew you wouldn't refuse him, so he spoke to you first.

---

* On May 30, 1925, workers and students, demonstrating in Shanghai's British concession in support of striking textile workers, were fired upon by British police. Many were killed or wounded.

I think he shouldn't go; it'll be dangerous. But he says you've already agreed."

"I don't think it'll be very dangerous." The father walked up to his son as he spoke and looked at him carefully. So you've reached the stage of taking part in campaigns, he thought. Is it just as an amusement or do you really . . . ?

"Suppose they arrest you?" the mother asked Xiang. "What will you say?"

"I'll say I only came to watch," replied the boy. Again he smiled shrewdly.

"You see!" the mother turned quickly to the father. "They have their alibis all prepared. They're organized I tell you. They even expect a clash with the police."

The father said nothing. His son broke the silence.

"They told us not to carry much money. They said don't bring any paper or pencil."

"You mean the school told you to go?" asked the father.

"No."

"Well then, who did? How do you know there's going to be a mass meeting at the Chamber of Commerce today?"

"The school hasn't formally told them to go," said the mother, "but it's encouraging them. They won't be marked absent. Some of the teachers are going too."

"But we're not going together. Our teachers will be in a different group."

"Ah!" The father looked at the mother. Evidently she had guessed right. The students expected a clash with the police. And how could it be otherwise? This was Kuomintang China, 1936!

Her ironing finished, the mother disconnected the electric iron. "I still feel he shouldn't go," she said. "He's too young."

"Make me some fried rice and eggs, will you?" the boy urged. "My group is meeting at twelve."

"Isn't it twelve yet?" asked the father. Xiang usually didn't come home for lunch until noon.

"They let them out an hour early today," said the mother. "It doesn't count as a cut either." She went into the kitchen.

Staring at his son, the father recalled that May Thirtieth eleven years ago. Xiang was only two then. He had just learned to walk. The evening of the day Nanjing Road was dyed with blood, Xiang's mother and two of her girl friends went to a mass meeting outside the Chamber of Commerce to demand that all shops close in protest against the massacre. When she returned, she threw her arms around the baby.

"There were elementary school students in the rear of our detachment," she said agitatedly. "The mounted police broke through our front ranks; many children were ridden down. I saw one little boy — he couldn't have been more than twelve or thirteen — fall beneath a horse's hoofs. Luckily one of our flying squads picked him up in time. I thought of our Xiang. Let's hope when he grows up the world will be different!"

Thereafter every time there was a demonstration, every time school children were struck with whips and trampled under horses' hoofs, the mother would come home and crush Xiang to her bosom. Each time she would passionately repeat the same prayer.

Recently, she saw some pictures of students who had

been wounded in the demonstration in Beijing on December 16, 1935.* She showed the pictures to Xiang.

"Look at that boy with the bandaged arm, Xiang," she said. "He's not much bigger than you! Ai! How can they treat children so brutally?"

And now Xiang too was taking part in campaigns. Countless children who were no older than Xiang eleven years ago, today like him, curious and full of excitement, were about to join in a demonstration for the first time.

Though the thought disturbed the father, it somehow gave him a certain amount of comfort.

He and the mother sat watching Xiang wolf down a bowl of fried rice and eggs. The father felt he ought to say something to the boy, but he didn't know where to start. How could he make him understand? Xiang was only a child after all.

The boy's mother spoke first. "If there's a parade after the meeting I don't want you to go along. Do you hear, Xiang?"

Xiang concentrated on shovelling down his rice.

"Your mother's right," the father agreed. "Your lungs have only just recovered. Too much walking is bad for you. If they rush you and scatter the parade in some part of town you don't know, you'll get lost. How will you find your way home?"

The boy had been eating quickly, with a shrewd look in his eyes. But at this point he retorted in an aggrieved tone:

"What are you afraid of? If I don't know where I am

---

* On December 16, 1935 over 30,000 Beijing students, led by the Chinese Communist Party, staged a gigantic demonstration demanding that Chiang Kai-shek "stop the civil war; unite to resist Japan!"

I can ask! I can take a rickshaw!" Then he held out his hand. "My fare money?"

The father gave him the twenty cents and Xiang left. The mother stood at the door until Xiang went through the gate at the end of the lane.

"You shouldn't have let him go," she said reproachfully as she came back into the room.

"If we didn't let him go this time, next time he'd go without telling us."

"But he's so young," she sighed.

The father shook his head and lit a cigarette. His mind went back to that unfinished article. He had to hand it in tonight.

The house seemed unusually quiet as they ate their lunch.

"At first I was thinking of going with him," said the mother, half to herself. "I figured if there was a parade after the meeting I'd bring him home. But then I decided I'd better not go. I'd be sure to meet a lot of people who know us, and he probably wouldn't agree to came back with me anyway. . . ."

The father laughed loudly. "Of course not. He wants to go with the masses — not be tied to his mother's apron strings!"

"But he doesn't understand anything. He's just thinking with his heart. It's blind courage. You ought to teach him."

"How? Teach him what? Shall I tell him to avoid useless sacrifices? He's too young. He probably wouldn't understand that." Again he gave a loud laugh, but the skin of his face was taut.

They talked no more of Xiang during the remainder of lunch.

After he had lit a cigarette and was slowly pacing the floor, he stopped several times to glance at his wife. There was an excited flush on his cheeks. Finally he came and stood before her.

"I'm afraid it won't be until Xiang has a son of his own in school that mass meetings will stop being dangerous. China's revolution is a long hard struggle."

"I know Xiang is going to be very brave. I wouldn't worry a bit if he were twenty. But he's only thirteen! I wish he were twenty right now!"

"Don't worry. Sometimes the days go very quickly."

The father and mother smiled at each other, their eyes a bit moist. Then their smiles became happier, more natural.

The afternoon was over before they knew it, but after six time started to act very peculiarly again — now dragging, now fairly racing. The boy's mother began considering where to make inquiries and wondering whom she should ask for help.

By eight p.m. the father was worried too. A friend came to call, bringing with him a number of leaflets he had received at the mass meeting. He said there hadn't been any clashes. Xiang's mother felt somewhat relieved.

But then she thought of other things to worry about. "Did he get lost? Suppose he was run over by a car?" To a mother a child is always as helpless as a new-born lamb.

It wasn't until about nine fifteen that the boy finally returned. "Where did you get these?" he cried the moment he came in the door and saw the pamphlets lying on the table. He quickly brought his own set out of his pocket.

His parents burst into laughter and his mother took him by the arm.

"How was the parade? Tell Mama all about it."

"We marched to the graves of the May Thirtieth martyrs. Then we wanted to go to the North Railway Station, but troops blocked our way and we broke up. My feet don't hurt a bit." He produced a slip of paper printed in words of red.

"These are our slogans. We really shouted them today!"

Shanghai, June 1936

Translated by Sidney Shapiro

Liena and Jidi

"IT'S so small and it's got emerald-green eyes, and they're so bright, and I'm sure it understands what you say. It's got tight, black hair all over."

The girl dashed running and jumping into her mother's room, indicating with gestures as she spoke the size of the puppy.

It had taken them only one day after moving into the courtyard to discover that it was inhabited not only by at least five nationalities but also by a number — it was hard to distinguish how many — of varieties of "dumb friends". The courtyard faced west, and its three main rooms at the front were occupied by the Uygur landlord as a sort of two-storey suite. Two storeys are two storeys; I say "sort of" because in the manner of the local architecture the upper storey was not for occupation but for storage, as for instance of hay in the winter, and had no doors or windows. More care was taken downstairs, where there were floorboards, double-glazed windows and quite a wide corridor. The thirty yards or so between this building and the main gate formed a long, narrow yard, on the north side of which, facing south, was a row, about a dozen rooms in length, of single-storey Western-style houses; the girl's family lived in the four rooms at the eastern end of this row. Across the passageway that led to the lavatory were another two single-storey rooms, smaller and in the local style, one of which housed the servant and the cook, while the other was the kitchen. It was in the servant's room that the girl had discovered the "little thing with emerald eyes", of whose origin she knew nothing, nor how long it had been there.

The mother was not greatly affected by the news of an extra dog in the servant's quarters. The courtyard was always full of them, wolfhounds, lap-dogs, Mongolian and Tibetan dogs and all their mongrels, racing about noisily in the newly thawed slush. In the dead of night, all it needed was one bark to elicit a vast wave of all their different voices, which so annoyed the father that he quipped to his friend Zhang, "We've got an ethnic exhibition here and a zoo into the bargain. Look at them all, cows, horses, chickens, sheep, dogs, and so many breeds of dogs you'd think they'd been recruited for a show."

But the children were highly delighted. Soon after the girl's discovery, the boy had come up with a background for the "little thing with emerald eyes".

"The quartermaster says the orderly picked it up in the road," he said ponderously, entering his mother's room, "but actually it's probably stolen; the orderly won't let it out of his room for a second."

The orderly, a man in his fifties, had been "in the service" for many a year and had, by his own account, served quite a few of the top brass. He had been seconded to the family by the adjutant because he was "clever". He had seen the world; he had been to Lanzhou. "That's the spot," he would exclaim with a sigh whenever Lanzhou was mentioned. "There's nowt here. You can't compare it!" To him, Lanzhou represented China, nay, the world. He had got by in the army, and would dwell with gusto on how in those "glorious days" he had made off with people's things scot-free.

So no one doubted it when told that the dog had been stolen by the orderly.

But it was certainly a very interesting creature. The orderly had a good eye. Both children passed on "intelligence" and egged Mother on to go to the kitchen and have a look. The little thing crouched on the orderly's pallet. It didn't bark when it saw strangers come in, it just stared at them dejectedly with its emerald eyes, and when they came near, it would lie down slowly, snatching the odd glance.

"Poor little thing!" said Mother. "See how it's trembling."

It trembled more violently when she stretched out her hand to it, but calmed down when it realized that the hand was not going to hit it. Slowly it raised its forequarters, stuck out its nose and sniffed softly, whimpering but still with dejection in its eyes.

"Sit! Sit!" rapped out the boy, taking a step closer.

The little thing looked at Mother with its head on one side and shot a glance at the girl, as if entreating them to say the word that would rescue it from its plight. When this was not forthcoming, it tucked in its front legs and sat up of its own accord with a wronged air, but the emerald eyes were full of tears, and the almost round, slightly concave face wore an expression of despair.

"It's too distressing to watch!" murmured Mother as she turned to go.

As if it had actually understood, the little thing straightaway put out its front legs and lay down, whimpering again softly and sadly.

Wang, a soldier whose job it was to bring round the water, stood by the glowing coal stove masticating his shrivelled, toothless mouth. "Pup wants to go home," he said after a while. "Pup misses his old master." He sighed.

The girl told her mother later how the little thing had trembled dreadfully when it saw the orderly and sat up straightaway when he told it to, not lying down itself after a while as it had done before, but crying as it sat; he must have beaten it cruelly.

"But then it begs other people to be sent home," she said. "That's why it whimpers. It's asking to go home."

"Wait till Father comes home," said the boy. "We'll tell the orderly to take it back. It's immoral to steal people's dogs."

"That's no good," the girl countered. "He'd just get rid of it somewhere else. He wouldn't take it back, would he?"

"Why not ask around," said Mother, "and find out which of the neighbours has lost it, then tell them to come and identify it and take it away?"

2

It was in the morning, perhaps two days later, that the original owner of the little thing eventually arrived, a Soviet woman who lived near the Soviet consulate over the main road. The little thing barked for joy when it heard her voice some way off, and as soon as she was there in front of it, it was up on its hind legs, wagging its tail and pawing at its not uncorpulent mistress, barking its head off and putting out its tongue to lick her hand.

It also expressed its goodwill towards the girl by licking her hand too and gambolling about her feet whimpering.

A woman of the "naturalized nationality" from the same courtyard played the interpreter with her broken Chinese. It was with difficulty possible to extract from her disjointed monosyllables and their accompanying gestures the following meaning: Thank you; her little boy loves the dog very much, so thank you.

But the same afternoon the Soviet woman was back again, carrying another dog and with a real interpreter. It too had tight, black hair all over and was not much bigger than a cat, and when it was put on the table stood motionless, casting furtive glances of its brown eyes at the strange room and the strange people. Brother to the "emerald-eyed little thing", it was, according to the translator, only just a month old, and she had brought it round in recognition of the restoration of its lost elder brother.

Mother had never intended to have a dog, but the Soviet woman, through her interpreter, expressed a great deal of gratitude and asked her time and again to accept it. And so it stayed.

"Now," she told her daughter when she had seen off the visitor with a farewell handshake, "it's yours to look after. And it's no easy matter training a dog."

The girl chose the name of Liena for the puppy.

The children were impatient to teach Liena his manners, but there was a lack of response that argued both laziness and feigned stupidity. When you stroked his hindquarters to make him sit up he could indeed do so, but he lay down again as soon as the hand was removed. He seemed not to understand commands, and if you made as if to hit him he put on a wry face and awaited the blow dully, glancing furtively at you all the while.

The old orderly disliked Liena, who he said had a "thieving look about him".

A couple of days or so later the children's interest in Liena was just on the wane when all at once old biddy of a Kazakh woman — heaven knows who she was, but the girl often saw her on the wooden bridge over the ditch outside the main gate, and despite a lack of articulate communication they expressed their civilities with a smile — came by carrying a puppy, which her manner seemed to imply she wanted to give to the children. They "spoke" to each other in gestures of the wish to decline and the desire to give until the happy advent of the Uygur landlord, a *baye* (man of means) with a modest command of Chinese, who made up their minds for them to keep the dog, which he said she had brought them because she could see that Liena was not up to much, and anyway she had quite enough at home as it was.

"Big!" he said, indicating the size with his hands. "Big! This year, next year, this high. This high, good, good puppy dog, you know!"

Since the girl already had Liena, the new arrival was assigned to the boy, who estimated from the landlord's words that this new dog was akin to Caicai, the great foreign hound with the tight, light-brown coat that belonged to their neighbours the family of Department Head Chen, and of which the boy was fond. He was only too happy to make the puppy his own, and gave him the name of Jidi, which he found in a book.

Jidi was then the same size as Liena. Despite his fluffy, light-brown curls, he had a pointed muzzle and broad ears that hung down beside his eyes. Impassive and seemingly uncomprehending, he had virtually expressionless, indeed timid, grey eyes. Liena took sole possession of the bowl at mealtimes, denying access to Jidi, who would crouch to one side waiting for Liena to finish so that he could come and get his leftovers.

Witnessing this injustice, the boy sometimes pulled Jidi up to eat with Liena, but the weakling still would not eat, and as soon as the boy's hand was removed he would retreat and crouch silently to one side with his head cocked, watching until Liena walked away satisfied, whereupon he would come forward.

Jidi gave such a wretched look that as his protector the boy sometimes felt rather annoyed.

3

The days were already warm in Dihua* in May, and the ubiquitous post-thaw mud was almost dry. Jidi's and Liena's voices mingled with those of the motley canine crew that raised its racket in the yard. They were good-looking pups by now. Liena, fully grown, was still no more than two feet long with short legs, a perfectly round body and a high sheen on his tight black coat. He was still one for furtive glances, and although he fell short of his brother's variety of expression, there

---

* Urumqi.

was an extremely knowing look on his face. Most of his fellows in the yard were of the wolfhound sort — the naturalized lady had one that was frankly the size of a calf — toughs that sprawled lazily in front of their owners' doors and from time to time paced ostentatiously up and down the yard with an air of supreme foresight and experience. Nevertheless, every day saw several outbreaks of loud barking, whether in a wrangle over a mutton bone fortuitously grubbed up from the scrap heap or at someone else's dog that had stolen in and made off with a monetarily worthless rag or board, whereupon Liena would jump up in haste from where he lay on the carpet indoors, dispose his short legs in a businesslike manner and start barking away in the house. In a flash he would be in the yard showing his own indispensability by pushing between all those great wolfhounds and jumping and yapping as keyed up as could be. Quite unaware of his existence, they loosed their assault only after an exchange of baying from battle-charger positions; then, however, Liena would weave his way between their lanky back legs bustling the busiest and barking the loudest and without the least sense of his own inferiority.

As for Jidi, he had now outgrown Liena in both height and size, and could run and jump faster and further with tall, vigorous legs and a lean, tight-flanked body that showed how handy he would be at chasing foxes and hares in the woods; yet he understood for all that the rule that "first through the monastery gate is the greatest" and followed Liena's lead. Whenever there was a sudden barking in the yard and Liena dashed outside officiously, Jidi would get up lazily, stretch lazily, pause for what seemed a moment's reflection and then walk quietly out. For all that he was slower off the mark than Liena, once in the yard a few bounds brought him into the thick of the fray, when his boyish impudence would assert itself in earnest and he would play his tricks on them silently and indiscriminately without even ascertaining which belonged to his own yard and which was an intruder; frequently he would bound back and forth over the wolfhounds' heads, sometimes biting their ears in passing. The toughs thus baited would leap up to try and catch him, but he would dash mischievously out and away then stop and give a couple of barks, as if to say, "You can't get me!" He would amuse himself with such tricks until the intruder withdrew of his own accord, chased to the gate with a volley of barking by tubby, waddling Liena like a victorious commander-in-chief, and only when Liena lurched back would Jidi follow him into the house.

"Liena's a grown-up already," Mother would say, "and Jidi's still a silly boy!"

But Liena was not totally devoid of naughtiness, though when he had learnt his lesson he bore it in mind. One fine morning, as if by prior arrangement, the pair of them set about rummaging through the scrap heap in one corner of the yard, ignoring all calls to come away. Liena then trotted up with a nonchalant air and jumped up to lick his masters' hands, while behind him Jidi dodged into the dining-room and in a flash was lying ensconced in front of the fire refusing to budge.

"Well I'm blowed, so that's what the treasure is!" said the boy, when he had dragged Jidi away to reveal the smelly piece of hairy sheepskin he had been hiding. "What do you want with that?" He held it in front of Jidi's nose then held him by his pointed muzzle and gave him a few raps on the head. Instead of putting up a struggle, Jidi just lay on his side with his back legs pawing the air aimlessly and wagging his tail — his old tune when he had taken a beating. Liena, realizing the game was up, got quietly into his kennel and wouldn't come out for the life of him when the girl called him, but eventually he couldn't stick it out and emerged with his head hung low and his face a picture of ill fortune.

The hairy, smelly sheepskin was thrown out. The dogs lay on the carpet, neither betraying the slightest concern. A while later, however, Jidi was gone; he was not in the yard, and he was not at the gate. It was assumed that he had gone to look for trouble in someone else's yard, and to everyone's surprise he was finally found in front of the dining-room fire, laying there snugly with his muzzle on the floor and his eyelids shut pretending to be asleep. He refused to be coaxed up, and when he was dragged up, why, there was the smelly sheepskin glaring up from under him. Why he hankered so after a fetid piece of skin that lent itself to neither food nor play none of them could imagine. Mother took pity on him. "Let him have his way," she said. But the boy demurred and once more threw the smelly thing away, giving him a beating into the bargain. He was blazing mad when two days later he found him lying on top of it again, but Father, Mother and the girl just laughed.

"He won't get it back this time!" said the boy furiously.

He ordered Jidi to pick the smelly skin up in his mouth and come outside with him, but Jidi refused to budge and had to be dragged forcibly out of the gate by his ear. The boy dropped the skin into the ditch outside and made Jidi watch the object of his affections float off into the unknown. That is what it took to break him of the idea.

Mother and the others thought it cruel to deprive him of his beloved plaything and expected a stretch of moping; but not Jidi. In the twinkling of an eye he was bounding out into the yard again to play tricks on the wolfhounds.

"When it comes down to it," agreed the girl, "he's still young and he acts like a baby."

Still, it was easy to account for Jidi's mischief. His breed was not used to domesticity as Liena's was. Probably his parents and brothers were with the Kazakh family in the mountain wilds, and if Jidi had not been given away he too by now would probably have been giving play to his natural gifts by accompanying the flocks and racing the high-headed thoroughbreds among those wild mountains and forest glades. As things were, it was only through a smelly piece of sheepskin with the wool still on it in this tiny courtyard that he could try to exercise his keen sense of smell and his skill in the chase.

4

It was a day of dizzying, stifling dry heat that hinted at the approach of the Turfan wind. Bewhiskered Kazakhs and Uygur girls with masses of small plaits, patterned dresses and tall leather boots sat and squatted in twos and threes on the railing of the wooden bridge over the ditch outside the main gate after lunch, cooling them-

selves in the willows' welcome shade. Dogs of all sizes
frolicked by the roadside. Clever Liena was waiting at the
gate to greet the boy and girl, who were returning from
a friend's house nearby. They paused on the bridge
to chat with one of the Uygur girls in ungrammatical
Russian. Suddenly, as if spotting something of interest
over the main road, Liena wrenched his rotundity into
action and hurtled across the road. He was halfway
there when the great lorry bore down at speed from the
north. The boy scarcely had the time to catch a glimpse
and blurt out "Oh no!" before their ears picked up
Liena's agonized shriek above the din of the street.
The dust cleared to reveal Liena in the middle of the
road, struggling to get up. A cart that was passing the
bridge stopped the children from rushing over. When
it had passed, Liena had already dragged his hindquarters to the bridge and taken shelter under one of its
planks. The boy scrambled across to him and put out
his hands to pick him up only to have his fingers bitten.
"Liena!" he cried despite the pain. Liena relaxed his
grip, and gingerly the boy picked him up. The rear end
of the tubby form was visibly flattened, but there was
no blood to be seen, and the girl took Liena in her
arms with an involuntary tear.

"Puppy dog," rasped the old Kazakh nearby in discordant Chinese, "no good now."

They carried Liena home. Mother found him a soft
cushion. Whining painfully and unable now even to
drag himself one step, Liena just watched them nurse
him with his expressive brown eyes. Jidi walked back
and forth around Liena and his nurses giving occasional
yelps — obviously he too realized what had happened.

"What are we going to do, mother? What are we going to do?" asked the worried girl.

"It's probably not serious," said Mother. "There's no blood, which is curious. Yet his back end's been flattened. I shouldn't think he'll die."

They nursed him attentively. Mother was matron. They fed him milk and moved his kennel into the dining room. The boy found out where there was a veterinary hospital, and when Father came home from the office they carried Liena to Father's gig and drove there. The vet said that there were no internal injuries, but that the hip might be broken and that there could be lameness or paralysis even after full recovery. At the hospital they smeared his hindquarters with a thick layer of ointment and artificially induced him to pass water.

They returned twice to the hospital, and gradually Liena improved. He no longer whimpered, he could eat, but a knock on any part of his rear end produced a howl of agony.

A fortnight later he was actually able to crawl along dragging half his body. By that time drinking milk all day long had filled out his chest, but his back end was disproportionately small, and a little later he could stand but only hop with his hind legs together, not walk.

With the first flurry of snow, Liena was walking and was not in fact paralysed, though he did seem a touch lame when he got up to speed.

Henceforth he did not venture alone on to the main road and escaped hurriedly in through the gate at the distant sound of a motor. Inside the courtyard, though, he was just as much a dynamic force as ever, in among the wolfhounds when they fought, limping with his hind legs as he barked and jumped with his air of indispensability, and he even still played the leader to Jidi, who deferred to him at mealtimes as before.

5

Jidi's ruling passion was going out with people. Whichever member of the family went out of doors, Jidi wanted to go too. Once when Father had gone to the nearby Number Nine Guesthouse to see a friend who had recently arrived from the interior, the first thing he saw upon entering the main gate was Jidi leaping and bounding about all over the yard, having evidently shadowed him then sneaked in first.

There were some young chickens in the yard, which Jidi took to be there for his own benefit, to be scared into flurried and disorderly flight. Father had no choice but to call for a rope and have him tied up, though his loud antics still terrified the friend's child. When his master disappeared, he went wild, setting up a clamour of misery and turning all his efforts to ridding himself of the constricting rope by walking backwards and clawing at it with his front paws while barking loudly. When at length this had no effect, he lay on the ground and hung his head despondently, feeling no doubt that all was up and that he had fallen into the hands of the foe.

Father had Jidi untied when he was ready to go. Jidi took the removal of the rope as the knell of doom and trembled all over with fright.

"You should have seen him tremble," he told his

wife and the two children when he got home. "He's never been like that before."

The shaft-horse of the gig that waited in the yard every morning to take Father to the office was quite a young blood too, and Jidi liked playing tricks on it. He would bound around it barking then leap on the gig and from there on to the horse's back. At last he got kicked, which put him off fun and games for the space of two days.

After lunch one day when Father was going into town to the office and the gig was flying over the frozen snow that carpeted the ground, he became aware only as they were approaching the town gate that Jidi was bounding along behind them as pleased with himself as could be. Fearing that being so far from home he would lose his way on the return journey or that failing that he would come to grief crossing the defended territory of one of the local canine residents, Father told the driver to slow down to let Jidi jump aboard and took him to the office.

Jidi in the gig lacked refinement and kept climbing up on to the box all the way to the cultural association, where before the vehicle had come to a firm halt he leaped down and darted in through the main gate for all the world like a regular visitor. Father hurriedly told the driver to keep an eye on Jidi and not let him run about, but Jidi had vanished. Not until much later was he found mounted once more on the gig as if waiting to go home. It appeared that after a brisk tour of every room in the large building, which had brought to light nothing at all diverting, he had reverted impatiently to thoughts of home. But Father had another hour to put in, during which time Jidi made umpteen trips to his office, on each occasion lying on the floor and barking as if to say, "Aren't you coming yet?" There was nothing for it but to tell someone to take him to the porter's lodge and mind he didn't break out.

After this experience, Father told the orderly to stand guard over Jidi every time he left the house lest he follow again. The first time he was held back and the second time he could not be found anywhere as the hour approached but was spotted racing after the gig when it had gone some way, whereupon it was stopped and he was grabbed and taken home. On the third occasion they were pulling out of the gate when the driver, peering anxiously about, saw Jidi crouching in the grocer's to the left of the gate, his head cocked and apparently unaware of the emerging gig. This proved to be deliberate, for they had not gone much more than ten doors down before he was bounding along again. Once more he was with effort apprehended and transported back in custody.

Next time he got craftier, secreting himself early in a distant shop and concealing himself ingeniously so as not to be discovered. He appeared only as they entered the town, running alongside with his tongue out in a show of exhaustion. He was allowed to jump aboard, but only to be shut in the stables upon arrival at the bureau, a term of confinement which appeared to teach him a bit of a lesson, for after this he abandoned the idea of following the gig to town.

6

Next year when the spring thaw had made an inch or so's thickness of mud, affairs called them away from

the city. As for Liena and Jidi, the only proper means
of disposing of them that they could come up with was
to find them a decent home with other people. Before
the "August 13 Incident"* in Shanghai they had had a
white cat, a present from friends, which they had had
a hard time disposing of too when the fall of the city
had started them on their itinerant life. They had still
had relatives there, and it was to some of these who
enjoyed keeping cats and dogs and who were unlikely
to leave that they had given it. Father had gone to say
goodbye to these relatives when their berths for Hongkong were booked, and Mother had asked how the
cat was, saying that the children would have shed a few
tears over it if they had been in Shanghai too.

Now that the time had come to bid farewell to two
other dumb friends who had virtually become part of
the family, Mother cast her mind back, overcome with
sentiment.

"I wonder if the little white cat's still alive," she said.
"Father said when he saw it last that its hair had lost
some lustre. There were plenty of people who would
sometimes treat cats and dogs badly —the servants, the
maid, the chauffeur. But the minute we thought about
it we knew they were the ones, because the old lady
was so sorry for the little thing."

Her words called up in each of them gloomy recollections of the lean years and the wandering life. Yet
Father was also reminded of how, when they had left
Hongkong, the boy had handed him the English car-
toon books he had collected over the year neatly par-

---

* August 13, 1937, when the Japanese invaders launched their
attack on Shanghai.

celled up to be sent for safekeeping to a close Hongkong friend, saying, "I know I'll be grown up before I get another look at them, and I may not like them any more, but I hope they keep them anyway so that I can read them again." As Father thought of this in connection with how to deal with the dogs, his feelings then mingled with his present gloom, and he thought, looking at his boy and girl, how very lonely their childhood had inevitably been, and was profoundly sorry.

"I was alone in the house," Mother went on, "the day that the Nationalist Army retreated west of Shanghai. You and Father had gone to Changsha. It was raining, and aeroplanes were circling west of Shanghai. The cannon fire never let up for a minute. I turned on the radio and listened to the broadcast with a weight on my mind. The cat was my only company. It crouched on the table by the window as if it was listening to the wireless too. It made such a deep impression on me. I'll never forget it."

As they talked thus of old times, Jidi lay on the carpet, and Liena hooked his front paws over the girl's knee with a knowing expression.

She took his head in her hands and drew him to her. "You're going to be given away tomorrow," she said agitatedly. "Do you know that?"

The boy smiled through his misery and sauntered off.

It was eventually decided to give Liena to a friend in the theatre and Jidi to Department Head Chen's family as a companion for Caicai. Chen, who was fond of hunting, would appreciate Jidi, of whom indeed he had spoken highly.

Liena, as being the more intelligent, was to be sent off a few days beforehand to see if he would settle in.

Mother and the children took the gig to see to this personally, while Father was to go round to his theatrical friend the following day to see how things were going. When they learned by telephone that Liena had missed his old family the first day and run away only to go back because he didn't recognize the streets, Mother and the children insisted on going to take a look at him. At the theatre Mr Zhu shut Liena in his room with his wife to look after him. The minute Liena heard their voices outside in the yard he barked out loud, ran to the door and scratched at it with his claws. When he was let out, he leapt around the three of them preventing any of them from taking a step in any direction. He stood up to lick their hands, whined affectionately and continuously and even shed tears. Mother and the children were miserable, but what was there to do? They told Mr Zhu to lure him back away and fled homewards.

They dared not go to see Liena again after this, but some days later the boy went into town to do some shopping and saw Liena crouching beside the crossroads looking worn out. It seemed he had run away the day before, spent the night out, would not go back on account of the unfamiliar streets and had lain down there, probably in hope of seeing Father's gig drive by. The boy took him barking in loud protest back to the theatre; but again, what was there to do? Mr Zhu was a most reliable new master, they would definitely take care of him, and also they had children.

With all this behind them, they decided to leave Jidi till the last day.

Jidi kept up the search for his companion for days, but eventually seemed to realize he would never find him and lay debilitated on the carpet all day. When they took him round to the Chens' on the last day, he went quietly, and when they arrived and put him indoors he lay down listlessly; only when Mother and the children took their leave of Mrs Chen did he jump up in surprise, but he made no great effort to go, pessimistic fatalist that he was!

With the dogs disposed of, they hastened to pack, for they were leaving the next day, albeit bereft.

A year later, as refugees from Hongkong arriving in Guilin, Father and Mother learned from a letter posted by the children in the northwest border region that the Dihua theatre troop had fallen foul of a rigged court case, and this led them to thoughts of Liena.

"I wonder how he's getting on?"

"I wonder if Jidi got away at the Chens'?"

And when they heard soon afterwards that Chen had left town:

"I wonder how Jidi's getting on?"

Mother thought again of the white cat and heaved a sigh.

Guilin, 1941

Translated by Simon Johnstone

Frustration

THE April weather really was going too far. Within thirty-six hours it changed drastically. People had no sooner shed their furs than they had to dig out their summer clothing. This sudden attack by Heaven caught Mrs Zhang completely unawares. She was furious. As she sorted through her trunks she cursed everything she could think of.

The first trunk mainly contained her husband's winter clothing, made at a time when he wasn't quite so stout. You can't beat those Hankou tailors, mused Mrs Zhang, absently turning up a few garments. There's real skill! Her face was hard. Praising the Hankou tailors was equivalent to reviling their local brethren. Although she had been living in Chongqing for more than four years, she had never been without Shanghai servants, many of whom had also moved west up the Yangzi River when the government transferred its wartime capital to Chongqing. Actually she had nothing against the local tailors, but when she was in a temper no one could escape her ire. Suddenly, she frowned. Abandoning the poor tailors, she directed her wrath against a new target.

Those rice-stuffing policemen! She pulled out her hand and shook it vigorously, as if shaking from it something unclean. They act so important. First they come and make me fill out a Stolen Property List. Then two days later they come again and make me fill out another. Then they disappear like a rock dropped into the sea — not a word out of them. You'd think their only job was recording thefts—not catching thieves!

Mrs Zhang giggled, puncturing her rage. Wearily, she sat down on a chair. To the Chongqing maid servant who had been watching her, expressionless, she said:

"Open the Young Master's trunk."

Probably out of sympathy or, to be more accurate, because she thought she ought to say something to indicate her concern over her mistress's predicament, the maid, while hastening to comply, remarked with a smile:

"The thief who stole your trunk ought to be shot! Of all the trunks, he would pick the one with Madam's spring gowns!" She was an honest woman of about forty who was quite anxious to learn to speak like some of those clever maids she knew.

Mrs Zhang apparently didn't hear her. She was still muttering about "rice-stuffing policemen", and her eyes were fixed on the open trunk with her husband's winter suits. It was bad enough losing the trunk, but worst of all the trunk was full of spring clothing, and it was all *her* clothing, and now the weather had suddenly turned warm. If tomorrow were just as hot and she had to go into town, what could she wear? And she positively had to go into town tomorrow. . . .

I had a couple of beige gowns in another trunk, but which trunk was it? brooded Mrs Zhang. She began to feel very warm. She hated the police for delaying her. If they hadn't been so confident in their assertions that they would recover the trunk, she would have had new spring clothes made already.

Bolt after bolt of material paraded past her mind's

eye, trailed by a row of prices. When she had spoken to her husband about it, he had heard her out, only to say negligently, "It's still cold anyhow and money's a little tight this month. . . ." Now that remark again flashed through her brain.

"I'm suffocating!" she cried angrily, leaping to her feet. In three steps she rushed over to the maid, snatched the Young Master's trunk from her hands, dumped it like a Customs inspector, then stirred through the pile of clothing on the floor with her toe.

Stormily Mrs Zhang tore through all the trunks, her rouged face bedewed with perspiration. But at last she had to admit defeat. "That means I've left two items off the Stolen Property List. . . ." she muttered weakly. She didn't have the courage to think any more about the miserable affair. Mrs Zhang looked at the tumbled disorder of the trunks and smiled a cold smile.

She went back to her own room, determined not to waste any more energy. When her husband returned she would see about the next step. To amuse herself, she opened her case of cosmetics. By various clever means she had managed to obtain quite a good deal of this precious imported merchandise, most of it before the Pacific War started in 1941. In other words, she got it cheap. Her slim fingers nimbly arranged the paints and powder in neat ranks, and the sight of them comforted her. Gradually the round, square, oval, many-angled, flashing crystal bottles and jars transformed themselves into little zeros that streamed from the end of a number in a long train, making quite an astronomical figure.

If I tried to buy this now at present market prices. . . . A faint smile appeared at the corners of Mrs Zhang's mouth. Even if I had the money, there's no place to buy it! Of course we have everything here in the interior, but even with a wad of money you have to know where to look. A merchant is doing you a big favour just to admit he's got the stuff. . . .

The practical problem of the moment, as if jealous of her satisfaction, again thrust itself into her consciousness, and her brows abruptly puckered into a frown. Mrs Zhang's face became very grave. Quite a number of her stolen gowns could not be replaced at any price— or at least it would require an enormous amount of prestige and pull to buy others like them, to say nothing of the long row of digits that would be needed to make up their purchase figure.

The wealthy young girls and matrons of her acquaintance used many devious methods and expended much effort to get their hands on adorable items like Mrs Zhang's cosmetics. She recalled the eldest daughter of the Wang family. The girl was an expert at the game; she could give lectures on the subject. The tricky business deals that Miss Wang had personally handled could fill a book. It had never been necessary for Mrs Zhang to engage in such activities. She had a substantial reserve of "merchandise" to begin with. What's more, her husband as an industrial engineer had good connections, and had been able to replenish her stock from time to time when the international lines were still open. But now a wretched thief had collapsed a big corner of the material goods edifice Mrs Zhang had been so carefully building the past four years!

Other things he didn't touch. No, he had to take all my spring gowns, fumed Mrs Zhang. May he die a lingering death! . . . But she no longer hated the thief so much that she could have swallowed him down in one gulp. Her mood was now tinged with melancholy. . . . And the Old Lord of the Sky is adding fuel to the flames—turning the weather so hot all of a sudden. Aiya, it's enough to suffocate a person! . . . Through the window she could see a fiery sun blazing down with a menace that seemed to be directed at her personally.

Mrs Zhang closed her eyes. Better just stay in bed all day and pretend to be ill, she thought. The black flower embroidered on the border of the somewhat worn nightgown in which she was clad winked at her insultingly. Mrs Zhang sighed. Her eyes drifted back to the array of cosmetics on the table. She remembered how Mrs Li had been attracted by one of her lipsticks and hinted at it several times; but she had pretended not to understand. If the acid-tongued Mrs Li should learn of the fix she was in, the remarks she would make would be just too horrible to imagine!

The heavy steps of the Chongqing maid entering the room startled Mrs Zhang from her contemplations. Annoyed, almost distracted by the problems confronting her, she only glared at the maid, but said nothing.

"Shall I put these things back, Madam?" asked the maid in a loud coarse voice, poking her toe against the trunk heaped with Mr Zhang's winter clothing.

"Mm," assented Mrs Zhang listlessly. She closed her eyes in vexation, but the troublesome problems continued to press down on her relentlessly, this time in the form of zeros, now big now small, one within the other, flying wildly in all directions, till Mrs Zhang was quite breathless. Three thousand? Not enough? — an imaginary opponent argued with her. Well then, how much altogether? What! Why that's enough for a four-foot lathe! . . .

Mrs Zhang's eyes flew open. What ever made her think of that? That was what her husband had said ten months ago when they estimated the value of her collection of cosmetics. Of course he was being a bit sarcastic.

It was at this moment that the maid set up an excited cry, "Madam, Madam! I've found one! Isn't this one?" She thrust a kingfisher blue gown under Mrs Zhang's nose.

Mrs Zhang couldn't restrain a smile of joy. She forgot that she shouldn't act like a poor relation in the presence of the maid, and seized the gown eagerly. Controlling herself with an effort, she assumed an indifferent air, shook out the gown and carefully examined it. Her face fell. Any theatrical company's wardrobe mistress could tell in an instant what year the gown was made.

"Where did I ever get a gown like that?" Mrs Zhang started to say, then corrected herself, "What's it doing in his trunk, wrapped so carefully, as if it were something precious?"

"Madam," persisted the tactless maid, anxious to display her zeal, "what do you call this material? It has a beautiful sheen!"

Ignoring her, Mrs Zhang smiled bitterly. That gown had its memories. Usually her recollections went against the stream—from the present back to the past. But today she started from the beginning. She remembered when she got married, right after the Japanese attack on Shanghai in January 1932. The next few years passed quickly, then the fighting began again. Step by step her little home had retreated with the government west up the Yangzi. Finally, four years ago, they had settled here in Chongqing.... The gown had been made for her trousseau but the tailor had cut it poorly and so she had never worn it.

If I hadn't been in such a whirl the past few years, I'd have given this antique away long ago, thought Mrs Zhang. With a sigh she tossed it back into the trunk.

But when the lid of the trunk banged shut, Mrs Zhang turned quickly to the maid.

"You'd better take it out again. Put it on the bed."

Perhaps she could have it altered and get by with it for the next few days while she was having new gowns made, thought Mrs Zhang. Her nose tingled and tears came to her eyes. She was suffering, really and truly suffering for the first time since the war began.

That evening, after Mr Zhang came home, they were visited by their neighbours Commissioner Li and his wife. From the difficulty of buying pork their talk rambled to prices in general. It seemed to Mrs Zhang that Mrs Li's sharp eyes were ceaselessly examining her from head to toe as if seeking a flaw. What's more, Mrs Li was dressed in sharkskin. Was she showing off especially for Mrs Zhang's benefit?

"It was hard to get toothpaste in the city yesterday," said Mrs Li, her eyes sweeping from the faces of the two gentlemen to Mrs Zhang's profile, then travelling downward. "Today every single shop, big and small, tells you flatly—Sorry, all sold out! Those merchants are a shrewd lot. They won't sell a scarce item till its price goes sky high!"

"Oh," said Mrs Zhang. She was quite upset. Maybe she's going to ask me if I don't feel warm, wearing such heavy clothing, worried Mrs Zhang.

Commissioner Li laughed. "But when someone they know comes in, they always manage to produce some—for a consideration, of course."

"Everyone knows that," Mrs Li glared at her husband. "It's just such a nuisance finding someone they know!" Then she smiled and asked Mr Zhang, "Why doesn't someone open a toothpaste factory here? Unfortunately that's not in Mr Li's line, otherwise—" She smiled again.

"It's not so simple," Mr Zhang replied thoughtfully. "You have to have lead-foil tubes, and for that you need lead. But by the time your machines are ready to go into operation perhaps you find it more profitable to sell the lead than to make tubes out of it."

"I don't believe it!" Mrs Li's eyes again darted to Mrs Zhang. "Boats rise with the tide. Why can't you do the same?"

Mr Zhang only smiled bitterly and looked at Commissioner Li.

The official nodded his head. "It's not simple," he confirmed with the utmost gravity, "not at all simple. The world of commerce is in a state of constant fluctuation."

But Mrs Li was never one to concede anything. She laughed coldly. "Constant fluctuation, piffle! The market's always going up. That kind of fluctuation any idiot can understand. It's not like our April weather. Now there's something that really fluctuates!" She turned to Mrs Zhang with a smile. "Don't you agree, Mrs Zhang? Cold one minute and hot the next, changing a dozen times a day. You go mad trying to keep up with it."

Mrs Zhang's nerves were ready to snap when Mrs Li

addressed her. It wasn't until Mrs Li finished that Mrs Zhang was able to relax. Strange. She was like a soldier going into battle for the first time; after the initial volley she became calmer. And with her mind under control, she could make her mouth obey her will. Her reply was quite casual.

"Yes, indeed. The best thing to do is just ignore it. Mark my words — tomorrow will be cold as usual."

"Aiya, what am I going to wear!" cried Mrs Li with unexpected vehemence, as if flinging down her last card.

Startled, for the moment Mrs Zhang didn't know what to say. Fortunately, Commissioner Li changed the subject. "Do you hear any news from your home town?" he asked Mr Zhang.

"Nothing lately."

"Who controls the town now?"

"First it was occupied by the Japanese. Then the guerillas took it back." His head to one side, Mr Zhang reflected, then continued, "It must have been six months ago, the enemy moved in again. Probably it's still in their hands."

"Was any of your property damaged? What about your house?"

"I think it's still intact."

"Then you've got nothing to worry about," Commissioner Li said firmly. "What's already been destroyed —well there's no use talking about that. But from now on you can be sure of what remains."

"Oh?" Mr and Mrs Zhang exclaimed together, the wife with joy, the husband rather sceptically.

Commissioner Li smiled. Before he could elaborate, Mrs Li took the floor.

"It's something he's heard. The Japanese devils know they're going to lose in the end, that at the peace conference we're sure to present them with a big damage bill. If they burn anything else now they'll just be making things worse for themselves. Even the Japanese devils can figure that much out."

"Of course that's only an opinion, but it's not without reason." Again Commissioner Li smiled. "Otherwise why do you people in industry keep talking about taking over the enemy factories in China? After all the damage they've caused don't you think we're going to make them compensate you?"

"Naturally we want to be compensated." Mr Zhang's voice rose a little with excitement. "There are figures to prove how much public and private enterprises have been damaged. There are even approximate figures on the extent of damage to the ordinary people's homes and property. But the fact that we want compensation is one thing; whether the enemy feel they'll have to pay the bill and so stop acting like barbarians is another. I think the Japanese devils won't quit until we drive them into the sea. The Japanese warlords will be savage to the end. They'll burn and steal and loot, they'll behave worse than ever. They know that they, the handful of warlords, won't have to foot the bill. It's the Japanese people who'll be made to pay."

"Won't quit until we drive them into the sea—Ha, ha, ha!" Commissioner Li burst into hearty laughter. No one understood what was amusing him, but as usually the case when loud laughter is suddenly injected into a conversation, the serious atmosphere eased. Mrs Zhang added a finishing touch.

"I don't know what those Japanese warlords can be

thinking," she said with a lazy sigh. "They're sure to lose. Why do they insist on dragging the thing out?"

"It won't be long now," Mrs Li assured her. "Do you know, Mrs Zhang, there's a new game that you play with numbers and the alphabet. If you do it with 1943, the word comes out in English—'Victory'. We're going to have victory this year and everybody can go home!"

Mrs Zhang was delighted. She insisted that Mrs Li demonstrate immediately, and promptly produced the necessary matchsticks. Standing beside the table, the two ladies manipulated the matchsticks in a demonstration of their deep concern over the outcome of the war.

The two gentlemen began to chat about the present state of industrialization.

"China must industrialize, no question about it," said Commissioner Li in a burst of enthusiasm. "State-owned heavy industry, privately-owned light industry—that's the only answer. We must make a long range plan, the sooner the better. One of the most cheering symptoms today is that everyone's eyes are looking toward the future, everyone is talking about national construction! Everyone is planning how to make China completely industrial. . . ." Counting on his fingers, he enumerated the number of articles dealing with "National Construction" in recent newspapers and magazines—at least fifty in the past two months.

In a low voice, he continued solemnly, "That's not to be sneezed at! It's the biggest fruit the war has brought us. If it weren't for the war there wouldn't be nearly so much enthusiasm for industrialization. . . ."

Mr Zhang listened in silence, thinking of the many difficulties that harassed him—the shortage of raw materials, of capital, of technicians, heavy taxes, how to keep production going. . . . And so Commissioner Li's beautiful picture of the future didn't glow before Mr Zhang's eyes with quite the same lustre.

"But we have problems," he muttered, almost to himself. "How do we solve them? . . . Everybody ought to concentrate on that."

"Ah—yes, that's as it should be," Commissioner Li said quickly. Mr Zhang wasn't sure whether he was referring to having problems or the need for everyone to concentrate on solving them. But the commissioner then switched back to the April weather and Mr Zhang had to shelve the case as unsettled.

By the time the minute hand of the clock had moved another four or five numbers, both hosts and guests felt they had nothing more to say. The visitors took their leave.

It was still only about eight p.m. and Mr Zhang took from his portfolio a large pile of letters and charts. He studied them, raising his head from time to time to stare into space while tapping the table lightly with a crayon pencil. He always did this when wrestling with knotty problems, and a technician not particularly skilled in administrative matters is very likely to run into problems, extremely troublesome problems. After tapping the pencil a while, Mr Zhang slowly shook his head, pushed the sheet of paper in front of him away and stood up with a sigh.

He looked around the room, as if searching for someone to whom he could talk. At times like this he always wished there was someone to whom he could unburden himself; but there never was, or by the time someone showed up he had already lost the desire. Today, however, perhaps his opportunity had come.

Just as he began looking around, his wife entered. He put down the crayon pencil and, drumming on the table with the knuckles of his left hand, said:

"When Mr A recommends raw materials, Mr B says they're no good. When Mr B recommends raw materials, Mr A finds fault. When we go out and buy materials on our own, the two of them jump all over us. . . ."

Mr Zhang sighed and rubbed a hand across his face. He was about to go on when his wife interrupted.

"What's that noise? Can it really be rain?"

There was indeed a sound like rain pattering against the tile roofs, rising and falling in intensity. Mrs Zhang was beside herself with joy. "Good, it's raining! Good!" she kept repeating. "Now it'll turn cold. . . ."

"It'll turn cold," Mr Zhang echoed. He smiled a lonely smile and sat down again at the table. He didn't know or care why rain should make his wife so happy, nor was he interested in whether it was actually raining or not. All he knew was that his wife's mention of rain had washed away the words he had been about to speak.

Mrs Zhang's joy was short-lived, however. The pattering noise she had heard through the window had already changed to a series of hard sharp taps. "Oh," she said, disappointed, "it was just neighbours shuffling their mahjong pieces!" Only then did her husband's previous remark register in her mind. Turning to him, she asked, "Who jumps all over you?"

Mr Zhang grinned weakly. "People with too much energy."

Mrs Zhang seemed to be listening with only half an ear. Her eyes gazed vacantly. After a while she queried softly, "Will there really be victory this year so that all of us can go home?"

"Naturally that's what everyone hopes."

"Then it's not definite?"

"I'm afraid it won't be so soon."

"Next year, maybe?"

"That's more likely. But it's no use asking me. I don't know any more about it than you do. The optimists figure it shorter, the cautious ones think it'll take a little longer. Actually, they're just like you and me. No one can predict for sure. It isn't some tangible object that we can measure exactly."

Mrs Zhang listened silently. Then she sighed and said, "If I knew that we had to spend the rest of our lives here, I could settle down to it. But we don't know how long we'll be here. I'm always thinking about going home, but nobody knows when that day will come. That's the hardest part of all. Every day is harder to face. Even the weather tortures you here. One day you're sopping wet, the next day you're scorched."

"We've stuck it out so long. Just be patient a little longer —"

"Everyone is trying to be patient," Mrs Zhang interrupted. "It's easy enough to say, but when it affects you personally, how can you help being aggravated? Like the weather, for instance — turning so hot all of a sudden. Is it any wonder I'm upset?"

Mrs Zhang felt she had made her meaning sufficiently clear. It was now up to Mr Zhang to offer the solution voluntarily. She was thus retaining her self-respect while at the same time giving Mr Zhang a chance to display his sense of responsibility. But this time she miscalculated. Mr Zhang failed to respond. Again he

picked up his crayon pencil and drew a fat envelope
out from the sheaf of papers.   The envelope contained
a large blueprint which Mr Zhang spread on the table.
Mrs Zhang had no choice but to set forth — in a detail-
ed manner with figures attached — the proposal she felt
should have come from Mr Zhang.

Noting the figures on a sheet of paper with his crayon pencil as she spoke, Mr Zhang silently waited until
his wife finished, then added and checked the column.

"Why," he laughed, "that's enough to buy a four-
foot lathe!"

These words, although spoken in jest, cut Mrs Zhang
to the quick. The aggravation she had suffered all day
brimmed to her eyes, but she managed to retain her
control.   Turning her face away from him, she said hotly, "Again that four-foot lathe! Very well, what if it
is? If those clothes hadn't been stolen at least I wouldn't
have kept them idle, and paid rent besides for a place
to keep them idle in! And tell me this — did your precious lathes ever make you rich? You were running
your own business three years ago, but what are you
doing today? Playing messenger boy for someone else!"

When she was angry, Mrs Zhang didn't care how her
words stung. Of course the cataclysmic change that had
taken place, the difference between their position three
years ago and now, was certainly no less painful to Mr
Zhang than to her.   But that was her way of expressing
herself, and whenever she mentioned their decline, there
was always a note of reproach in her voice — no, say
rather a cold outright sneer.

But her husband would not strike back and Mrs
Zhang couldn't work herself into a real fury. She looked

at him. He was still bent over his blueprint. It seemed
to Mrs Zhang that she was losing ground.

"What about it?" she demanded formally. "Am I
right or aren't I? Did your lathes ever make you rich?"

Mr Zhang raised his head and faced her helplessly.
"You're quite right." His smile was bitter. "But what
I did was also right! It wasn't the fault of the lathes
that I didn't get rich. The reasons were quite complicated. But you wait and see. Sooner or later those lathes
will make a big show again."

"Fine. I'd like nothing better. But when that happens
I don't want them, and you, to be earning money for
somebody else."

"What's the difference?" Mr Zhang forced a laugh.
"We'll still be increasing national production."

His self-mockery displeased Mrs Zhang — if it was
self-mockery; and if he were talking seriously, she was
even more revolted. Glaring, she stabbed again:

"I'll wait and see. But I'm afraid by the time your
lathes finally make a big show they'll be ready for the
scrap heap!"

The shot went home. Mr Zhang sighed deeply and
crouched closer to his many lined blueprint. The lathes
that were the only vestiges of his glory of three years
before had been idle for more than six months — that
was fact.   Rather than sell them at a sacrifice he was
paying rent for storage space — that was a fact too. And
finally, though he would never admit it, the dismal
thought his wife had just so poisonously expressed often
stole like a black shadow across his heart — that was
even more of a fact. The lines of the blueprint danced
and wavered. Mr Zhang strained to keep them steady.
Things are sure to get better, he thought. They must get

better. They will, I'll stake my life on it. It's only a question of time. . . .

A slip of paper attached to a corner of the blueprint caught his eye. In addition to some numbers, the slip bore five or six bright crimson signature seals attesting the importance of the document. They also showed that the blueprint had been travelling for a long time from department to department through miles of red tape. The time it had spent touring from the bottom to the top and then back down again to Mr Zhang was already longer than it had taken to draw the print. How long a road still lay ahead of it before it passed through the hands of a certain engineer to the workers and shop technicians Heaven only knew!

Some day there'll be fewer people putting seals on blueprints and more people drawing them, thought Mr Zhang, his heart beating steadily. There's bound to be a day when specifications won't have to make so many detours, when the big wheels of industry will turn day and night, turn in an orderly co-ordinated way. That day must come. I'd give my life to make it come, no matter when. . . . His heart seemed to be pumping with increased vigour. Slowly he raised his head and took a breath.

He met his wife's eyes, only this time he read her involved thoughts with the same keenness that he read a complicated blueprint. "The weather's warm," he said slowly. "You'd better make some clothes quickly. We'll manage about the money somehow."

"It's all right," she replied. "I've found a gown that I've never worn. I can get by with it for a while if I have it altered." Though she spoke without rancour, she couldn't control a sudden tickling in her nose. She quickly turned her head to avoid her husband's eyes. She felt frustrated. There was an empty and yet comfortable sensation in her heart. Her urge to weep mingled with a sensation of relief. It was rather like her feeling when they left their comfortable home in Hankou's "foreign settlement" and started up the Yangzi toward the interior.

Once more a pattering could be heard through the window. But now besides the neighbours' mahjong pieces, something else was contributing to the sound. After listening carefully for a moment, Mrs Zhang laughed with innocent pleasure.

"It's really raining! Oh, this April weather!"

She lightly flitted to the window and closed the shutters to keep the rain from blowing in on her husband.

April 26, 1943

Translated by Sidney Shapiro

The Beancurd Pedlar's Whistle

WAKING this morning I heard the beancurd pedlar's whistle outside the window.

That whistling always makes me feel rather distracted.

Not that its plaintive sound makes me, a wanderer, homesick; no, an outcast like myself has no home or country, so such refined sentiments as homesickness hardly apply to me.

Nor did that solemn, stirring trill, like an old reed-leaf whistle on a smaller scale, remind me of other scenes which had vanished like clouds. No, the past had left only a faint scar, long since covered over and wiped out by grim reality and the gleaming future.

So this distraction of mine is hard to describe. Yet each time I hear this whistling I cannot suppress a sense of recurrent distraction.

Last night at the night market I had a similar sense of bitterness.

Whenever I go to the night market and see the mats spread over the muddy ground with wares and salesmen crowded on them together, the ragged pedlars crying their wares in the freezing wind, I feel an indefinable distraction. Is it pity for them? I know that pity would mean contempt. Then do I sympathize with them? It's

---

The following essays were translated by Gladys Yang.

more than that. At heart I admire their honest approach to making a living, yet, to some extent, I think it too crude. From the eloquence with which they crack up their wares I sense their wretchedness. I seem to see their hot breath congealing in the sky into grey clouds.

But they have no whistles. No underground sound like this, which seems as if muffled in a jar or struggling out from beneath some heavy weight, to symbolize their life.

The whistling rent the frozen air and passed outside my window. As I listened intently I felt I had read volumes in that monotonous sound.

I flung back my bed-curtain to gaze up at the sky behind the house. What did I see? Only a vast white expanse of melancholy mist.

1929

Mist

MIST cloaked the mountains opposite my back window.

I don't know the names of these mountains. The night of my arrival I saw lights on the highest peak like a diamond tiara. As my room had no electricity at that time, each evening I sat quietly in the dark staring at that stretch of light halfway up the sky, which reminded me of a fairy tale I had once read. Indeed, that neat formation of three dimly separate tiers of fireballs set off against the fearsome black peaks in the background could not but give rise to fancies out of this world.

By daylight, though, they were nothing out of the common. Of this range of five or six peaks about the same height only the westernmost had buildings on it, the rest had nothing but trees; and the highest peak in the middle had a big patch of water on it like a scabby head.

Now as usual the morning mist cloaked everything, even the telegraph poles a slight distance away.

Gradually the sun struggled out of the thick mist. And what a pitiful sun! Its light was so faint. Then it too hid itself to let the sea of thick white mist swallow up everything, engulfing the earth.

To hell with this mist which blots out everything!

Naturally I also dislike cold winds, snow and ice. But they are preferable to mist. Cold winds and icy weather can be lethal, but they also stimulate men to take action and struggle. Mist, mist simply makes you wretched, dispirited and enervated, as if you had sunk into a bog and longed to struggle out but were unable to.

Towards noon the mist turned into a drizzle like a curtain hanging all the time over the window. Twenty to thirty feet away one could see nothing but clouds which still covered everything, but not like mist. There was no wind. Yet the withered lotus stems in the pool in front of the door shook suddenly from time to time, then red carp frisked about cleaving the surface of the pool — so still that it had seemed stagnant.

I wonder if the red carps' abnormal behaviour was due to unbearable boredom? For my part, in the absence of bright sunshine I would prefer wild wind or pelting rain, I have no patience with this drizzle which after the melancholy mist hangs all the time like a curtain outside the window.

December 14, 1928

The Rainbow

IMPERCEPTIBLY, golden-red sunshine spread over the northern peaks. But in front of my window light rain still fell steadily.

I had heard that the weather in these parts was not too good. Did that refer to sunshine on one side like this and light rain on the other to spatter you with mud? It was much like the rainy season in my old home. The sun comes out and at the same time it rains.

But two nights ago there had been a heavy frost with a temperature of forty degrees Fahrenheit.

At all events sunshine was welcome. I sat by the south window reading a play by N. Evreinoff. This was the third time I had read it. Still I didn't know whether I should hate or love the hero Paraclete who stood for an adviser and benefactor, and the five others in the cast who represented different sides of his character.

Wasn't this much like today's weather combining rain and shine?

I laid down the book and stared eastward at the distant peak bathed in gold by the setting sun, and my thoughts flew far away. The white buildings on the peak seemed to me like medieval forts whose occupants should all be knights in armour or slim alluring beauties.

But hadn't warriors like European knights once ridden roughshod over this area? Over a century ago in the one-time capital enfolded by these mountains hadn't there been warriors wielding iron maces? Didn't the aftermath of those days still swirl like an underground spring through this prosaic town?

I lowered my head sunk in dreams.

When I looked up again — ah! A brilliant rainbow had cut through the blue evening sky. I had no idea when it had appeared; but now it was like a bridge, arching from behind the white buildings on the east peak to a slightly higher emerald peak to the north. Ah, rainbow! The ancient Greeks said you were a goddess, a symbol of lovely hope, on your way to Hades to fetch back spring!

But rainbow-like hope also causes men too much distress.

Then I seemed to see a knight in a coat of mail and iron helmet appear on the bridge in the sky. Was he searching for the fair lady to whom he had vowed to be true? Was he sweeping away injustice from the world? Or was he a predator relying on his powerful connections?

By now it had grown dark. My table lamp suddenly lit up, and I roused myself from my dream.

He may seem a medieval knight standing on the rainbow bridge and holding high some fancy banner, when actually he is simply seeking the lime-light or waiting for the highest bid. There are probably not a few new knights of this kind in our present "new Dark Age".

March 10, 1929

An Old Country Gentleman

> "If there were no so-called God,
> we would have to create Him."
> — Voltaire

FRIENDS! This is something that really happened in a certain village, township and province.

Early that morning the red sun rose in the east, the air was fresh and cool. There had been a thunderstorm during the night, and the hollows in the street's flag-stones were still little puddles. An old country gentleman in a jiesan gown* was standing on the stone steps in front of his house. Tweaking his beard with one hand he was looking up leisurely at the drifting clouds, more carefree and content than even immortals.

The old fellow was slightly eccentric: he liked to talk nonsense and tell white lies. When others were taken in he stood aside and laughed up his sleeve, claiming that this was his best secret way of prolonging life. He was a humorist.

This morning as he watched the drifting clouds seriously, not considering a fabrication, a young friend suddenly accosted him, respectfully clasped both hands in greeting and called:

---

* A woollen gown with a light skirt sewn on to the dark upper-part, worn by some of the literati.

"Good morning, Old X! They say that clap of thunder last night split open an old scholartree outside East Township — that old tree beside X Bridge."

X Bridge? That big three-arched bridge six *li* from the market town! Old X rolled his eyes and answered without reflection:

"That's right. A monster had its den under that tree by the bridge."

His startled young friend stared at Old X's sallow face, not knowing what to make of this. But Old X went on, as if talking sanctimoniously to himself:

"Well! It's a good thirty *li* from X Bridge to Snail Sands. If that monster struck by lightning could get that far, it was really fearful, fearful."

Catching on, the youngster hastily asked:

"Old X, was there some evil spirit beneath the scholartree?"

"There certainly was! After last night's thunderstorm, a big python dropped out of the sky on to Snail Sands. Thicker than a barrel with a head like a wicker basket, it covered at least half a *mu* of the field where it dropped dead. My small son often goes to X Bridge, I'm ashamed to say. He was lucky not to have been eaten up by it. Now that the python's met with retribution I must go to Snail Sands to see just what happened."

"Yes indeed. But it's no joke walking over twenty *li* in hot weather like this."

With that the youngster clasped both hands and left. Old X watched him till he was out of sight, then laughed to himself as he savoured this joke and went back in to the house.

By the afternoon Old X had completely forgotten this

business. When he strolled to the teahouse as usual, everyone there was discussing the death of a huge python in Snail Sands. Then he recalled the trick he had played that morning and couldn't help smiling as he listened to their talk. But presently he stopped smiling to concentrate on listening. The talk was so circumstantial! And one speaker, his head covered with sweat, claimed to have just been to the scene.

"Did it really happen?" Old X wondered, tweaking his beard. He suspected that there were grounds for what he had told his young friend that morning. He didn't believe that he could have made it up.

After hearing the others out, he stood up.

"I heard about this too this morning," he said. "I thought it was a rumour. Since it's true I must go there to have a look."

Many other customers agreed with him. A crowd of them flocked out of the teahouse to head towards Snail Sands west of the market town, with Old X leading the way.

March 16, 1933

The Incense Fair

AFTER Clear and Bright* our market-town always had an Incense Fair which lasted about half a month in all.

Most of those who went there were peasants. The fair was held in the temple of the local deity. In the old days when the countryside was still idyllic this Incense Fair was the countryfolks' "carnival". Because the weather was fine in the twenty days from Clear and Bright to Grain Rains,** that was a time for enjoyment just before the busy "silkworm season"; so the peasants came to this fair partly to pray for good fortune (a good silkworm harvest) and make offerings to the gods, partly to prepare themselves for the hard work ahead. It was both a pilgrimage and a spring outing.

So eating and enjoyment figured most prominently at the Incense Fair. Tea stalls were set up by a show ground for jugglers, acrobats, performers of martial arts, tigers, dwarfs, string puppets, operas played by women, or peep-shows — the huge square covering fifty to sixty *mu* in front of the temple was packed. The temple stocked herbal medicines and pear candy, coloured paper, various toys made of paper, clay and metal, "candle mountains" like clusters of stars. The smoke of camphorwood incense brought tears to your eyes, and on

---

* From about April 5 to 20.
** From about April 20 to May 5.

the hard hassocks whole rows of people kowtowed. Inside and outside the temple the sound of voices, gongs and drums, children's little trumpets and whistles blended into a din which carried three *li* away.

That was the lively Incense Fair I went to as a child. There I not only learned to appreciate our "national arts", I also made the acquaintance of tigers, leopards, monkeys and pangolins. So this Incense Fair was a carnival for children too.

After the Revolution* the Incense Fair was banned for several years "to root out superstition". The left side of the temple was taken over by the Public Security Office, and on one corner of the square in front a bamboo fence was put up — it was said for a park. A sign "Centre for Improved Silkworm Strains" appeared on the lefthand hall.

But starting last year this "superstitious" Incense Fair was suddenly sanctioned again. That gave me a chance to relive the old dream of my boyhood, and I went off cheerfully to the fair with three younger girl cousins who had been born too late to go to that lively Incense Fair.

Though the weather was perfect, "business" was very slack. Though there were more people than usual in front of the temple, the atmosphere seemed gloomy. I heard unexpected gongs and drums. But they sounded monotonous. Black Dragon Pool in front of the temple was as limpid as before, but the stage behind the pool was in a state of collapse, its beams exposed to the light of day like the ribs of someone lean. It was totally different from the Incense Fair of my childhood.

---

* The 1911 Revolution which toppled the Qing Dynasty.

Anyway we went to have a look at the only place where gongs and drums were sounding. I expected to find jugglers who would be wretched players too. To my surprise, however, it was the Nanyang Martial Arts Troupe. One performer was the strong man who "slept on nails", who had been written up in the sixty-second issue of the Shanghai *Liangyou Pictorial*. So this was no obscure group of travelling players. Yet their tickets sold for only sixteen coppers.

There were very few spectators, less than two hundred. (When I went in there had been only fifty or sixty.) Although the performers seemed rather disappointed, they conscientiously put on the half dozen acts advertized: circus stunts, cutting through barriers of swords or fire, tight-rope walking, displays of strength. . . . They said "Few people have come to today's first performance, but we're going to do our best." They had at least thirty people, men and women, old and young on their three boats!

It seemed to me that the acts of this Nanyang Martial Arts Troupe were actually much better than the boxing, peddling of medicine and so forth of the old Incense Fair. Had they come a dozen or so years earlier, the place would probably have been packed out. Yet today's first performance had only two hundred spectators. There were virtually no peasants — those most in evidence at previous fairs.

I later learned that the revival of this Incense Fair had been promoted by some small shopkeepers in town. They had hoped in this way to attract customers to improve their business, but they too were disappointed.

July 15, 1933

Before the Storm

FIRST thing in the morning I walked to the small stone bridge. Its stones were still warm to the touch. There had not been a breath of wind all the day before. Towards evening thunder rumbled, with still no wind, and the night had been even closer than the day. Just before daybreak two or three people were still lying on the bridge — perhaps they had heated the stones by sleeping there.

A grey curtain shrouded the sky. The sun could not be seen. Yet the might of the sun seemed to have penetrated that grey curtain to press straight on your head.

There was not a drop of water in the stream, and the clay in the middle of its bed was cracked like tortoise shell. In the fields countless ditches seemed to have opened up — over two feet across, could you deny that they resembled ditches? That pallid clay was just about as hard and dry as cement. As if even after one night it had still not spat out all the heat absorbed during the day, and now its long mouths were exhaling something like white smoke.

Anyone standing on the bridge felt as if all his pores were blocked up, as if his stomach was churning, about to vomit.

This morning the sky remained shrouded by that grey curtain, with not the least rent in it, no movement either. There may have been some wind beyond the curtain but, covered as we were by it, when we dropped a chicken feather off the bridge it didn't flutter airily away. As if living in a vacuum tube men stretched out both arms and breathed in hard, but all they inhaled was hot acrid stuffness.

Sweat kept oozing, oozing out, but it was like glue making you sticky all over and encasing you in a shell.

By about three in the afternoon people were gaping like fish out of water. Suddenly a rent appeared in the grey curtain overhead! A genuine rent! As if gashed by a gleaming knife. But after being gashed the curtain closed up again as if never cut, not allowing a breath of wind through. Presently lightning flashed and another rent appeared in the grey curtain. But what was the use of that?

It seemed a giant hand holding a huge flashing knife was trying to rip open the curtain from outside, seemed as if the giant's roars of rage were coming nearer and nearer, as the whole sky was lit up by that flashing knife and the thunder of the giant's roars came from outside the curtain.

Abruptly both the flashes and roars died out, leaving the dense grey curtain through which no wind could pass.

The air was now twice as stifling. The curtain was twice as dense and dark as before.

You might guess that now the giant outside the curtain was wiping his sweat and resting; you foresaw that he would return to the attack. You waited desperately, waited for the lightning flash of his big knife ripping open the grey curtain, the thunder of his roars.

But as you waited, waited, flies flocked round. They

flew out from dunghills, droning, to surround you and sting your sticky skin. One golden fly with a red button on its head like a high official, having just glutted itself in a cesspool chose to squat on the tip of your nose.

Mosquitoes came too as you waited. Buzzing like old monks chanting sutras or old scholars intoning the classics. The flies brought you infectious diseases, the mosquitoes frankly wanted to drink your blood.

You leapt up wildly waving a rush fan, but as soon as you drove away the insects on one side, another horde attacked on the other side. In response to your yells they simply droned and buzzed.

The cicadas on the treetops outside were shrilling, "You're done for, done for!"

With no more sweat to shed, your parched mouth ablaze and your hands limp, you felt the end of the world could be no worse than this.

But abruptly a flash of lightning shed a dazzling light on each corner of the room. The giant outside the grey curtain tore it to shreds! Thunder rolled as he roared in triumph. The howling wind blocked outside the curtain for two whole days swept down hotfoot, exceeding the speed limit. The cicadas stopped shrilling, the flies fled, the mosquitoes went into hiding, and people felt as refreshed as if stripped of their shells.

Wham! Wham! Wham! The giant's knife flashed through the sky.

Boom! Boom! Boom! Please speed up and roar more deafeningly.

May the thunderstorm sluice the world, making it clean and cool!

September 20, 1934

Evening

THE sea, dark green, was not smooth; files of small waves, too many to count, were on the march as if crying, "Left, right — left" on their way to the sea-wall shaped like the mouth of a trumpet. They crowded forward to break against the beach. Then their troop scattered, spraying angry white foam, while the file behind caught up and charged in its turn.

A few white gulls darted past, their wings skimming the waves, which were becoming increasingly angry.

The wind sounded its bugle. Sounded the charge. The small leaping waves looked like big eyes flashing golden light. The whole sea was a mass of leaping golden eyes. Clarion battle cries rose up from below the sea-wall.

And rank upon serried rank of this sea of leaping golden eyes, each angrier than the next, each a deeper blood-red colour, stretched to the horizon to form a wash of ruddy gold. Above this was half a fiery red setting sun.

Half the sky, blazing red, pressed heavily down on the rays of the setting sun.

The setting sun, struggling angrily, seemed to be saying:

... Ha! I've already completed today's historic mission, completed this day's course. Now, now is the time for me to rest, the time for me to die. Ha! But I am also nearing the start of a new life. Tomorrow I shall rise in all my might from the other side of the ocean to give you light, warmth and happiness.

. The wind soughed.

The wind carried all over the world the declaration of the undying sun. The highest peak of the lofty Himalayas, the vast Pacific Ocean, dismal little old villages, and cities congealed in silver light — the setting sun sprayed them all with blood-red flames.

Two or three gulls cleaved the sky which was gradually growing brilliant.

The wind flew off with the setting sun's declaration.

As if suddenly melting, the countless dancing golden eyes of the sea flattened out into a huge dark green face.

In the distance sounded a solemn, stirring reed flute.

The dark curtain of the night, soon to descend heavily, had not yet descended.

The wind which had flown off somewhere abruptly came back, this time as if sounding a tattoo on a drum. No, not just wind but thunder. The wind had brought thunder.

The sea heaved again, the wave leapt up and crashed.

A storm had come to the night sea.

November 20, 1934

Footprints on the Sand

HE was walking, all on his own, on the beach that evening.

Everything was hazy, he could simply make out an expanse of white which he knew was the beach, and the pitch-black ocean where a storm was brewing.

A spark of light in the distance was a lighthouse.

He was using the fire in his heart to light his way, but could see no farther than two or three feet ahead. He picked his way carefully.

All of a sudden there was a flash of forked lightning. It lit up a dark mass not far ahead — the "Kingdom of the Night" or some demon's fort?

He saw too that the sand about ten feet away was covered with crisscrossing, overlapping footprints.

Aha! Now he knew what to do. Quick! He jumped for joy, meaning to follow those footprints surely left by passers-by.

He braced himself, rekindling the fire in his heart.

He bent down to identify the crisscrossing, overlapping footprints by the faint light of that fire.

But he gave an exclamation of dismay.

These were obviously the footprints of birds and beasts crisscrossing and overlapping. Large, small, new and old, there was no knowing how far they stretched. And he stood all alone in this vast sea of animal imprints.

He stood there uncertainly, having lost his nerve, the fire in his heart grown fainter like a pale yellow fuzzy moon, unable to light up even two steps ahead.

So, his head in his hands, he sat down on the sand.

He sat down intending to wait till dawn. Sure that among those crisscrossing, overlapping footprints of birds and beasts there must be men's footprints too, which would lead him to a broad highway and the warm, lighted homes of men. If he just waited patiently till daybreak he'd be able to make them out.

He waited patiently, head in his hands, not even glancing at the distant lighthouse. He believed that in this fearfully dark night he was right to wait patiently. And yet —

Boom! Boom! A weird sound made his hair stand on end. Not the rumble of thunder, nor the roar of the sea. Looking quickly up he saw a host of demons, green-faced and long-toothed, trooping out from the black waves, each with a knife in one hand, in the other a gold ingot smelted from a black human heart. They were frantically searching for victims.

Behind these demons he also saw bewitching mermaids with long flowing hair and high, rounded breasts sitting on the pebbles of the beach and singing songs to enchant men.

He closed his eyes, realizing that he had been wrong to wait. Using his last ounce of strength he rekindled his inner fire, meaning to find a way out. But now sparks of light flew out from the black mass. More and more of them! These sparks formed a ball, then a line, finally forming the glittering large characters: Bright Road.

Ah! Ah! he exclaimed in relief.

Now lightning zigzagged again across the sky. Shaped like a saw it was going to saw the dark sky in half. By its light he saw clearly over there demons who looked seven tenths human, each holding a long weapon which he suspected was a human bone emitting from its tip a green ghostly fire. It was this ghostly fire that had formed those scintillating characters.

The lightning also revealed that there were indeed human footprints among all the other imprints on the ground. Some had been trampled over and smudged, others were still clear and looked new.

His heart leapt up as if it had doubled in size and gave out a much brighter light. He saw that some of the footprints, though they looked human, had actually been made by monsters wearing men's boots, and beside them were the footprints of small children. They had trapped some innocent children!

But under the overlapping footprints of beasts and demons masquerading as men he discovered true human footprints. And these were heading in the same direction, their ranks closing the farther they went.

That increased his confidence and made him give up the idea of not leaving till daybreak. By the light of the fire in his heart he carefully identified the genuine human footprints in the mass of crisscrossing prints, then resolutely set forth.

November 20, 1934

On Landscapes

THE evening before last I saw a trailer of *Wind and Clouds over the Pass*, which reminded me of the desert beyond Monkey Gorge. That is no Gobi Desert, simply a nameless dot on the average map, yet its borders are invisible to the naked eye and when the sun is overhead at noon the glare of light reflected from it is dazzling. There are no undulating sand dunes and not an adobe hut in sight, nothing but an expanse streching in all directions, so flat that you cannot even find wells connected by underground channels. Its colour is so uniform that if you spot the bones of camels or horses their faint whiteness has long since blended into their vast surroundings, so lonely and still that the only sound is the hot air crackling like fire. But you cannot say there is no "landscape" here. When a black speck appears on the horizon followed by others to form a line, a file, and when a breeze sets the bells of this caravan tinkling, carrying that ding-dong tinkling to your ears, and finally when that orderly formation of proud camels plods calmly yet resolutely closer and closer till the leading camel's oblong crimson flag flashes into your view and your ears are filled with the dingdong euphony of bells large and small — at such a time you may say nothing but are bound to feel: how magnificent, how enchanting! Here is Nature at its most monotonous, yet the addition of human activity changes it entirely to make this a genuine landscape. Nature is great, but mankind is even greater.

And that reminds me of another scene, the "loess steppe". Most of the hills there are bald, yet their tiers of terraced fields make them look like leprous heads with sparse brownish hair. Those neat fields of long-stemmed plants in particular, like troops drawn up for review, have their own distinctive charm as they sway in the evening wind. Even finer are nights with a full moon in a sky so blue that it appears transparent. When the moon rises apparently just a few feet over the peak, seen from a distance the dense millet on the heights stands up like bristling hair, and just at this point two ox-horns grow out of the mountain's back, then whole oxen appear as well as men shouldering ploughs. Not many, just two or three, with perhaps a child tagging behind. They come slowly down, silhouetted like scissor-cuts against the blue sky, black hill and silver moon-light. A bucolic poet seeing them would think them a superb subject for a poem. Nor is this all. These peasants coming home at night send simple songs with gay rhythms drifting down from the hill top as they disappear into the valley below, leaving the blue sky, bright moon, dark hills behind. But their songs linger in the air.

Another time. Another place. Sunset in the hills where the parched yellow earth is puffing out the heat sucked in during the day while the stream is racing as if to sweep away the pebbles in its shallow bed. At this hour a troop of people in the valley are coming back from work, talking cheerfully in at least seven or eight different dialects. Suddenly, singing the same tune, they burst into a rousing song. Their gay laughter falls on the water and seems to make it laugh too. Look at their hands: this one usually holds a palette, that one yesterday fiddled the accompaniment to the "Song of Production"; this generally holds a woodcut knife, that pens magnificent writings true to life. Now, however, all are callused from gripping the wooden handles of hoes and spades. At the foot of the hill they are stopped by another group. A blazing bonfire has been lit here, and many artists' hands have already cooked golden millet and emerald rape. The sun has disappeared behind the hills, its afterglow filling the sky, the stream is splashing more loudly, throwing up more white foam as it falls on the rocks. They dip their feet in the stream to wash off the yellow dust or scoop up handfuls of water to wash their faces. In this place, backing on to the hills and facing the water, tranquil Nature and men brimming with vitality make up an entrancing picture.

Here the blue sky, bright moon, bald hills, drab loess and shallow stream seem the most appropriate background, not to be altered. Nature is great, mankind is great, but greatest of all are the activities of men filled with high ideals.

We have all seen couples, one wearing a Western suit and leather shoes, the other with permed hair, a long gown and high-heeled shoes talking intimately on a seat in a shady corner of a park. But suppose one rainy day you passed between a turgid brown river and a rugged cliff, your horse wading carefully into the muddy water, unable to avoid stumbling. Suppose all around was still, grey-brown with no vivid colours, and then abruptly looking up you saw high on the cliff some natural caves like small rooms on the third floor where two people were sitting side by side clasping their knees.

Only from their different hair styles could you make out that one was a woman. Driven there by the rain they had probably chatted long enough and now had opened a notebook which both were reading, their heads close together. . . . If such a scene met your eyes, wouldn't it intrigue you much more than a couple nestling on a seat in a park to whisper together? One glance at the two in the park and you would assume that they were lovers, but here on such a dull rainy day on a lonely barren mountain with primitive caves, it would strike you as a "miracle" to find two such people adding colour to Nature. Whether they were lovers or not was beside the point. You saw two people full of vitality who clearly understood life's significance and under no circumstances would be apathetic or bored; still less could they seek excitement from foolery. No matter what happened they would be able to cope, to live in peace and content. But what enabled them to achieve this?

However, to get back to landscapes, it is people who make a landscape, for without them there is nothing to admire. Besides, if dynamic men were not the masters here, what would make the place memorable?

Or take another example. If you agree that twenty or thirty peach trees rate as an orchard, there is such a peach orchard here. The blossoming season is over, now green leaves fill the boughs without a single peach. An old millstone is an ideal round table. A few feet of broken tablets or one stone from an old flight of steps make splendid teapoys. Rocks large and small are at hand to serve as stools — and these stone stools appear as luxuries. These strange furnishings are essential because there is a teahouse here. In front of the orchard the local people have grown long-stemmed buckwheat, hemp and millet. The buckwheat is in flower and seen from a distance looks like a rosy carpet, the hemp and millet seem screens round the carpet's edge. Sunlight filters through the leaves to mottle the soil and stone furnishings with gold. Occasionally an insect chirps in the grass, or the horses tethered to the trees at the orchard's edge crane their heads to scratch them against the bark and start neighing, maybe in delight. You may say, "It's not bad here." Yes, this place meets the requirements of a "landscape". Yet this may not be all. Under the fierce sunlight on the steppe people like to rest here in the shade out of doors, and so someone started this teahouse; this is how this "scenic spot" came into existence. But it would be ridiculous to consider twenty or thirty peach trees, a millstone, a few feet of broken tablets, buckwheat, hemp and millet — things you can find anywhere — as the chief requisites of a scenic spot. China is so vast, there are countless scenic spots much more beautiful than this, which is nothing to boast of. So we should look at it from a different angle. Please take a seat and have a cup of clear tea and twenty cents worth of dates in this Peach Orchard Teahouse. If young women attract you most, all right, there are three or four over there, one of whom has probably just received a little money from home and is treating her friends. A few others over there round another stone table have substituted the books they have brought for dates and tea. Then there are two dashing youngsters who have travelled "the most difficult road in the world" and are now sitting quietly, looking as refined as young ladies. In a mixed group some are sitting, others squatting to have a philosophical debate, punctuated with roars of laughter, while on a long bench beside them lies someone with a book over his face. Enough, no need to look farther. In short there is a special atmosphere here, but nothing out of the way. People come here to relax after tiring work, to sip tea if they have money, or simply to chat. From the viewpoint of idlers who merely want to kill time, sitting here is uncomfortable, the refreshments are too crude and simple, and there is nothing to amuse them; so at most they come once — a second visit would bore them. But those who don't know what it is to kill time find this simple green shade delightful, and so this peach orchard has won quite a name.

That is why this "landscape" lives in your memory. The radiant noble-mindedness of mankind makes up for the poverty of the natural world, adding form and content to the scenery. Men create a second Nature!

My last recollection is of North China in May. At dawn when the window paper glimmered and silence reigned, a clarion call rent the air. It suddenly reminded me of the first photograph I had seen in an album the previous day: the grey figure of a young bugler blowing his bugle silhouetted against a silver background. His squared shoulders and arched brows showed stern resolution, courage and keen vigilance. I admired the photographer's skill and pondered that picture. In this morning's bugle call I also heard stern resolution, courage and keen vigilance. Throwing on my coat I went out to have a look. The air was very crisp, sunrise covered the hill on the left, on the peak of which stood the young bugler. The morning sunlight irradiated his temples. But what made me exclaim in amazement was a soldier with a rifle not far from him, who stood solemnly like a statue facing the east. The morning wind blew the red tassel of the bugle, the only thing that moved; and the glittering bayonet on the soldier's rifle was the only rigid object in the rosy sunlight. I was transfixed by the sight. The two men seemed to me the personification of our nation's spirit.

If you call that another "landscape", it was a genuine one, the greatest of the great!

December 1940

In Praise of the White Poplar

THE white poplar is really remarkable, I salute it.

As your truck bowls along the seemingly endless steppe a big yellow-green patchwork rug flashes into view. The yellow is virgin soil heaped up millions of years ago by great natural forces to form the crust of this loess steppe. The green, the result of men's toil to conquer Nature, is wheat fields blown by the breeze into green waves — showing the aptness of the men of old's phrase "a sea of wheat". If not coined by a genius it demonstrates how well our language has been refined. Yellow and green lord it here, stretching out on all sides as broad and smooth as a whetstone. If not for the distant peaks shouldering each other, which the naked eye could tell were beneath your feet, you might forget that you were driving over the steppe and such epithets as "grand" or "great" might spring to your mind. At the same time, though, your eyes might grow rather tired, so that shutting them on the "grandeur" and "greatness" around you might secretly start feeling — "monotonous". Yes, a bit monotonous, isn't it?

The next moment though if you look up abruptly and see a row — no, just a few or a couple of trees standing proudly erect as sentries, what would become of your boredom? For my part I exclaimed in surprise.

The white poplar is the most common tree in the northwest, yet a really remarkable tree.

It is an aspiring tree with a straight trunk and straight branches. The trunk is usually about ten feet high, as if man-made, with no lateral boughs for ten feet, and all its forked branches thrust upwards close together, as if man-made too, forming a cluster with none straying sideways or at an angle. All the broad leaves too rise upwards with hardly one slanting let alone drooping down. The bark is a glossy silver halo tinged with light green. This tree remains stubbornly erect even when crushed by the wind and snow of the north. It may measure no more around than a bowl, yet it strains upward to attain a height of ten or twenty feet, reaching unswervingly for the sky and defying the northwest wind.

This is the white poplar, the most common tree in the northwest, but by no means a commonplace tree.

It doesn't look as if dancing with curved, circling branches, and you may not think it beautiful. If beauty means dancing or straying sideways, the white poplar isn't a good daughter of trees. But it is sturdy, upright, simple and serious, without lacking in warmth, not to mention that its fortitude and stubborn erectness make it a man of honour among trees! If you cross the steppe as the snowdrifts start to melt and see a poplar or a row of poplars proudly erect on the flat plateau, you can hardly feel that these are simply trees, for their simplicity, seriousness and fortitude must surely symbolize to you the villagers of the north, reminding you of the sentries throughout the enemy rear proudly erect as white poplars, firm and unyielding as they guard our land. And surely you will go on to reflect that these closely-knit boughs and leaves of the aspiring white poplar symbolize the spirit and determination of those fighters in the North China plain who are with their blood writing a new chapter in our history.

The white poplar is a remarkable tree. Being so common in the northwest it is no more highly regarded than the peasants of the north, but it has the same immense vitality of those peasants who can never be ground down or crushed. I salute the white poplar not only because it symbolizes our northern peasants, but even more because it symbolizes the simplicity, fortitude and aspirations needed in today's struggle for national liberation.

Let those diehards who look down on the common people admire a rare tree like the straight, beautiful *nanmu* and despise this common easily grown white poplar. But I am loud in my praise of the white poplar!

March 10, 1941

Mountains and Rivers of Our Great Land

THE people of the northwest steppe cannot imagine life in the Taihu "lake district" south of the Yangzi. "In spring in the south grass and flowers shoot up, and orioles dart through the air," so the saying goes, but this hardly conveys what it's like there. The northwest steppe dwellers with no network of waterways may be told that streams run behind the southerners' houses so that, standing at the back door (the door of the water pavilion), you can draw up a pail of water, or waking at midnight can hear oars creaking past; but they find this difficult to visualize.

Someone who has never been to the northwest — or north Henan or south Shaanxi — probably assumes that those rivers whose names are marked on ordinary maps must be real rivers, at least much larger than the "havens" and "inlets" of the lake district which are not shown on most maps. At least they assume that these rivers flow all the year round and are navigable. A friend of mine once went to Kaifeng in the winter and standing on the dyke had no idea that this was the dyke of the famous Yellow River, for when he looked down he saw just a few trickles of water flowing through the brown mud. He asked, "Where is the Yellow River?" How was he to know that those trickles were the Yellow River? In fact in the low-water season the Yellow River is reduced to a few trickles.

Most of the northwestern rivers marked on the map grow just as shallow in winter as the irrigation ditches in the south. Put down a few stepping-stones in the shallow parts and you can walk across.

The River Urumqi is known far and wide, but when I saw horse carts driven through it I was staggered. And if I hadn't seen with my own eyes students roll up their trousers to wade across the Yan, I would have marvelled too, as the River Yan is clearly marked on the map.

But in summer when in spate these rivers are really impressive. Once the water rose in the upper reaches of the Yan, and a huge, heavy boulder to which the Women's College had fastened its pontoon bridge was swept over a hundred feet downstream.

Simply flying over it you can't understand exactly what the "northwest steppe" signifies. Simply travelling on the ground you may understand more specifically without grasping the "overall picture" (if I may borrow this term.)

You can see from the plane's altimeter that you are more than three thousand metres above sea level, but looking down through the window, ha! how clearly all the towns are spread out to your view. Then you realize that underneath is the steppe. But only when you have to walk over it can you supplement this knowledge.

You may not believe that you are not on level ground. Aren't there level fields and undulating seas of wheat as far as eye can see? However, if you strain your eyes to the distance, isn't that mountain range at the horizon also level with your feet? Sometimes it may strike you as even lower. If your truck happens to reach a gap with a deep precipice below it, a precipice at the middle height of the steppe, then you should really understand at last why the steppe is called a "high plateau".

This is not something you could dream up out of the blue.

The elder son of the Xie family compared snow to "scattering salt", whereas his younger sister* said it was more like "willow-down dancing in the wind". Her comparison has always been considered more beautiful. Of course "Willow-down dancing in the wind" sounds very charming; but they were speaking of snow south of the Yangzi. Her brother's comparison would have applied to the north. Of course sometimes big flakes fall too like "willow-down", but more often the snow here is "scattered salt".

When you walk in felt boots over the drifted snow it swishes like crisp dry powder, absolutely as if it were "salt". If you are out in the open and everything is white, the normally rutted dusty roads seem level and firm as a whetstone, and skimming lightly along in a one-horse sleigh you will feel really cool and refreshed — for indeed the air is as pure as if it had been filtered.

Once I saw a stretch of white far off in the Gobi and was amazed to think it had snowed in May, but it turned out to be a salt lake!

August 19, 1941

---

* Xie Daoyun, a fourth-century woman poet of the Eastern Jin Dynasty.

Night on Mount Qinling

SETTING off at three in the afternoon our truck broke
down with a flat tyre after only a dozen or so kilometres.
There were twenty-three of us aboard. Though we
hadn't much luggage we were carrying two tons of cotton. (According to a rule made the previous year, all
army trucks going south had to transport goods, either
public property or merchandise.) There was nothing
wrong with the engine, but we were overloaded and the
tyres were old.

So everyone went into action. The truck was jacked
up and the flat tyre removed, but it was no easy job
getting off the iron hoop round the outer tyre. The
driver nicknamed Darky was strong enough to lift five
hundred pounds, yet it took him about twenty minutes
to cope with that stubborn hoop.

The truck set off again uphill in top gear, Darky's
hefty hands keeping a firm grip on the steering-wheel
while the truck creaked and groaned. In his rather awkward Mandarin he commented, "We're too heavy!"
There were snowdrifts on Qinling and its ranges seemed to stretch away for ever. The truck inched upwards,
wheezing. And dusk crept up from the valley. Then
the truck stopped abruptly and Darky jumped down,
bent forward to listen and inspect the engine. Confound
it, another flat tyre and some engine trouble. "Well?"
asked the escort jumping down too. Darky shook his

head. "No good. But it doesn't matter. We'll make it somehow to the top, then see." "Can it be repaired?" "Sure."

By the time we reached the top a full moon was overhead. There were two inns there as well as a thatched cottage, not yet completed, so food and shelter would present no problem. Accordingly we stopped there.

First we were divided into three groups and assigned different tasks. The first group was to find sleeping quarters, the second to unload the truck, the third to eat.

Though the unfinished cottage, our makeshift lodging, had no doors or windows fitted, luckily it had a thatched roof. The floor was damp and cold, for the top of Mount Qinling was near the snow-line. Luckily there was straw, left over no doubt from the roof. So we laid straw on the ground and spread our quilts over it. There was no wind, but the cold cut our faces like wind. The moonlight was extraordinarily brilliant; distant ranges stretched on both sides at our feet.

Six of our party of twenty-three were girls. Some people would have to work all night repairing the truck. And stopping in such a wild place we might need to post sentries too.

Thereupon more tasks were assigned. Five or six men would be enough to help with repairs; two sentries would be posted at a time for a two-hour shift, four shifts in all. No girls were chosen for any of these duties. But W and H asked to join in. So an extra sentry shift was added. Two people turning in first lent their fur coats to the sentries.

From the little noodles shop we bought two dollars' worth of firewood and lit a big bonfire. By its light they started to repair the truck. The heads of the different groups issued further instructions: "When it's your turn to sleep, go ahead, but don't undress." But even if this hadn't been a precaution, not everyone could have stood the cold all night undressed on the top of Qinling in a thatched cottage like that, where the cold made our noses smart and the temperature was undoubtedly below zero.

Lying there and looking outside, the moonlight on the road seemed like hoarfrost, the sky was a deep blue, the sparkling stars extraordinarily bright. The sound of the men repairing the truck carried faintly to our ears, interspersed with their laughter and talk. Some time later peasants driving horses and carts also passed intermittently. The crack of their whips sometimes sounded like rifle shots. Under the moonlight a figure walked past our cottage then presently returned — it was one of the sentries.

"I wonder if any party like ours ever spent the night here on Qinling before?" I gave free rein to my fancy, my eyes moistening — perhaps stung by the cold, on my face a faint smile.

Muffled thuds could be heard. They were hammering the tyre to test whether enough air had been pumped in. I had a mental picture of two short energetic youngsters. Brought up in luxury, throughout this trip they had been most lively and cheerful.

Faint voices could be heard. Opening my eyes I saw that the moonlight on the road had been replaced by the light of early dawn, and the silvery laughter of girls was approaching. People had crowded round the bonfire where some fuel was still left. The truck was reloaded. Its windscreen had frosted over, forming a beautiful pattern. A pan of water was heating on the fire. The frost on the glass was wiped with a steaming hot towel, but it froze over again. Darky and our escort took it in turns to crank the engine but couldn't get it to start — the petrol had frozen too.

Brrr! Night on Qinling was so cold! Only now did we realize that last night's temperature had dropped below zero. This discovery seemed so intriguing that everyone laughed and talked gaily as we fetched straw to thaw out the engine.

First published in April 1943

Afterword: This records how the writer, after travelling from Yan'an to Xi'an in the early winter of 1940, took an army truck from Xi'an over Mt. Qinling. When first published some sentences were cut by the KMT censors, the original manuscript has disappeared and I can no longer remember the details clearly, so can only leave it like this.

November 13, 1958

Recollections of Hainan

WE visited the "End of the Earth".

It had been my habit, before visiting any scenic spot or historic site, to first read up in some thread-bound book what the men of old (most of them of course men of letters) had written about that place in inscriptions or travelogues.

Later experience taught me that this was not a good plan.

When I read earlier inscriptions or travelogues I was quite carried away, as if enjoying the pleasures of travel from my couch; but this meant that arrival in the place itself was rather a let-down (not a complete disillusionment), for I felt I had been taken in by those magnificent descriptions. For instance, before visiting the Seven Star Caves in Guilin I read a good many poems and travel accounts in rhythmical prose from the *Records of Guilin*. But as soon as I entered the caves I realized how awesome are writers' pens — they can make something commonplace seem miraculous.

So before this visit to the "End of the Earth" I deviated from my usual custom of busily making "mental preparations".

Still I had certain preconceptions. The name of the place prepared me to find a promontory jutting out into the sea, with surging emerald waves blocked by the shore.

But I was wrong. It wasn't like that at all.

The "End of the Earth" is simply a couple of dozen paces from the highway. Of course the sea laps its boulders, but there is nothing like a "promontory". I can understand why our forebears thousands of years ago gave it this name; but now that man is bound to conquer Nature and this highway encircles the island, linking up Nada and other places of interest as well as salt fields and iron mines, how can this still be called the "end of the earth"?

To my surprise, the shore really had huge strange-shaped boulders. We looked at those two high boulders close together, worn smooth by the wind and waves. The gap in between, large enough to admit a man, was carpeted with fine sand. Several feet away emerald waves lapped the foot of the rocks. We joked: It's too bad we're old now, or we'd certainly sit in that gap talking sweet nothings for hours.

But those strange boulders reminded me of Su Dong-po's poem "Mount Zhaner":

Towering up through a narrow gap into space
This outdoes all other mountains.
Look at the roadside rocks,
Left over by Nü Wa when she mended heaven.

Up to fifty years ago, anyone reading these poignant lines would surely have heaved a deep sigh. In the *Qiongzhou Prefectural History of the Dao Guang Reign* (1821-1851) I read in the section "Banished Ministers" that during the Tang Dynasty ten officials had been banished here, and another ten in the Song; while from "Working Away from Home" I learned that there had been one official sent here in the Sui Dynasty, twelve in the Tang and twelve in the Song. In the Ming Dynasty there were twenty-two banished officials and officials who had come from other parts of the country. Weren't all those men "roadside rocks" which could have "mended heaven"? Of course, when Su Dongpo wrote that poem he had no idea that after him five famous Song officials would be banished here, their crime being to have opposed peace talks and urged resistance to the Jin Tartars. Among them were Li Gang, Zhao Ding and Hu Quan whose names were known far and wide. When the Song court moved south, these five celebrated officials were not used to "mend heaven" but banished to this island where "the earth sinks to the southeast" as "roadside rocks"*. For centuries since then readers of this poem cannot but sigh in sympathy.

Hainan Island began to be opened up in the Han Dynasty. I won't venture to make wild claims for the Hans as to how well they administered this pearl of the South Sea. But even if the Han rulers simply regarded this as a treasure island where "each fountain gushed wine, and each tree when shaken shed coins", at least they did not use it as a place of exile for criminals. It was probably during the Tang Dynasty that the emperor began to prize the island; but the Song Dynasty was worse than the Tang. In Emperor Taizong's edict banishing Lu Suoxun to Yenzhou we read: "Let him be spared extermination of his clan and simply be banished to the wilds." Obviously the second Song em-

---

* A myth tells of the fight between two gods in which they knocked over a pillar supporting heaven, so that the southeast of the earth subsided. The goddess Nü Wa carried rocks to mend heaven, leaving those not used by the roadside.

peror considered banishment to Hainan as one degree less severe than wiping out a man's whole family, for the island was regarded as a "sinister garrison area".

Not until the people took over political power was Hainan Island transformed. Seeing over the Xinglong Farm, I recalled the island's history and that poem by Su Dongpo. Xinglong is a big farm run by overseas Chinese. To see over the whole farm takes a couple of days even if you go by car. Today many tropical crops formerly unknown there have been brought in from far away. Like the farm workers here, whose ancestors or parents fled to distant foreign lands as menials they have now returned to our great island in the South Sea not as "roadside rocks" but to "mend heaven".

We drove along a highway between leaping foam-capped waves and huge flat paddy fields. Now at the end of the lunar year, aren't the peasants in North China preparing their New Year wine, or in snug rooms working out the year's harvest and planning to battle for a larger crop next year? Not only in North China, the peasants along both banks of the Yangzi have just finished one campaign and are preparing for the next. But here in Hainan we see level fields of tender green paddy seedlings — a truly amazing sight.

On both sides of the road also grow endless clumps of grass. These dense clumps have small white flowers like fluffy balls which cover them like an awning of clustered pearls and from the distance seem a length of white silk.

I suddenly remembered the poem "Duck-feet Millet" written by Wang Zuo in the Zheng Tong reign (1436-1450) of the Ming Dynasty. I asked our escort Comrade Bai Guang, "Is that duck-feet millet?"

"No," she said. "It's called aeroplane grass. There was duck-feet millet by the road just now."

How novel — aeroplane grass. After further questioning I learned that this aeroplane grass can be found everywhere and is used as a fertilizer. I asked what duck-feet millet was used for now. She said, "As fodder. But we have better fodder than that."

I told her that a Hainan poet in the Ming Dynasty had written a poem in praise of this duck-feet millet because in those days the common people ate it as grain. The poem read:

> All the five grains nourish life
> And not for one day can men go without them;
> Who knew that besides the five grains
> Are other plants to sustain life.
> Far away south of the great sea
> Where the sun sets and a lone gull vanishes,
> There are bountiful crops
> Of this special plant.
> This plant sprouts like ducks' feet,
> Gradually frogs' eyes protrude,
> Then it seems a scatter of tiny pearls
> Grown on a crooked hairpin.

See what a vivid description this is of duck-feet millet. No wonder it made such a deep impresssion on me that I mistook aeroplane grass for it. But the poet wrote not only in praise of duck-feet millet. Please read his last anguished lines:

> In the third month there is famine,

Tax-collectors roar like thunder;
The small crop reaped in the third month
Is barely enough to give the tax-collectors.
In the eighth month another famine,
The crops still green in the fields.
The big harvest comes this month,
And counting on it the people have no fear.
In a million homes in Hainan
All are haggard, poor and ill;
Each time a famine comes
This herb keeps them alive;
They eat cakes made from it
With enough to spare to brew liquor.
It not only tides them over
But serves as their staple food.

Judging by this poem, none of the common people could eat even a fraction of their harvests small and large; and it was often duck-feet millet that kept them alive.

However, Wang Zuo wrote another poem called "Tiannanxing":*

Look at the Tiannanxing
Found in all books on herbal medicine;
Grown in the South Sea
It saves men in time of famine.
In the eighth month the wind blows,
Every face is haggard;
But the sprouts from its tubers
Fill their baskets.

---

* Tiannanxing, literally "sky-south-star", is the plant listed in the *Materia Medica* as *Arisaema japonicum* or *Arum pentaphyllum*.

In other words, after the main harvest in the eighth month the peasants' crops were taken away and they had to rely on duck-feet millet and Tiannanxing. Wang Zuo ends on a note of wry humour:

This wonderful plant grows beyond the sea;
Does anyone on the Central Plain know its taste?

May 13, 1963

Mao Dun, Master Craftsman of Modern Chinese Literature

Fan Jun

LITERARY innovation in modern China has been closely linked with the awakening of the Chinese nation epitomized in the May 4th Movement of 1919, which put an end to the dominance of classical language and tradition and heralded the advent of modernism. Modern literature was thus the product of a growing ideological awareness of modern ideas about democracy, socialism and the role of literature itself. The corruption permeating society and the danger the nation faced, as well as the revolutionary fervour to which these gave rise and which had its own roots in the May 4th Movement too, occupied the attention of the majority of writers, who consciously or unconsciously joined the revolutionary struggle by taking up their pens to analyse social reality. It was against this socio-historical background that the revolution began to influence literature directly and profoundly and determine the direction in which it would develop, conferring on it a historical character foreign to its precursors. Mao Dun, a versatile talent, was active during this process.

Fan Jun, 55, born in Zhejiang, is a research fellow in the Literature Research Institute of the Academy of Social Sciences in Beijing.

Mao Dun, whose real name was Shen Yanbing, used this pen-name when he began writing in the late 1920s. He was well known both nationally and internationally as a writer, but was at the same time a social activist. One of the earliest members of the Chinese Communist Party, he began revolutionary work in the mid-1920s and continued to take an active part in social and political struggle throughout his life. But it was literature which he made his career, one in which he achieved splendid things. National liberation and social progress were the constant goal of his writing. In him were combined the social activist and the man of letters, the writer and the revolutionary. It is nonetheless in the establishment and development of modern Chinese literature that his contributions were greatest and where his far-reaching influence can be felt today even after his death. He was truly one of the great men of modern Chinese literature.

I

When Mao Dun was born on July 4, 1896 in Tongxiang, Zhejiang, the last feudal dynasty, the Manchu Qing empire, was on the verge of collapse, and the people of China were seeking liberation and a way to change their society. His home was on the southeast coast close to Shanghai, in that economically and culturally developed area where advanced science and thought were first introduced from Japan and the West. His father was a doctor who sympathized with the doomed Reform Movement of 1898, and consequently Mao Dun grew up in a relatively free and progressive atmosphere, reading books that would never have found their way into the hands of a child in a feudal family, among them popular novels whose wealth of social content at once instilled in him a love of literature and a democratic consciousness. His political zeal was further fired by the Revolution of 1911, which finally toppled the ailing dynasty, and he began to busy himself with propaganda work; a protest against the autocratic nature of his middle school got him expelled.

In 1916, as the ideals of the May 4th Movement were crystallizing at last, Mao Dun graduated from the preparatory course at Beijing University, went to work for the Commercial Press and began to write. He formed eclectic intellectual habits at these two institutions, which despite being tightly controlled by conservative interests were respected as disseminators of advanced ideas in both science and politics.

His early writing was aimed predominantly at the young and preoccupied with the nature of ideological enlightenment, so that when Hu Shi, Chen Duxiu and Lu Xun began to promote the literary revolution through the columns of their magazine *New Youth*, they found in the young Mao Dun a ready response. In January 1920, he began to experiment with literary innovation as editor of the "New Trends in Fiction" feature of the magazine *Short Story Monthly*, which by the end of the year he had taken over and transformed thoroughly. From this he went on to join with Zhou Zuoren, Ye Shengtao, Zheng Zhenduo and others in founding the Literary Research Society to put his ideas into practice by promoting realistic literature that mirrored life. He was not only the society's active organizer but also the elaborator of the theory it stood for. His management and advocacy gave *Short Story Monthly* and the Literary Research Society alike a modern flavour all their own which destined them to be enormously influential.

His articles from these years reveal a keen concern for the freedom of youth and the liberation of women. It was after the 1920s that he began to be drawn to Marxist theory and the ideals of the Russian Revolution, which were just then becoming known in China, and this led him to direct involvement with the Chinese communist movement. He was never exclusively concerned with literature. The outbreak of the First Revolutionary Civil War (1924-27) rapidly disillusioned him with the "enlightenment" of the early post-May-4th literature, and he began to call for "great changes". As one of the first writers to combine proletarian Marxism with literature, he helped to make the step from literary revolution to revolutionary literature. In 1930, he joined the China League of Left-wing Writers, which for a time he led in this spirit during what many historians have called the "red 30s". He added lustre to that turbulent decade with a phenomenal output of original writing and criticism, working in close association with Lu Xun and Qu Qiubai. His novel *Midnight* was universally regarded as a prime example of revolutionary literature and was enthusiastically received by writers themselves and the reading public, soon achieving international status with translations into English, Russian and German.

In 1937, the War of Resistance Against Japan broke out, which was destined to last for eight years and be followed by another three years of the War of Liberation, a turbulent period during which Mao Dun was constantly on the move from place to place in an attempt to evade the ravages of the invaders as well as the persecution of the Kuomintang government. He lived in Urumqi, Yan'an, Guangzhou, Hongkong, Wuhan, Changsha, Guilin and Chongqing, and as a council member of the All-China Federation of Writers and Artists for Resistance Against the Enemy he continued his work of writing, criticism and translation, besides editing literary journals — *Literary Front* was one of the most important magazines of the war of resistance — and the literary supplements of several newspapers.

With the death of Lu Xun in 1936, Mao Dun and Guo Moruo became the most prestigious and influential writers in China. Mao Dun devoted himself to the twin tasks of making literature contribute to national liberation and winning acceptability and popularity for it with the public at large whilst at the same time exploring the theoretical and creative possibilities of a distinctively Chinese literature.

The Yan'an Forum on Literature and Art, held in 1942, encouraged much new writing in the liberated areas; full of admiration for the new literature, Mao Dun embodied its principles in his own work in the Kuomintang-controlled areas, extending his endeavours beyond the literary field into the forefront of the ideological struggle for national freedom and democracy against world fascism.

For a long period after the founding of the People's Republic of China in 1949, Mao Dun was a leading figure in government cultural institutions and in other literary and artistic bodies, interesting himself particularly in cultural exchanges with foreign countries and the defence of world peace. At the same time he kept up his theoretical work and literary criticism, writing voluminously on new writers. His contribution to the world-wide debate on socialist realism of the late 1950s was *Notes of a Night Reader*, a summary of world literature down to modern times upholding realistic writing and the socialist path.

During the "cultural revolution" Mao Dun, like any other honest writer, was persecuted into silence. He was over eighty by the time the storm passed, and began to concentrate on his memoirs, which when finished ran to tens of thousands of words, an invaluable document for the study of his life and work and the political, literary and social history of modern China, besides reviving the tradition of literary memoirs, which had been in abeyance for many years.

Mao Dun died in Beijing on March 27, 1981. On his deathbed he donated his royalties to establish an award for novels to encourage young writers.

2

Mao Dun's greatest achievement was his original writing. His first novel, *Disillusion*, created a sensation in the literary world, but unwilling to restrict himself to a self-made mould, he sought painstakingly for "a new method of expression which better fits the temper of the times".

He wrote altogether seven novels, six novellas, over fifty short stories, one play and ten collections of essays, through which he wanted to "describe the social phenomena of China on a grand scale" and "record some aspects of the heroic drama" of modern Chinese history. In this he succeeded.

His novel *Frosted Leaves Are as Red as Flowers in February* paints a picture of Chinese society from 1911 to 1919, presenting the rise of the young revolution. His long novel *Rainbow* reflects the stormy period from the May 4th Movement to the mid-1920s, while the *Canker* trilogy — *Disillusion, Vacillation* and *The Search* — records the First Revolutionary Civil War from its origins to its failure. *Midnight,* "The Shop of the Lin Family" and "Spring Silkworms" show urban and rural class struggle during the Second Revolutionary Civil War and the growing threat to the nation, strikingly reflecting the life-and-death struggle between opposed social forces.

The Story of the First Stage, Manning the Post and *Training* are stirring works that mobilized the nation for the war of resistance, whereas *Decay* and *Before and After the Qingming Festival* expose the darkness of Kuomintang rule after that war reached its stalemate. His stories from the late 1940s reflect the spectrum of tendencies on the eve of the national victory of the War of Liberation. Taken together, these works form a historical picture of the changes in Chinese society throughout the first half of the twentieth century.

If one work must be singled out, it is surely *Midnight,* set in semi-colonial Shanghai, which with its grand design summarizes the plight of China in the 1930s and the ineluctable failure of capitalism there.

Mao Dun attributed his popularity in part to his willingness to tackle "grand themes which others hesitate to write about" and to the centrality in his work of relationships between and among the people, whereby characters are portrayed in terms of the sum total of human relationships in society.

His broad social palette was unusual among contemporary writers. Perhaps his most successful characters are capitalists, industrialists, businessmen and the educated young women known as "women of the times". He is as at home with the widest of themes and the most intimate of details and never lapses into superficiality, describing for instance the love of a boy and a dog in "Liena and Jidi" as sincerely as he would the fate of a nation. His essays, commentaries and lyrics, too, range from gentle poeticality to stirring calls for revolution and hopeful visions of the future with uniformly brilliant versatility.

3

At the same time as being a writer, Mao Dun was a literary theorist and critic who spent much more time on these pursuits than on fiction throughout his sixty-year career. Literary criticism played a great role in establishing the new literature after the May 4th Movement, and Mao Dun was a path-breaker in this regard.

Modern Chinese literature needed extrication from traditional Confucian restrictions and resistance to the temptation of art for art's sake; there was a genuine desire for literature that would reflect social reality and the sufferings of the nation. Hence among the many divergent trends which were pursued at the time, the one which eventually took root and developed was realism. This was a feature of articles in *New Youth*, a central tenet of the Literary Research Society's call for "literature for the people", and a point repeatedly stressed by Mao Dun himself from the very beginning. Literature must show concern for the people; literature must portray the people and have the ability to guide them. The time was ripe for such ideas, and they rapidly caught on. Mao Dun's stand on revolutionary literature, people's literature and socialist literature never wavered, and in this he can be taken as representative of the mainstream of thought on the subject throughout the period during which he was active.

However, being the experienced artist that he was, Mao Dun did not neglect literature's aesthetic role at the same time as he was stressing its social function. "Literature", he wrote in his first article on literary innovation, "is the product of ideology — there is nothing wrong with this. But the constitution of literature relies entirely on art". Although a steadfast proponent of realism whose ideas stemmed from 19th-century realist critical theory, he was not blinded to the limitations of early realism nor prevented from deriving nourishment from other literary trends like romanticism and more advanced realism, especially factors in them which strengthened the function of realism as a reflection of reality. This flexible attitude to realism is instanced in his enthusiasm for Soviet writing in the wake of the October Revolution, which he said, "presents faithfully all aspects of this great and memorable age." Mao Dun's mind was open and abreast of the trends.

A major part of his theoretical work was literary criticism, wherein he proceeded with keen observation and profound knowledge to analyse a writer's work ideologically and artistically in the context of the movement and the history of literature. He was often the first to discover new writers, new works and new trends, grasping their character and appraising them objectively with a foresight that demonstrated his sagacity as a literary historian.

He established himself during the early 1920s as the chief literary critic in the Literary Research Society by a series of articles on new books. He was the first fully to understand and appreciate Lu Xun and was warm in his praise of that writer's "My Old Home" and "The True Story of Ah Q" immediately they came out. When Lu Xun published *Call to Arms,* Mao Dun was quick to point out that the book laid a solid foundation for the modern Chinese short story. Mao Dun's work on Lu Xun is a mine of information for the study of that writer.

"We desperately need," wrote Mao Dun in 1936, "earnest and down-to-earth critics, who must firstly know the actual needs, secondly study and discuss more often the actual problems in creative writing and thirdly endeavour to learn from life."

Mao Dun's contribution to literary criticism is on a par with his original writing but has been neglected in the past. It is only in recent years that greater scholarly attention has been paid to his influence as a critic.

4

With great zeal Mao Dun also studied, wrote about and translated foreign literature and made annotated selections from the Chinese classics.

He translated from 1916 on, specializing in Russian and other Eastern European literature, though he is believed to have translated over thirty years works by at least sixty writers from twenty-five countries, beginning with some two hundred short pieces which appeared in *Short Story Monthly* in the first five years of the 1920s.

In a short period in the late twenties and early thirties he wrote ten books on foreign literature, including *The European War and Literature, Modern Literature, Six European Writers, An Outline of Western Literature* and *Famous Literary Works of the World.*

In 1934, he and Lu Xun founded *Translation* magazine, which carried translations of foreign literature and was the precursor of the present-day *World Literature.* After the founding of the People's Republic he edited *Chinese Literature.* In the study and translation of foreign literature he was also a pioneer.

Although Mao Dun spent less energy on classical Chinese literature than on foreign literature, his annotations are particularly useful for the young beginner. Of especial note is his research into Chinese mythology, which stands alongside Lu Xun's study of Chinese fiction and Zheng Zhenduo's study of Chinese popular literature as an academically valuable breakthrough in a branch of learning.

"We believe," he wrote early on, "that Western and classical Chinese literature can help us create the new Chinese literature. . . . We want to use the old literature as material for our study, investigate its characteristics and combine them with those of Western literature to create a literature of our own." Elsewhere he says, "Our purpose in writing about Western literature is to familiarize the reader with Western writing and art but also with modern ideas from the rest of the world, and this purpose deserves careful attention."

Mao Dun was one of the most outstanding writers of 20th-century China, and his influence has been immense. During a writing career of over sixty years he produced a wealth of literary works which have inscribed his name indelibly in the modern literary history of his country.

Translated by Niu Jin

目　　录

茅 盾 作 品 选

熊 猫 丛 书

*

《中国文学》出版社出版

（中国北京百万庄路24号）

中国国际图书贸易总公司发行

（中国国际书店）

外文印刷厂印刷

1987年第1版

ISBN　7-5071-0000-6/I.1

00400

10—E—2130P